A DEEPER DIVE

by Deborah Madar

NFB
Buffalo, New York

PRAISE for Deborah Madar's CONVERGENCE

"With taut prose and vivid detail, Madar creates both the internal and external world of three very different characters – a recently divorced, passive college professor; her troubled and troubling student; and her long-forgotten college boyfriend, now a married glazier haunted by his stint in Vietnam."

"This is a gripping tale, perfect in its pacing, authentic in its detail, and haunting in its perception."

"You will never forget Charlotte, Leigh Ann, and Phil! Author Deborah Madar seamlessly transports us, the readers, to small town America and throws us in the midst of these people, their complex lives and their issues."

"Madar writes beautifully, with conviction and compassion. This is a rare novel that I'll read again more slowly the second time around to savor the writing now that I know the story arc. Well done!"

"Convergence is a compelling read on two levels. On its surface it is an extremely well-written psychological thriller encompassing the lives and actions of its three main characters. On a deeper level it broaches the existential question of authentic versus inauthentic living, of the consequences of the choices one makes either consciously or by default. On both levels Deborah Madar hits the mark."

"What a great read! Deborah Madar's plot and character development are masterful. Convergence is a psychological thriller you will be thinking about long after you turn the last page. I can't wait for her next book."

PRAISE for Deborah Madar's DARK RIDDLE

"This book by Deborah Madar is a gentle nudge or maybe it is a sharp poke....a wake up call about the forces in our society that affect not only our young people, but our school communities, our towns and cities, and our families. It is beyond thought-provoking."

"I haven't cried in a couple of years. This book brought me to tears. It was emotionally draining. It also made me think."

"An engaging, cleverly designed plotline that addresses the haunting questions around inexplicable violence by young people. While exploring possible reasons, it does not fall into the trap of giving pat answers or pretending to know the unknowable. The characters are well developed and believable."

"Sooo good. Madar manages to weave family dynamics, school and community politics, tragedy and mystery into such a believable, readable and relevant tale for our times…It's been awhile since I "couldn't stop reading" - yet the further I went with Dark Riddle, the more I had to know now."

"Every page made me want to get to the next. I couldn't put it down. Madar did not disappoint. Can't wait for her next novel!"

NFB Publishing
119 Dorchester Road
Buffalo, New York 14213
For more information visit Nfbpublishing.com

This book is dedicated to the "wing women" in my life.
You know who you are.

"It's never too late to start over – it's never too late to be happy."

-Jane Fonda

PART ONE

March, 1997

Chapter One

THE MALL

Joanna wanted to murder her mother.

She often fantasized about the particulars, the wide variety of possible methods for doing the deed. The more violent and bloody the technique she imagined, the richer her daydreams became. Last month she had seen *Pulp Fiction* at the movies, and since then her menu of murderous means had elaborately expanded.

Even as a young child, Joanna had never been close to her mother. From her daughter's point of view, Grace had always been more involved with and more loving toward her precious twin boys. But last fall, Joanna's estrangement from her parent was solidified. Her mother had been hired by her daughter's high school as a teacher's assistant. Since then, a mere glimpse of the woman's face, arms, or swinging hips in the halls made the girl's stomach roil and her face burn with fury.

Within Joanna's very limited circle of friends, it was normal to hate your mother. At weekend sleepovers, inevitably a girl would declare that she detested her mom, prompting complicit head nods from the others. But Joanna recognized that she was different from these other sixteen-year-olds. She knew that her peers were temporarily irritated, annoyed, frustrated by their mothers. These terrible feelings would eventually pass. What Joanna harbored toward Grace was an unforgiving, murderous contempt.

Her shrink had told her that most teens felt this way about a parent from time to time. What she was feeling was normal, she assured the girl.

But *Madam Freud,* Joanna wanted to scream out loud during one of these sessions, *how many girls my age have to compete with their mothers for the love of a boy?* She pictured the therapist's sleepy eyes popping open if she ever confessed that little detail.

Where the hell was the bitch, she wondered. Tightening her grip on the mini-van's steering wheel, she focused her eyes on the main entrance to the Mill Springs Mall. The clock on the dash confirmed that musical practice started twenty minutes ago. Mr. Wells would definitely ream her out in front of the whole cast. She should have known that her mother had lied about the "quick errand" she needed to run. Lately, if her mouth was moving, the woman was telling a lie. But Joanna had not protested when she'd told her to pull into the mall. If she wanted to get any driving practice before she took her road test, she would have to put up with her mother's maddening whims.

In spite of her father's ridiculous warnings that the battery would die just so that she could listen to music, she started the mini-van and turned on the radio. *"That thing, that thing, thaaat thiiing,"* Lauren Hill's smooth voice sang. Opening the window a few inches, Joanna inhaled the late afternoon spring air. She turned the volume up to drown out the deafening noise of heavy equipment at work on a new parking lot behind the mall. Joanna leaned into the headrest, closed her eyes, and began to play The Game.

Whenever anyone, most typically one of her parents, made her wait, she established the guidelines of The Game. They would appear, she reassured herself, after the next red car passed. After this commercial. After the clock ticked off another three minutes. Now, she willed her mother to hurry out of the mall by the time the song ended. She clutched the steering wheel and sang the last line with the Fugees, but when she opened her eyes, her mother was not there. Joanna turned off the engine. She was gulping air now, the explosive hate for her mother making her sick to her stomach.

Pulling the keys out of the ignition, she threw them into her purse. She jumped to the pavement and slammed the car door shut.

"I'm going to kill her!" she said out loud.

CHAPTER TWO

HOME FIRES

DAN PHILLIPS SPED through the tall pines that lined each side of his curving driveway. It was more of a private road that led to the house that he had built four years earlier. When he reached the end of the driveway, he wiped his sweating palms on his jeans and turned off the ignition of the new Silverado. Squinting into the noonday sun, he looked up at the home's three stories.

Dan couldn't remember the last time he had left work before dark, and a shot of hot guilt prickled his scalp. It was this house that, as newlyweds, he and Grace dreamed of, saved for, designed themselves, and after two long years of construction, joyfully moved into. That crazy day had been their 12th anniversary, and until recently, Dan thought that they had come far in those dozen years.

They were kids when they married. He was nineteen, and Grace, pregnant with Joanna, was seventeen. In those days in that place when a girl was expecting, marriage was a foregone conclusion. There was no pre-marital counseling, no waiting to become your complete adult self before you made a lifelong commitment to a man, to a woman, to children, to a mortgage, to a pattern that would become your life. Two months after the wedding, in the tiny apartment over the noisy dance studio on Main Street, the young couple was joined by their infant daughter.

Grace and Dan had never lived anywhere else but Westfield. Their mothers had given birth to each of them in the same hospital on Central

Avenue. Now they were raising their three kids in the small town within blocks of both sets of grandparents. Neither he nor Grace had gone to college. Dan started working for Woodruff's Asphalt Company as soon as he graduated from high school. Ten years ago he bought the business from old man Woodruff, and he had expanded it to a full service contracting and construction business.

That was why Dan spent most of his married life working ten to twelve hour days. And when he wasn't working, he was attending village board meetings or Chamber of Commerce activities. Recently, he had been elected president of the County Board of Contractors. He did all of this for his wife and kids, he told himself, in spite of the fact that he was usually too exhausted when he was home to spend any time with them. His own father, who had died in his mid-forties, penniless and sick from alcoholism for most of Dan's life, had taught him through his own bad example that work and money had to come first in order to be successful.

Grace had the twins when Joanna was still a toddler, and the days and nights of his wife's early twenties were filled with the rigors of motherhood. The couple hadn't had the time or foresight to plan their lives, but by the norms of this small town, they were doing well.

One night a few months back as Dan drifted toward sleep, he felt the heat of his wife's body moving toward him. And then their shoulders were touching. Grace whispered his name into the darkness, and he rolled over and came face to face with his wife. "Are you happy?" she asked. Her question transformed his excited expectation of having sex, which didn't happen very often these days, to a cold rage. His quick temper had been a problem from the time he was a teen and he had the scars to prove it. Some of them were from combatants and a few had been inflicted upon him by his father, from whom he figured he got his own temperament.

It had been a decade since Dan had punched another human being, but he remembered clearly the exhilarating release. Now, he was a family man, a business owner, and a civic leader, so he curbed that inclination whenever he reached his boiling point. He had never been tempted to hit his children. Grace was the only one who pissed him off so much he would sometimes relieve himself in a fantasy of abuse. That night he stared up at the bedroom ceiling and fought the urge to grab her. Instead, he turned away from her and said nothing.

What a stupid question, he thought as he punched his pillow into submission. No, he wasn't happy. But that wasn't the point of living, was it? The point was to work so hard that you didn't have the time to think about such things. The goal was to get all the stuff that money and connections could buy and give it to your family, so that eventually, *they* would be happy. He tried to calm himself by breathing deeply and pretending that Grace had never spoken.

The truth was that, lately, everything Grace said or did or didn't do angered him. When they married, she had been so down to earth. Easygoing and content, her quiet ways had made him calmer than he had ever been. But since she had returned to college he watched helplessly as she moved away from her old self. Many husbands would have been pleased with their wives making an effort to improve themselves, but Dan felt resentful and diminished.

It wasn't just that she had fearlessly gone back to school, in spite of the fact that he disapproved. She seemed to be trying to remake herself. She worked hard to make healthier meals and to stick to an exercise program for the first time in her life. And it showed. She lost thirty pounds and paid more attention to how she dressed, trading sweatpants and sneakers for tight jeans and boots. In the hallway gallery of family pictures, each of their high school graduation pictures hung side by side. Recently, their son Andrew had stopped in front of Grace's photo and said, "Mom, you look younger now than you did back then!"

"Thank you, sweet boy!" she said, delighted by the compliment. Dan watched as she playfully clung to the thirteen-year-old. He clenched his fists in an effort to repress the urge to shout, GROW UP!, at both of them.

The truth that her husband had to face was that each day Grace was moving farther and farther away from him. And her involvement with their kids was waning, as he had worried it would when she said she wanted to go to school. "They hardly need me anymore," she told him after reading aloud the acceptance letter to the teacher's assistant certification program. "Joanna can barely stand the sight of me these days, and Zach and Andrew are so busy with their own lives, they won't even notice the few hours that I'll be gone."

Dan had to admit that their thirteen-year-old twins were happy boys. But he worried about Joanna. She didn't seem to have any friends that Dan was aware of. Most of the time she ignored her brothers and when she did pay attention, it was typically to blast one or the other with a surly comment. And lately, Grace especially seemed to be her nemesis, the target of their daughter's hostile glances and biting sarcasm. Still, Dan was not in favor of Grace going to college at this point in their family's life. But this new version of his wife didn't seem to pay much attention to what he wanted, and she completed the certification program in two semesters. The high school had been desperate for an aid in the Resource Room, and she was hired the day after she submitted her application. Last night, before she turned off her bedside lamp, he watched out of the corner of his eye as she poured over the state university catalogue. In spite of his disapproval, it seemed that she was forging ahead with her plan to get her bachelor's degree.

Dan got out of his truck and walked quickly to the front door, anxiety building with each step. Once inside, he was rushed by the two golden retrievers. "Back off, boys," he yelled as he turned off the security alarm. He blamed his wife for these spoiled canines. From the time they were puppies, the brothers had been insistent jumpers. "No barking!" he admonished them as he hurried to the spare bedroom that Grace had converted to her study.

On the desktop was her computer, the screensaver a picture of the Chautauqua Gorge in the fall. That figures, he thought. The Grace that he had married would have chosen a picture of their family rather than a landscape. His glance swept the space and he noted that there wasn't a photo of any of them in the room. He pulled open each desk drawer and flipped through the pages of her course notebooks, which offered nothing. Only her textbooks occupied the bookcase shelves, so he went back to the desk. He clicked on the mouse, but he couldn't guess what password his wife might have selected. His mounting frustration was soon transformed to the familiar rage. "Sit! Stay!" he shouted at the dogs as they tried to follow him out of the room.

He hadn't removed his work boots at the front door, and the loud stomping as he moved through the hallway temporarily quelled his anger. Dan glanced into the messy room his boys shared – he would give them hell when he saw them tonight, but he marched on until he came to Joanna's room. "STAY OUT!!!" warned the homemade placard she had tacked onto her door. His daughter had inherited his impatience and quick temper, he knew. A colicky infant and a temper-throwing toddler, he could count on one hand how many times he'd seen his sixteen-year-old smile since her troubled middle school days.

Dan turned the knob and entered his daughter's bedroom. A dozen or so stuffed animals, most of them missing arms, legs, or eyes were thrown around the room. They looked more like helpless victims rather than comforting companions. After a call from her guidance counselor explaining that Joanna was getting into verbal skirmishes with her classmates and her teachers on a daily basis, her parents had made a rare mutual decision to send their daughter to a therapist. The book she brought home after that first session lay open on the floor, the binding loosened as if it had been flung across the room. After nearly tripping over it, Dan picked it up off the rug. He snorted as he read the title out loud. "*How To Give Yourself a Break and Stop Hating Your Parents: A Teen's Guide.*"

He looked up at the two creepy posters hanging over her bed. Uma Thurman cooly dragged on a cigarette, staring at him dismissively. Next to her was a poster from his daughter's favorite movie, *Scream*. The terrified blue eyes belonged to the actress who had played the innocent Gertie in *ET*. That film used to be his little girl's favorite all those years ago.

On Joanna's unmade bed was the new Discman they had bought for her sixteenth birthday. Spilled out next to it were several CD's. Dan picked them up. The Goo Goo Dolls, Alanis Morrisette, Nirvana. He recognized the names, but he couldn't have told you a song by any one of them, unlike his wife whose musical tastes lately seemed to match Joanna's. There was no doubt that Grace was aging backwards in so many ways since she had started working with high school kids. He dropped the discs on the rumpled sheets and walked across the room to Joanna's desk.

He tugged on the drawer. Locked, of course. He should have known. What he was doing now was a total violation of the shaky trust father and daughter shared. Above all her many demands, Joanna insisted on privacy. As he anxiously rifled through her dresser, he realized he wasn't sure what he was looking for. Beneath a pile of sweatshirts in the bottom drawer, his fingers grasped a piece of twine. Three small keys were tied to the end of the string. Sure enough, the largest one fit the lock on the desk drawer. A partial pack of Marlboros and a blue leather journal slid forward as soon as Dan opened it. He hesitated for only a moment before inserting the smallest key into the lock on the front of the diary.

Scrawled on the first few pages were poems or song lyrics, Dan couldn't be sure which. Photographs from magazines displaying celebrities and singers were taped onto several pages. Joanna had pasted a blurry picture of herself sitting on a blanket at the shoreline in Barcelona. The scrawled caption above his daughter's image read: "Beached Whale."

A sadness washed over him. He knew what it was like to loathe yourself. And it appeared that others felt the same way about his daughter. He flipped to a page and read the label at the top. "Things I Have Been Called This Month." The list was heartbreaking and maddening at the same time. "*Nasty, Freak, Weirdo, Low-Life, Bitch, Cunt...*" On a few pages he saw nothing but "*Brad*" written dozens of times. A red ribbon marked a page with a cast list for *Grease*. In small print under Ensemble and highlighted in pink: *Joanna Phillips*. His daughter's name emphasized that way made Dan sigh in relief. Maybe she would emerge from this phase of her life and look back on it as a time when she was unhappy but had hung tough anyway.

He turned to the last page of the journal. As he read the words his daughter had scribbled, a blind rage consumed him. He stared at them and minutes went by as he attempted to breathe. He stumbled across the floor to his daughter's bed. He sat there for several minutes, his heart pounding so hard it hurt. When he looked down, he could see each beat making a visible vibration under his shirt. Was he having a heart attack, he wondered. He willed himself to take slower and deeper breaths and the pain gradually subsided.

But the pilot light of rage was ignited in Dan Phillips, and from that day forward he could do nothing to put it out.

"I will kill her," he said to the empty room.

Chapter Three

VANISHED

The phone numbers for her father's three worksite trailers were on speed dial, thank God. Joanna had no idea where he would be today, or any day, for that matter. Her fingers trembled as she pressed 1 on the car phone.

"Hello," a gruff voice shouted at her from the other end of the line. She thought it was Gus, the jobs foreman who had worked for her father for as long as she could remember.

"I need to speak with my dad. With Dan. It's Joanna." She was surprised to hear that her voice was shaking.

"Joanna? Oh, sure. Hold on, honey," the man said and roughly put the receiver down. In the background she could hear the sounds of heavy equipment and men shouting to be heard over the noise. Joanna struggled to calm her breathing while she waited for her father to come to the phone.

Forty minutes ago her anger at her mother had transformed to a fury with each quickening step she took through the mall's main thoroughfare. Turning her head from left to right, her eyes scanned each storefront. Where the hell was she? Joanna was already late for practice, and of course the selfish bitch had probably not given that a thought while she chatted with a neighbor, or no, more than likely with some of her mall rat students.

The Mill Springs Mall did not have an expansive footprint like those gigantic ones that you found in Buffalo or Erie. Still, Joanna's anxiety about being late to practice grew as she looked at the Sears on one end to the JC

Penny at the opposite end. Smaller shops lined the three hallways that intersected the main thoroughfare. She rushed past the first one that led to the food court; Grace hardly ate a thing these days. Waldenbooks was a place her mother frequented, and Joanna peered through the window. She could see all the way to the back of the store where the children's books were. No sign of Grace. Forget the Sharper Image. Bath and Body Works was a possibility. Joanna's allergies were triggered as she raced from the front to the back and then to the exit, with no sign of her mother. Nike. That's right! The twins had ordered new baseball cleats. Was she picking them up right now? Was that the errand she had mentioned? Joanna hadn't been listening. Her mother's voice these days triggered something awful in her, and as soon as she started talking, Joanna did her best to zone out. From the front of the store, she could see Troy Benjamin, their neighbor who had dropped out of college and was working there now. Joanna would not normally have spoken to someone like Troy. He was a loser but still way cooler than Joanna. But in her desperation, she practically sprinted up to him.

"Hi, Troy. Have you by any chance seen my mother?"

She could have been a Martian by the look he gave her. "Uh, who's your mother again?"

Embarrassed, her voice cracked as she said, "Grace Phillips?"

"Oh, yeah, course. Mrs. Phillips, Grace. She's a nice lady. No, sorry, I haven't seen her today. There's an order here for her, though," he said, bending down and shuffling through some papers under the counter. Joanna was gone by the time he looked up again.

Toys 'R Us to the right, Spencer's to the left; no, neither of these were likely places for Grace to frequent. Claire's, no, Grace thought the stuff they sold was chintzy, even though her daughter loved it. Camelot Music, no, Deb's Boutique, no, Victoria's Secret – yes, she could be in there! Joanna wove through the aisles filled with women and girls, none of whom looked like the gigantic posters of VS's fleet of supermodels. Up and down the narrow rows she went, glancing at the patrons who perused the shelves of thongs, crotch-less panties, and garter belts. No Grace anywhere. Sweating and red-faced the girl retraced her steps through the mall twice more, but her mother was nowhere to be found.

She must be back at the car by now! Of course! Breathing heavily from the exertion of her trip through the mall, Joanna pushed on the heavy main entrance door, and escaped the smothering warmth of the place. As she ran to the parking lot, she tried to comfort herself. She would play The Game! She laid out the rules. After thirty steps, she would close her eyes, open them, and then see her mother's silhouette behind the wheel of the van. Of course Joanna would be relieved, but she wouldn't show it. She would open the door and blast her mother with her fury. Thirty steps later, she was almost to the van.

Her mother was not there.

She looked at her watch and a flood of panic took over. They had been here an hour and a half for a fifteen minute errand.

She was sobbing by the time Gus picked up the receiver again. "I don't see him right now, Joanna. He had a meeting with some other contractors after he did an estimate for a job at noon. He's not back yet. Let me see if I can get a hold of him for you. What do you need, honey?"

"Tell him I'm at the mall! Tell him to come and get me at the mall! My mom is gone!"

Chapter Four

SALMON RIVER

Brad Childs was freezing. It was his own fault, but he was in a mood to blame this misery on his father. Yesterday, he resisted his dad's packing advice and left his cold weather gear at home. Standing at the river's edge twelve hours later, unprotected from the wind and pummeled by the late March sleet, Brad's face was a frozen mask of resentment.

His foul mood was exacerbated by exhaustion. Last night, he'd tossed and turned in the bottom bunk of the largest bedroom in the cabin. Throughout his childhood, the soft mattress lured him to sleep at the end of those happy days, but last night he was restless and agitated. Rolling over, he glanced at the clock radio. One-thirty in the morning and he was still wide awake.

When his father brought him a cup of black coffee at four AM, he drank the whole thing with his eyes shut. He pulled on his clothes and waders in the dark, and by sunrise, he was grudgingly following his father to the shoreline. From the corner of his eye, Brad watched his dad as he waded thirty yards upstream carrying the oversized salmon net.

For the first time since they had been coming to the river, his son had not joined him at the cabin's oak table last night as he worked on making and tying the flies. That had always been something father and son loved doing together, but Brad was so pissed at him, he kept the door to the bunkroom closed in protest. Now at the river's edge, he pretended not to hear his dad when he told him to be sure to rub some of the slimy salmon sac on his bait. Instead, he cast the line with the dry fly at its end.

Brad couldn't remember ever being this angry with anyone, and especially not with his father. Late yesterday afternoon, with less than a half-hour's notice, he'd dragged his son from their Westfield home three-and-a-half hours north to Salmon River. It made no sense to the seventeen-year-old. There were still five days of school left before Easter Break. His grades were not that great, and missing this much time wasn't going to help his third quarter average. The two colleges that were still interested in having him on their football squads weren't going to be impressed with this hole in his attendance record. But Ben Childs could not be crossed. He was the ultimate authority in Brad's family, and even though his wife had argued that Brad should not miss a week of school, the father and son were out the door and in the car heading north before she had finished trying to reason with her husband. Silently fuming throughout the ride, at dusk Brad found himself lugging backpacks, rods, and tackle boxes into the cabin his grandfather had built decades ago.

In the past, the family outings to the small lodge in Pulaski with the bountiful river running through the property thrilled Brad and his little brothers. He had inherited his father's and grandfather's love for the outdoors, and except for football, he loved sport fishing more than anything. When his grandfather was alive, he had shown the boys how to make and tie their own flies. The ritual of pulling on waders and casting his line gave Brad so much pleasure and contentment, just as it had done for their father when he came home from Viet Nam, his grandfather had told the boys. Now, the whole thing had become a time-consuming ordeal that Brad had avoided for the past couple of seasons, but yesterday his father insisted that the salmon were running like never before and that this sudden trip up north would be the best yet.

As a younger kid who had been diagnosed with ADD in elementary school, Brad found a welcoming calmness in the flow of the river and the fishing ritual. His father called it being in the zone. Standing knee-deep in the cool, clear water, Brad didn't think about how difficult school was for him. He forgot about the teasing and mocking, the calls of "*Hey, Ge-*

nius. Hey, Weirdo! "Hey, Faggot!" that came from the open windows of the school bus as he walked toward his house. All that misery was forgotten at the river. And the shaming stopped entirely the minute he caught his first touchdown pass. By the time he was in high school, his circle of friends grew, and he had lots of girls interested in him, too. He still struggled academically, but the newest prescription his doctor had put him on was helping him focus better. And since Grace Phillips had come into his life, everything about his world seemed perfect.

Wavering unsteadily in the strong riverside wind, he concentrated his thoughts on Grace. He was sure she was thinking of him, too, wondering why he wasn't in school. Brad pulled up his parka sleeve and glanced at his watch. His stomach flopped as he realized it was third period. The time of the day he looked forward to most. Until recently, it had been a whole hour spent only with her without having to worry about the questioning glances from kids and teachers, the ones they often faced as they walked down the hall together or stood at Brad's locker. And then just after Christmas break, their privacy was invaded by Jack Woodhall, a student teacher who had also been Brad's assistant coach on the football team. "He gives me the creeps," Brad told Grace.

"What do you mean?" Grace asked.

"He's weird. The team had to put up with him hanging around the locker room a little too long after practice, and now he seems to think he can interrupt my Resource Room time with you!"

Grace pressed her leg against his and her pine and soap smell enveloped him. "Oh, Jack's fine. He's just lonely, that's all. He and I have a couple of classes together at the college, and we talk during our breaks. He's very dedicated to becoming a good teacher."

Brad snorted. "He'll never be as good as you!"

When Grace had been assigned to be his aid at the beginning of the school year, she was the third one in his four years of high school. He was stunned by her beauty from the moment she introduced herself. "Hello, Brad." She put her hand out and he stood with his mouth open, staring.

"I'm Mrs. Phillips. We're going to be working together this year." He managed at last to clasp her hand in his and shake it.

"Phillips? Are you related to the twins?" he asked. He felt like an idiot as soon as the words came out of his mouth. What a stupid question! She was way too young to be the mother of junior high kids.

"Yes," she said. He loved the sound of her voice. It was soft and raspy at the same time. "They're my sons. And Joanna is my daughter. She's a sophomore. Do you know her?"

Dumpy Joanna Phillips was this sexy woman's daughter? Joanna was in his biology class. He was retaking it to change the D on his transcript at his father's insistence. When the girl sat down in the seat next to him that first day, he asked her to be his lab partner. Her face turned bright red and she nodded yes. From that day on he noticed that Joanna seemed to be everywhere he was. Whenever he caught her eye, she would look away. He'd glance over his shoulder and see her walking behind him in the halls, or he'd feel like someone was watching him, and sure enough, from two tables away in the cafeteria he'd catch her staring at him. She seemed like such a loner, and Brad felt sorry for her. He hadn't forgotten that feeling of being considered a loser. So during their labs, he would joke around with her, although he couldn't tell if she appreciated his sense of humor. Her face would turn bright red whenever he spoke.

"Yes," he said, staring into the smiling hazel eyes of Joanna's mother. "I know your dau…Joanna." He felt the old signs of shyness creep up his spine. He was practically tongue-tied in this beautiful woman's presence. Although Brad had a girlfriend, by October Grace was all he could think about. He told Annie Wentworth that he needed to break up with her to allow himself more time for football, and also, this would be his final year to get his transcript in order. But the truth was that by then there was no room in his life for anyone else but Grace.

School had always been a challenge for Brad. If it hadn't been for his athleticism, he would have probably dropped out in his junior year. Grace made everything about his subjects understandable and relatable, especially English, which he had hated since middle school. He actually raised his hand last week and offered an opinion. Of course, it was Grace's explanation as to why Hamlet did not kill the king as soon as he knew that his uncle had murdered his father. But she had made him understand how someone could feel conflicted, undecided, and so when he was called on, he said so. Mrs. Ruckland paused and stared at him for a second before she commented. "That's a very interesting, theory, Brad. Good thinking."

The first time he had kissed Grace was behind the screen that cordoned off a private study space in the Resource Room. He had followed her there, and when she turned from the desk where she had laid a stack of papers, he moved close to her and asked the question with his eyes. Seconds passed and then her silent answer sent an electric shock through his body. His tongue was deep inside her. Her arms around his neck caused his scalp to prickle, and radiating warmth traveled to every part of his body. He pulled her closer and breathed her in. He stroked her hair, her back. He was trembling. When the long kiss ended, he caressed her shoulders and then he turned her around. While he gently clasped her breasts and moved against her, he kissed the top of her head.

When he looked back on this first physical encounter with Grace, he marveled at how the awkwardness he typically felt in the beginning with girls was not at all a part of what he experienced when he was with her. These kisses and embraces came so naturally for Brad, who had been a virgin until one evening last winter at Lake Erie State Park. Just after the sun set, they made love in her car. Brad told her that he loved her that night. Since then, he had suggested several times that they meet at a motel in Buffalo, but Grace said that the time wasn't right for her to be gone that long. She was afraid her husband would become suspicious.

From that night forward, Brad spent much of his days and nights in a convergence of ecstatic love for Grace and a sickish sense of longing for her. It killed him anytime he had to be away from her, which was almost all of the time that he was not in school. When they were together, Grace insisted that they had to be more careful. Since that night at the park, he noticed that she often resisted his attempts at intimacy. When he asked her what was wrong she said that Coach Woodhall had actually questioned her about the amount of time she spent helping one kid.

And then the graffiti began to appear all over school. Carved into desks in the senior wing, spray-painted in red in the second floor boys' lav. *Grace sucks senior dick, BC is fucking Hot Mama, Brad is a mama's boy.* After that one appeared in foot-high letters in the locker room, Mr. Harding, the principal, called him into his office. Brad denied knowing anything about it, but still the bastard had called his parents to "make them aware" of these incidents. Ever since then, his father hardly let him out of his sight. And now he had practically kidnapped him and taken him to Salmon River.

He stayed inside the cabin while his father cleaned the catch. There was no television; his grandfather had been adamant about that. Old paperbacks lined the shelves of an oaken bookcase. Brad picked up several and glanced at the snippets of plot summaries on the backs, but he couldn't concentrate and the words made no sense. There was no mobile phone reception, and the landline had been disconnected after his grandfather passed away. Brad felt the panic rise. What was Grace doing right now? What was she thinking about his absence?

He began to pace. From the main room to the kitchen to the bunk room, he made a frenzied circuit. Finally, he threw himself down on the lower bunk. He turned to look at the old clock radio on the bedside table. Shit! It was only two o'clock! He was a prisoner in the place that used to set him free. The room was closing in on him. His father had been in such a hurry to leave home, Brad had forgotten his meds. Out of focus to the point of panic, he reached out to the radio dial.

For as long as the family had been coming here, the thing got only one AM station out of Syracuse. Static filled the space in the room and Brad turned the volume down on a local car dealership commercial. He tried to concentrate on the words in the stupid jingle so that he could stop the dread from rising further. "Breathe," he said aloud. He closed his eyes and because he had only had a few hours of sleep, he started to drift off. Corny pop music from the 50's and 60's soothed him, and he slept. He was dreaming of Grace, her eyes, her smile, and then someone called her name.

"Grace Phillips, 35, a Westfield resident, has been reported missing since Friday by her husband. State Troopers from the Syracuse and Buffalo barracks were dispatched to the small town in Western New York yesterday. The woman was last seen at the Mill Springs Mall by her daughter. The girl informed police that her mother told her she had a very quick errand to run. An hour later, the girl searched the mall, but could not find her mother."

Brad sat up and turned the volume to maximum. "The only trace of the missing woman is a high heel found near the mall fountain. Mrs. Phillips is five foot five with hazel eyes and dark hair. If you should have any information about her whereabouts, please contact..."

Brad bolted from the bunkroom and collided with his father. "Where is she???" he screamed into his face.

PART TWO

MARCH, 2017

CHAPTER FIVE

WING NIGHT

"YOU CAN DO this, Merrill!" Kate shouted over the Journey tune blasting from the jukebox.

"You *should* do this, Merrill!" Sherry said. "Look at everything you've accomplished during your career, all the research you've done for other people's projects."

Jenna leaned in and gave Merrill a meaningful stare, but her tone was gentle. "You gave Richard everything you had to give these last couple of years... It's your turn now."

Their Thursday night gathering at Larry's almost always proved to be inspirational in some way for the circle of friends. It was at this table three years ago over pitchers of Southern Tier IPA that Jenna had revealed her first piece of Lake Erie sea glass jewelry. Sherry had been in the midst of pouring their first round when she spied the dazzling red pendant. "My God, Jenna! Where did you get that amazing piece?"

"I made it," the retired chef and restaurateur said, basking now in the warm admiration of all the friends. The three women knew that Jenna had walked the Lake Erie shore for years, picking up the multi-colored little treasures and throwing them into an old pickling crock she kept by her back door. What they didn't know until that Thursday is that she had also put on her flippers and swum out to Van Buren Bay to harvest the hidden gems that hundreds of casual collectors would never find on the shoreline. She hadn't told her friends until that night that she had been taking a class in jewelry design at the Arts Alliance. The red pendant had been her first effort. From that point on, Jenna's "hobby" had turned into a highly valued artistic endeavor, as well as a very lucrative one, too. Her first customers were residents of the local lakeside communities, but after the launching of her website, she received orders from all over the country.

A few months after Jenna had revealed her jewelry-making pursuit, the four friends were once again gathered at Larry's when Kate announced that she, too, was exploring a post-retirement career option. She had decided that the occasional gig at jazz clubs in the area was not enough to feed her hunger to compose and perform music. The manager she had hired had booked her for several out-of-town engagements, and this spring, she would be going on tour for three months. The friends were happy for her, of course, even though they feared that she might not return to their small town life. But she did come back after that first successful tour, and when they met for wings she proudly revealed the recording contract she had landed. The friends were thrilled for her success and happy that she was still in her place on Third Street when she wasn't recording in Nashville or L.A. or doing business in New York.

Sherry, who had left the SUNY accounting office five years before to start her own theme-based travel agency, astonished Merrill and the others with her recaptured vitality. She had shed ten years since she had transitioned to this new job and lifestyle. Her business took her around the country and beyond to international destinations as she researched possible vacation sites for her clients.

Merrill's three best friends were women of a certain age who had entered Phase Three of their lives. And unlike far too many of their peers, they were more visible, more viable than ever. They had retired from careers that they loved or hated, and had forged new paths. On this particular Thursday night, Merrill looked around at each of the three, and she knew they were all having the best time of their lives. Maybe it *was* her turn, at least to try.

"*Don't stop believin'*" Steve Perry sang.

"Okay, which one of you chose this sappy song?" Merrill said. "It's going to take a lot more than believing in myself to pull this off."

"I'll help you with the technology end of things. We'll design a website for you…" Sherry said as she reached for her last atomic-sauced wing.

"And I'll compose a riff for your opening and closing. Every podcast has a signature musical piece," Kate said.

"Will you broadcast from home?" Jenna asked. "Maybe from Richard's studio?"

Merrill felt her face flush at the mention of her husband. The Shed, dubbed so by Richard, still showcased his paintings, photographs, and sculptures nearly three years after his death. His kiln had gathered a thick coat of dust. Merrill had just recently moved off the couch in his studio and back into their bedroom to sleep. "No," she said composing herself. "I'm pretty sure they'll let me use a little space in the basement of the library. There's a small storage room that will work, and since I've been volunteering there a couple of days a week, I have a key, so I can come and go as I please."

"All done, ladies?" their waitress asked, slinging cardboard containers spilling over with chicken bones onto her tray.

"Let's have one more round to celebrate Merrill's new journey," Jenna said.

Merrill loved the invincibility she felt when she was with these women. They had been as supportive as friends could be as she nursed Richard during his losing battle with ALS. They visited as often as they could, even near the end when other friends did not have the courage to witness the hell Richard and Merrill were going through. These women believed she had the strength to face those long days and nights, even though she herself didn't think so, and they had been right. And now they believed she could do this.

All Merrill knew about podcasts she had learned by being widowed and subsequently becoming a faithful fan of several. *Serial, This American Life, One Great Book, The Teacher's Pet, My Favorite Murder, The Dollop* were a few of her favorites. A voracious reader since childhood, lately she found it almost impossible to concentrate on the words on the page of a book.

Since Richard's passing, especially in the evening, Merrill craved the isolated intimacy of ear to headphone. These programs, each in their own way, gave her so much. They filled up some of the empty spaces that belonged to a widow who had loved and been loved. The hosts ignited her brain with ideas that she had never thought about, and they offered the what if's and the why not's that she and Richard had challenged each other with in the days when conversation had still been possible for him.

One recent evening when her youngest child had come for dinner, she shared with Jason how much she enjoyed spending her abundant free time listening to them. "I'm afraid I'm getting a cauliflower ear from the headphones," she said.

"I'll get you some nice earbuds," he said. From the time he was a preschooler, this boy, now on his way to thirty, had seemed to "get" his mother. Her daughters, each of whom lived hundreds of miles away, had been there for her and their father in those final days. Since then, they came home for holidays only, and spent the majority of those visits in Richard's studio, admiring his great talent while reminiscing about their childhoods, a time when they had basked in their father's love. Mickey and Dina shied away from Merrill, steering clear of her grief and loneliness, as though they might be contaminated by it. Jason, on the other hand, had become almost obsessively attentive to his mother. Recently, she had told him that he did not need to stop in so often or to call her daily. "You have a life of your own. I want you to enjoy it," she told him.

As he sat across from her in the breakfast nook, a combination of joy mixed with relief came over her son's handsome face. "Mom! You could do your *own* podcast! You were a college librarian doing the research for professors and students for about a hundred years! And now in your free time you're volunteering at the Prenderson Library. You've got the hard part down, lady!"

"No," she said, "I couldn't..."

But he cut her off quickly. "Yes, you could, Mom! The technology is really pretty simple, and I could help you with that..."

"Jason, you have a life…"

"Just until you learn how to do it yourself," he assured her.

That night after Jason left, she sat in her husband's studio and thought about her son's words. What he had said made a lot of sense. She already possessed the research skills it would take to delve into almost any topic. And because of her former profession she had become a decent public speaker, too. An advantage would be that during a podcast, she wouldn't be facing hundreds of college freshmen in the auditorium as she explained rudimentary research techniques. Besides, her days and nights were so long without Richard. What else did she have to do?

Merrill called Jason the next day. "Teach me how to be a podcaster, please," she said.

Chapter Six

PODCAST #1

"Yes, I do believe Paul and I were in love. From the first day we met."

Jenna, Kate, and Sherry sat at Jenna's kitchen table and leaned closer to the wireless speaker as they listened to the woman's wistful voice. "And in a very unique sense, we were still in love the day he died decades later."

"Hello, folks," they heard Merrill say.

"There she is!" Jenna said as Sherry and Kate high-fived one another. "Quiet! We agreed no comments until after," she added.

"Welcome to the first episode of my podcast. I'm Merrill Connor, your very excited and somewhat nervous host, coming to you from the basement of the Prenderson Library in beautiful Westfield, New York. Before we hear from my guest tonight, just a little bit about me. Research and digging have always been a passion of mine. As a research librarian for SUNY Fredonia for thirty years, I got to marry that obsession with a profession. I explored books and documents and sometimes primary sources to get the answers to the questions of students and faculty, and I loved my job. Now that I'm retired, I get to choose the topic to explore each week for this broadcast...oops, podcast."

Merrill paused long enough to take a sip of water. Her voice had stopped shaking, thank God. Her son had told her that in the future anything could be edited out if need be, but she felt pressure to get it right the first time. She didn't want to waste his time.

"Lately, I've been spending a lot of hours in the local history section of our fine library, and the materials I've found have given me a lot of fodder for excavating deeper. Tonight, with the help of Susan Brown Fortney, my guest for this first episode, I'd like to take you on a journey back in time, before I was born, but a time that some folks in Westfield might remember still. Back in 1943, when Americans were fighting against Hitler's forces in Europe and the Japanese in the Pacific, Westfield, along with dozens of other towns throughout New York State and the nation, employed and housed German and Italian prisoners of war. In those days, once our servicemen left their jobs to serve overseas, the Bertram Mill in Westfield stood empty. And so the plant was retrofitted as a dormitory to house the three hundred or so German prisoners who were brought to the states to make up for the labor shortage on our farms and in our processing plants. For this first episode of my podcast, I talked to Susan Brown Fortney about her very personal experience with one of these prisoners." Merrill pressed the link to her recorded interview with her first guest.

"Paul and I met on our family's farm, in our hayfield, to be specific," Susan said. "I was fourteen and up until that summer, my job was to drive our old flatbed truck while my brothers and uncles threw the heavy bales that would later be loaded into the barn for the livestock. That particular August day was brutally hot as August can be, and because my brothers and uncles were all overseas, my dad had hired five of the "campers," as he called them, to help. Paul Strouse was one of them. He was the tallest of the five men and very handsome. He had deep-set green eyes. And a wonderful smile. Our eyes met often that first day. I kept looking at him in the rearview mirror as I drove."

Merrill asked, "So was it love at first sight, Susan?"

"It was something I had never felt, before or since, that's for sure," her guest answered.

"Did you speak to one another? Or was that not possible due to the language barrier?"

"Actually, we didn't speak that day, even though I would later find out that Paul had a very good grasp of the English language. He had studied it in high school and in his first year of college. Academics ended for him, though, when he was drafted into the Wehrmacht, the German army."

"So after your hayfields were harvested, when was the next time you saw Paul?"

"Merrill, it's a good thing I kept a diary for years, including those days when Paul was in my life." Her laugh was warm and infectious.

"Would you mind telling the listeners your age, Susan?"

"Not at all. I'll be eighty-nine on my next birthday. I'm a lucky woman. The body is breaking down a little each day, but I've still got pretty good vision. And my diary fills in some of those memory gaps that come along. You were asking about the next time I saw Paul."

"Yes," Merrill said, "tell us about that, please."

"Oh, my God! She's a natural," Jenna said. There was a long enough pause for the friends to agree that Merrill was terrific.

"Well, that would have been during grape season," Susan continued, "and again, in spite of the fact that all of my aunts and cousins came to our farm to harvest the Concord grapes, we were struggling to get them all in and sent for processing. In those days, of course, the picking was done by hand with those old metal cutters, one bunch at a time. That next time that I saw Paul was on one of those beautiful September days that we get around here. The sky was blue and cloudless, and there was no wind in the vineyards. My mind was wandering as I basked in the sun. The work was hard, but hypnotic, and according to my diary, I was lost in some kind of daydream, when suddenly, there he was looking down at me and smiling. I'm sure I must have jumped, I was so startled."

'Ready?' he asked.

"I was so shy in those days and he had appeared out of nowhere, I couldn't say a thing. He pointed to the bushel I had been filling.

'Yes,' I stammered. "I was just overwhelmed by his beauty and kindness, and I wrote about this little exchange we had in true 1940's Hollywood style. I'm sure it's embellished, the way a fourteen-year-old might do, but in essence, I recognized that he was the first man that I had ever been attracted to in this way. The harvest went on for three more weeks, and during that time, I couldn't wait for the school day to end so that I could get to that vineyard. So I could see him again." The old woman's voice had become almost melodic as she continued telling her story.

"Did your family know that you were falling in love with this stranger?" Merrill asked.

"Oh, no! How could I possibly tell them? After all, our family, like most American families during this time, was torn apart because of Germany's actions overseas. My brother and several of my cousins were serving in the army on the European front. Paul was their enemy because of where he had been born. And I was very young. Too young by their standards to be in love with anyone. I couldn't possibly tell them what I was feeling. Only my diary knew."

"Susan," Merrill said, "please tell our listeners when it was that you saw Paul again after the grape harvest was over."

"Oh, months passed. I never stopped thinking about him, though. That spring, I started riding my bike the three miles to school so that I might catch a glimpse of him. The Bertram Mill was a few blocks from school, and for the entire month of May, I would ride past the barb-wired enclosed yard where the prisoners would sometimes be exercising. As I pedaled toward the Mill one day on my way home from school, I could see dozens of prisoners walking in the yard. The closer I got, the more I felt someone watching me. I was still pedaling when our eyes locked. I stopped and Paul came closer to the fence so that we could talk.

'What is your name, please?' he said immediately, as though he had been planning to ask me this since the grape harvest.

"Susan," I said.

A wonderful smile spread across his face. 'Susan,' he said. 'Beautiful.'

"My heart was pounding and I was shaking. I gripped the handlebars of my bike to steady myself. 'I have to get home,' I told him. I couldn't believe how my voice trembled. I don't even remember the ride back to the farm. But I do remember that each day after that I got up earlier and waved the school bus on. Even when it rained, I rode my bike so that I could ride by the Mill. Most days, Paul was not there, but when he was, he would try to get close to the fence so we could speak."

"What did you talk about, Susan?" Merrill asked.

"Well, our conversations were very short because the POW who was in charge of the men in the yard was constantly watching us. I asked Paul about his family. He asked me about mine. One day he looked at the books in my basket and asked me what I liked studying. Another day he told me he had loved school and missed it very much. I told him his command of English was amazing, and that Latin was my least favorite subject. But Merrill, please understand, Paul and I really didn't have the luxury of getting to know one another well. Some days, he wasn't in the yard, and I would be so disappointed. And when he was there, our conversations were limited to one or two sentences. And then I went to church one Sunday, and I discovered that there was a way to see Paul for a longer stretch of time and on a regular basis."

"Your heart found a way, right, Susan?"

"Well, my fifteen-year-old year old heart was in love for the first time, and so yes, my heart and mind conspired and found a way to see Paul. It was after mass that morning when I noticed a line of ladies and girls in the back of the church. A classmate of mine told me that they were signing up to serve meals to the German POW's in the basement of the church hall. I tried to hide my excitement as I followed her. When I reached the table, I found that there were still several shifts left, including some breakfasts and dinners. School was out for the summer, so I signed up for both, knowing I would have a better chance of seeing Paul if I did. "

"And did your plan work, Susan?"

"Oh, yes. I saw Paul several times during those meals. I made sure of that. And that summer is when our written correspondences started. Each time I came to his table on the pretense of clearing it, Paul would pass me a note, and I would leave him one. I still have those summer notes."

"Really?" Merrill sounded delighted. "How many are there?"

"Thirty or so. I keep them in plastic sleeves in a three ring binder, along with a hundred or so letters he wrote to me over the years."

"Amazing!" Merrill said. "What did you and Paul write about in those early days?"

"Well, at first, we shared details about our families. About our siblings, and what life was like at home. I told him about school, and I talked about what I wanted to do when I grew up. I had always wanted to work with children, and of course, as some of your listeners may know, I did become a teacher. Paul loved languages. And he eventually made a career as a linguist and translator. But that came years later. That summer, he was very homesick, but his letters to Germany and his family were often censored. I think those letters to me were his only outlet for sharing the sadness he felt being so far from home." Susan's deep sigh brought tears to the eyes of Merrill's friends.

As Susan told the story of their relationship after the war, how she and Paul stayed in touch for five decades, how each married, and as widow and widower, how they had reconnected in Paris fifty-five years after they had fallen in love, Merrill's friends were spellbound.

"Susan, how do you explain this connection that you and Paul had as young people up until his death last year? Here you were a young American teenager, and Paul was, let's face it, considered an enemy to everything you had been taught to believe in. And yet..."

"And yet, we loved one another," Susan said. "We were just a boy and girl in love. He was a person, not my enemy. From the beginning, I never viewed him as anything but a kind, intelligent, sweet human being. And our nationalities were beside the point. We loved one another and we became lifelong friends. It was one of the greatest blessings of my life, Merrill."

As Merrill brought the interview to a close, promising her listeners they could go on the podcast website to read several of Susan's "summer letters" from Paul, Jenna popped the cork on the prosecco.

"She's back!" she shouted to Merrill's cheering circle of friends.

Chapter Seven

BEGINNINGS, ENDINGS, BEGINNINGS

"Merrill, you were great!" Jenna lifted her glass and toasted to something the three friends had been praying for these many months. "To Merrill's podcast! To new beginnings!"

Merrill took her place in the circle, beaming. When Richard died, her heart and mind had blocked any expectation of happiness in her future. For two years, she was crippled by the loss. She could never have imagined during that painful time the joy she would feel tonight.

Richard and Merrill had met on campus decades ago when she was an English major and he was a grad assistant in the Art Department. Her roommate, a visual arts major, had invited her to the spring senior exhibit where three of her works were being showcased. Merrill had a final paper due in her American Lit class the next day, and she hadn't even started it, but she agreed to go for one glass of wine to show her support. True to her word, she had shown up, stared admiringly at her roommate's pieces for a few minutes, and plastic wine glass in hand, took the obligatory stroll around the circumference of the gallery. She was heading for the exit when she noticed a table in the far corner that held several wheels of cheese, baskets of crackers, and bowls of olives. The dining hall was closed and Merrill had not eaten a thing since breakfast. She made a beeline for the table, grabbed a paper plate, and began piling the little orange and white squares onto it.

"Does all this art whet your appetite?" Merrill twirled around and saw the source of the voice. She had seen this guy around campus and he was definitely her type. Muscular and long-haired. Big brown eyes. Faded jeans, white shirt, sleeves rolled up to reveal a green beaded bracelet.

"Yes, it does," she said. "Grab another plate and load me up, would you please? I've got a paper to write."

It was their first interaction and their connection was immediate. By that fall they were together all the time, and when Merrill moved to Buffalo for the Library Science program at UB, he loaded up his AMC Hornet, and joined her. From their tiny West Side apartment, he commuted to Fredonia for those two years. They were married the day after she received her degree. Merrill was hired as a research librarian at Fredonia for the fall semester. Throughout the decades, their love and marriage had fortified them as they raised their three kids and built fulfilling careers at the college. Many of the couples they knew at the beginning of their relationship were divorced by now, and those who had long-standing marriages like theirs had lapsed into a kind of numbing co-dependency. But the Connors had a fluid love that allowed their friendship to deepen and grow over those thirty years.

Early on, the symptoms of Richard's disease went almost unnoticed, but they eventually became hard to ignore, especially in his classroom. He joked about the weakness in his hands while one of his students took the remote from him and clicked through the slides of the art of Northern Italy. When his voice cracked and changed pitch in the middle of a lecture, he laughed it off, telling his classes that he was younger than he looked.

The diagnosis, when they finally got one, did not surprise either of them. It was the quick onset of the more debilitating effects of ALS that shocked them. When the muscles in his legs began to atrophy, Richard steered a shiny red scooter into the seminar room, his eyes conveying the good humor his students had come to expect from him. Many of them were upset when at the end of that semester he had turned in his retirement letter. The university council worked quickly to bestow upon him the Professor Emeritus status. "That's the college's version of a death certificate," he joked to Merrill.

"You'll have more time to work on your own projects now," she said.

"More time? Honey, if I could get that…" He smiled, but it tore her apart to see the tears shining in his eyes. Merrill took a leave of absence from the library to care for him. She wanted every minute of this last chapter to be spent in her loving company. She was a true fan of her husband's artistic talent, and now she was witnessing his drive to beat an ultimate deadline.

Although his preferred medium was sculpture, in his last year, that had become impossible. Instead, his final piece was a watercolor of a falling woman, tiny in relation to the deep blue ocean surrounding her. Merrill recognized immediately that Richard's subject was not a helpless drowning victim, but rather a free diver. Extreme athletes in every sense of the term, these divers from all over the world swam into depths that seemed impossible, with no breathing support or gear of any kind. The Connors had watched a Netflix documentary on the extraordinary competitors and from that point on, Richard could not read enough about the subject. When he'd finished watching all of the videos on YouTube, he started all over again. Merrill suspected that as her husband's body declined, he was more and more fascinated by these divers who challenged their own physiology. Diving to profound depths, holding their breath for extraordinary amounts of time, they defied their mortality with each leap into the sea.

Richard became totally absorbed in trying to capture this phenomenon in his painting, spending hours each day in the studio working on it. One day as Merrill walked quietly behind him with his lunch, she saw that his arms were at his side. His hands rested on the arms of the electric wheelchair he had finally accepted as his way to attain some mobility. She stopped and held her breath when she noticed that his shoulders were strangely hunched as he leaned toward the canvas, mere inches away from the painting. She watched, puzzled, as his head moved slowly, first up and down and then side to side. "Richard, what…" Merrill walked to the other side of the easel.

He opened his mouth and dropped the small brush into his lap. "Giving my hand a rest," he said dismissively as she continued to stare at him.

"Don't look at me like that, Merrill, please. I've always told my students to use whatever works. That's what I'm doing."

To the untrained eye, Richard's last painting was finished by the time he passed away two months later with the kids and Merrill by his side. But to his wife, the work seemed incomplete. There was something about the diver's body. The position of her left foot raised almost parallel with her nose as she held the crouched position, her right foot and her arms outstretched. The dive was not quite final. The woman was suspended in the bottomless blue sea. It seemed that she would be diving forever.

Merrill didn't tell her family or her friends this, but the painting terrified her. In spite of its negative power, she spent hours staring at it. She could relate to the ever-falling body, to the diving down, always down. When Richard died, the heavy grief that sat on her chest day and night smothered her every passion, her own desire to live. She went back to work for a couple of months, but everything about the familiar campus tore open the deep wound of her grief on a daily basis. In the staff cafe, through the throngs of students heading to their classrooms, walking through the aisles of the library, she looked for him still, but of course, he wasn't there. Merrill applied for retirement at the end of that semester.

She began to spend all of her waking hours in her husband's studio. It became impossible for her to fall asleep in their bedroom. Most nights she curled up on the old sofa that the dogs had claimed during the days when her husband could still work. During Richard's decline, she had somehow managed to stay focused on him and his needs and refused to succumb to the depression that many caretakers of ALS victims dealt with. But after his death, she plummeted into despair. Her kids were so worried about her, they each offered to move in. But that was the last thing she wanted. Merrill did not want to be distracted by anything or anyone. She wanted to give herself over to the terrible sadness that engulfed her.

Her son and daughters were helpless in the presence of this ghost who had been their vibrant mother. Grieving themselves, they were relieved when one night while they were at their mother's place, Jenna, Kate, and

Sherry banged on the outside door of the studio. The dogs went wild with barking, and wouldn't stop until Merrill let the women in. Technically, it wasn't an intervention, but a week later, her three friends joined her at a grief support meeting at the community center, her first time outside of the house in months. From that point on, one or the other of them picked her up and went to the group with her. Months later, when she claimed she had taken everything these other grievers had to offer, they were ready for her. Kate handed her a card with her psychiatrist's number. "You earned a lifetime of great medical coverage from the college," Kate said. "It's time to use it."

Merrill could hide for the most part in the group situation, but she was resistant to facing this shrink on her own. She made the appointment anyway, mostly to prevent the annoying phone calls and her friends' frequent and unannounced drop-ins. The doctor suggested they begin with twice a week sessions, and by her second month in therapy, she insisted to her kids and her friends that she would drive herself.

By the second anniversary of Richard's passing, she was beginning to crawl out of the immobilizing sludge of depression. Until the sessions with her psychiatrist began, she had felt invisible and worthless. But lately, she told her friends, she was starting to feel a pulse. She began to face the fact that although Richard was gone, *she* was still alive and healthy. Besides, the three women would not leave her alone unless she reconciled herself to that and all of the possibilities that came with the realization. And here they were tonight, two years later, surrounding her with love and support and raised glasses. "I have an announcement," she said, looking from one to the other as she spoke. "I've decided on a name for the podcast."

All three women responded at the same time, their eyes on their friend. "What is it?"

"The inspiration comes from Richard's last painting. I'm calling it *A Deeper Dive,*" she said.

CHAPTER EIGHT

A DEEPER DIVE

MERRILL TOOK A sip of wine and looked at the expression of expectation on each friend's face. Having given birth to her new venture with the encouragement of these "midwives," it made sense that naming it would be done while in their company. "I've been doing some research in our local history archives, and they're overflowing with potential subjects. But I want the podcast to delve beyond the surface of the available facts," Merrill told them.

"Like you did tonight in your interview with Susan!" Kate said.

Before Merrill had time to respond, Sherry said, "Ah, I get it! *A Deeper Dive*. That's brilliant, Merrill!" With every encouraging phone call and all the Thursday night conversations at Larry's, Sherry made an effort not to patronize her friend. Torn apart by her own ex-husband's infidelity followed by an ugly divorce, she understood loss. And she recognized when people were bullshitting her about how "sorry" they were. Her enthusiasm for her friend's new path was genuine.

"I'm going to aim for doing live interviews whenever possible. The Prenderson director has been wonderful. He's letting me use that little storage room in the basement after the library closes, so I have a place to bring my interview subjects. The elevator came in handy for Susan when I interviewed her last week."

"Fantastic!" Jenna said. "You were great at asking Susan just the right questions and giving her the space to not only answer, but to go beyond."

Merrill took a deep breath and reminded herself once again how lucky she was to have these women in her life.

Her first podcast and the women's encouraging critiques marked a turning point for her. As the sun came up each morning, for the first time since Richard's passing, she was eager to get out of bed and start her day. Over the next weeks, she spent hours doing background research on her upcoming topics. Although most of the time she could be found in the stacks of the local history section of the Prenderson, when she went to the grocery store, the dry cleaners, the bank, she was greeted by people she knew and a few strangers too. "Great podcast, Merrill."

Kate and Sherry's businesses and artistic endeavors often took them out of town, but when they were in Westfield, their monthly podcast listening parties were at Jenna's house. Merrill's friends continued to be delighted with her new-found passion and the part they had played in making it happen. They were elated when Kate's original jazz piece, "Free Dive," played before the opening segment of podcast number two. From that episode forward, it became a mainstay.

"She's so good!" Jenna said, after Merrill had explained to her listeners the title she had given to her project and how this broadcast would be a deeper dive into chapters of their local history.

"Shhh!" Sherry was particularly interested in tonight's topic. She had done some research of her own on the nearby town of Brocton's mayor, Phillip Worley, who, while he was in office in the mid-sixties, was discovered to be a three-time bigamist. Because of her own cheating ex, Sherry was fascinated with this infamous philanderer. Merrill had given Sherry a heads-up about her interview with the politician's granddaughter.

"I'm not sure what he told my grandmother," said Laura Penn, responding to Merrill's question. Merrill said nothing, waiting out the seconds in silence. "As far as my mother and her siblings know, Grammy was clueless about his other two families. One was in Albany and the other in New York City, and in those days, even more so than today, that distance was prohibitive. They believe Gram died certain that she and Papa had had an ideal marriage. But I'm not so sure."

"I can see you're tearing up, Laura. Take a moment," Merrill said.

"I'm sorry. I was very close with my grandmother. She was amazing. A role model for me and my sisters and to think that he..." The woman paused and Merrill's friends were again impressed with her well-placed silence. "Is there anything worse than a loved one betraying your trust?" Laura asked Merrill and all of her listeners.

"No," Sherry said aloud. Turning to the group she said, "This is what makes Merrill so good. She shows you the way to the minds and hearts of the people she interviews. And that leads you to go inside your own. I'd be a fan even if she weren't my friend."

One of Kate's favorite episodes of *A Deeper Dive* was with a California woman. Cheryl Taylor was an expert on Spiritualism who Merrill had tracked down, even though she herself was a skeptic regarding psychic powers. But Kate was a devotee of the Lily Dale culture and belief system. Several times a year, she would book a reading with a medium there.

Because of the geographical challenge, Merrill broke with her favored routine of live interviews and instead, recorded her phone conversation with the author, an expert on the subject. "Spiritualism," Merrill began, "in the 1920's and '30's was followed and practiced by many Hollywood types, is that correct, Cheryl?"

Her guest picked it up from there. "That's right, Merrill. Studio heads and movie stars were captivated by séances and readings with these mystical types. And apparently, Aidie Livingston, from Westfield, New York, was one of the most sought-after mediums of her time."

"Amazing!" Merrill said. "What can you tell my listeners about her, Cheryl?"

"She was an incredible character. Aidie was a poor immigrant from Hungary who grew up to rub elbows with the rich and famous in America. Charlie Chaplain, Ava Gardner, and Tallulah Bankhead were among the many Hollywood stars who consulted her before they accepted a movie role. And her persuasive powers with many actors went beyond professional advice into their personal lives."

"Did she travel all the way from Westfield to Hollywood to consult with them?"

"Initially, no. At that point in her life, she rarely left town for any reason. Because of the time zone difference, the celebrities often came to her in the dead of night. By rail, by private planes, oftentimes when they had been in New York City doing a play, they would hire cars to come to her in Westfield. But eventually, Aidie moved to Hollywood where her wealthy clientele lived."

"Did she use a crystal ball?" Merrill chuckled softly. She was having a hard time being objective and muting her skepticism on this topic. She and Richard shared the belief that there was more than likely nothing awaiting a person when he or she died, except an opportunity to support the flora and fauna left behind.

"Sometimes, yes, other times she used tarot cards. But most of the time, she held a piece of the person's jewelry in her own hand during one of these sessions."

"I see. Go on, Cheryl."

"She read tea leaves, too. That's why Aidie was responsible for several highly visible celebrity divorces at the time. She could see their partners' infidelities in the bottom of a cup."

"And she had their trust to the extent that they would divorce their spouses?" Merrill sounded shocked.

"Oh, yes. And it wasn't just matters of the heart she delved into. She also would advise them on their financial holdings. And this is how smart, or conniving, depending on your viewpoint, Aidie was. She made her fortune this way."

"Truly?" Kate's brow wrinkled in concentration as the expert answered Merrill.

"Oh, yes. The investments she encouraged a certain segment of Hollywood royalty to put their money into were undertakings she was very much involved in. The owners of these enterprises cut Aidie in on the action when she brought a stakeholder to them. She would often invest her own money in these very companies."

"Ah, ha! So she was a shyster as well as a Spiritualist," Merrill said. "Just how wealthy did she become?"

"Very," Cheryl Taylor said. "Until the stock market crash in '29 ended that. Aidie came back to Westfield in 1930 and moved in with a cousin. In 1932, she died penniless."

Merrill couldn't help herself. "I guess she should have seen that coming, no?"

Everyone in Jenna's living room exploded with laughter. Everyone except Kate.

Cheryl Taylor's amiable chuckle soothed Kate's ruffled feathers. "So Merrill, let me ask *you* a question."

"Go for it," Merrill said.

"You live less than thirty minutes from one of the oldest and most venerable Spiritualist communities in the nation. Have you ever had a reading in Lily Dale?"

"I haven't. Should I?"

"You absolutely should!"

"Yes, she should," Kate said, "and I'm going to make sure that happens."

Chapter Nine

RIDING WITH KATE

Kate turned the radio down as Merrill buckled her seat belt. "Are you ready to have your mind blown?" she asked her friend.

"I'm ready. And I can already make a prediction before we even get to Lily Dale."

"And what would that be?" Kate asked.

"That in a couple of hours I'll be saying, 'I told you so' to a dear friend."

"You can be quite the smartass for a librarian, you know that, Connor?" Kate said a silent thank you to the universe that she could once again pull her friend's leg without worrying that Merrill was too fragile to take the ribbing. This repartee had been a part of their friendship for years, and Kate was happy to have their good-natured joshing restored.

"Kate, you know how I feel about this Lily Dale hocus pocus. But for your sake, and even more so for the sake of doing primary research for the podcast, I do thank you for being my tour guide today," she said, reaching out to pat her friend's hand.

"Fantastic! An ethanol-free gas station in the middle of nowhere," Kate said as she made a sharp right into the County Seat Kwik Fill.

"This isn't nowhere," Merrill admonished her friend. "It's beautiful downtown Mayville!" As Kate eased the sports car up to the pump, Merrill jumped out and said, "I need water. Do you want something?"

"Brought my own," Kate said as she held up what looked like a gallon-sized YETI with "All that Jazz" sprawled across it.

A family with five young children cut Merrill off as they raced each other to the door of the convenience store. "Sorry," their haggard-looking father said as he passed her, taking longer strides to catch up to his kids.

"No problem," she said, wondering what it would be like in this day and age to raise such a brood.

As she held the door open for them, something affixed to the window caught her eye. In the middle of the gaudy beer and cigarette ads was a scotch-taped 8X10 piece of paper. Taking up the top half of the crude poster was one word. **MISSING**. Merrill stopped and read the rest of the notice. *Sarah Ingham, 15 years, last seen, September 6th, in Mayville. If you have any information about her disappearance, contact Samuel Ingham on Open Fields Road.* At the bottom of the page was a blurry photo of a young Amish girl. Her hand was held up in front of her face, obscuring all of her features except her eyes. Was she waving to the photographer? Or attempting to cover her face? Merrill had a vague recollection that Amish folk did not permit themselves to be photographed, so perhaps that was the reason.

"The poor kid," Merrill muttered as she walked into the store. She did a quick calculation. Today was September 8th. Missing two days. Her scalp prickled as she contemplated the possible explanations for the girl's disappearance, all of them horrifying. On her way out of the store, with the large family pushing and shoving each other behind her, she resisted the temptation to take a picture of the poster with her phone.

"Everything okay?" Kate asked as Merrill slid down into the soft leather seat.

"Yes," she answered, attempting to shake off the feeling of uneasiness the poster had given her.

As they rode, Merrill and Kate admired the perfect fall afternoon. The leaves on the trees were just beginning to turn, hinting at the future golds, reds, and oranges that would emerge soon. The maple and oak branches reached up to the blue sky and seemed to touch the expansive white clouds. "No power lines, just Mother Nature's beauty everywhere you look," Merrill commented.

"That's why I'm going to take the back way," Kate said as she swung a quick right onto a partially paved road. Her red Z4 climbed the knolls and hugged the curves through Amish country. At the crest of a steep hill, a buggy full of Amish teenagers blocked their way, and Kate slammed on her brakes. She pulled the car over to the shoulder and the women waved as the youngsters passed them. "Kids!" Kate said, shaking her head.

Merrill leaned back against the seat and closed her eyes. The third anniversary of Richard's death was next week. She missed him terribly, but as each day passed, the jagged edge of grief dulled somewhat. Her friends, her work for the library, and the podcast were crucial in restoring her sense of well-being. As the sun shone down on her, she said a silent prayer of thanksgiving. Just then, Kate nudged her shoulder. "Hey, don't fall asleep," she said. "You're missing the beautiful scenery!"

Merrill opened her eyes in time to see the pasture of grazing cows and horses ahead. Kate slowed down, and the women smiled as they watched a very new foal trot by his mother's side. Behind the creatures stood a large red barn with a handcrafted sign that read EGGS. "These are the views I miss when I'm in the studio in L.A. or Nashville," Kate said, speeding up again. As they drove, they saw more white farmhouses with buggies in the driveways. They passed iron-framed signs advertising a quilt shop, a black-smith's barn, and a produce stand. "Slow down, please. I could use some veggies," Merrill said.

Kate parked the Beamer in front of a quaint wooden farm stand. When they got out of the car, they were delighted by the sight of two beautiful children, a boy and a girl, neither of them older than seven or eight. They stood at silent attention behind a handcrafted oak counter as the two women selected peaches, melons, late season corn, and herbs. "Yum! Who made the pies?" Kate asked the small cashiers, picking up a blackberry one before either could answer.

"Our Grohs-mammi...our grandma," the little girl said, translating for Kate's benefit.

Merrill juggled the produce as she approached the counter. Before she set it down, she was startled to see the same poster she had seen at the convenience store. The eyes of Sarah Ingham seemed to stare back at her once again. The little girl took the melon and the corn from her, her serious expression out of sync with her young age. "Do you know Sarah?" Merrill asked. The child lowered her eyes and then turned to look at the boy.

He nodded and said, "Der Gschwisderkind."

"Our cousin," the little girl said.

She wasn't sure why, but at that moment, Merrill felt that she urgently needed to have that piece of paper. "May I have this?" she asked.

"Ya," the little girl said, handing it to Merrill. From under the oak slab, the little boy pulled out another one and placed it carefully on the counter.

Kate insisted upon paying for all of their purchases, and as the children put the produce in her shopping bags she asked them, "How do you say thank you?"

"Denki," they said in unison.

"Denki," the women called back, walking to the car.

"That might not have been the best idea," Kate said as she loaded their purchases into the BMW's trunk.

"The pie, you mean?" Merrill asked. Her friend had been on a diet throughout most of the three decades she had known her.

"All of it," Kate said. "We may have wilted basil and warm pie by the time we leave the Lily Dale grounds."

"No worries. They'll be fine. We'll be out of there in an hour's time," Merrill said.

"No way," her friend answered. "How do you expect us to have readings in fewer than three hours?"

"Hmm," Merrill answered. "We'll see. What do you make of this?" she asked Kate as she slid in behind the wheel. She passed the piece of paper to her friend.

"Sad," Kate answered. "The community must be desperate to find her, although I'm guessing they probably haven't notified the police. They typically handle legal matters themselves," she said, passing the poster back to Merrill.

"Do you think she was taken?"

"Who knows? Maybe she just ran. She's too young to be on a Rumspringa venture," Kate said. "That happens when a sixteen-year-old begins dating and other "explorations," if you get my gist. Maybe she didn't want to wait another year to have an adventure." She handed the poster back to Merrill.

"How do you know so much about the Amish?" Merrill asked her friend.

"We had an Amish cleaning lady…in my first life, that is. I'm sure I drove her nuts with all the questions I had about her culture. I was so bored in those days. In the long run, Greg did me a huge favor when he left. I was so blocked creatively and in every other way while we were married. So instead of playing and composing on my weekends back then, I pestered Corrine about what her life was like."

"That sounds like you," Merrill said, folding the piece of paper and putting it into her bag. The car dipped smoothly over the next rise, revealing the noonday sun shining brilliantly on Cassadaga Lake. "Ooo, that's a great shot," she said. Merrill reached for her phone in time to capture it.

Kate didn't respond. Merrill turned toward her friend and noted the look of intense concentration on her friend's face. She had seen it many times before and it meant that she was hell-bent on something. Sure enough, she ignored the yellow light at the intersection of Route 60 and turned left. "Almost there," she said as she followed the signs to the gates of Lily Dale.

CHAPTER TEN

MEDIUM

KATE PULLED THE BMW up to the white iron gate of the Lily Dale grounds. "Good afternoon, ladies." The pleasant man in the booth took their entrance fee and handed them two pamphlets. "So the best things in the Afterlife are *not* free," Merrill joked as she put her credit card back into her wallet.

"Don't start," Kate said. "You promised you'd keep an open mind."

"I will, I will," Merrill said, although for most of their trip, her mind had been somewhat preoccupied. Since opening the convenience store door, she had been mulling over the many reasons why Sarah Ingham could have disappeared. This brand of gnawing curiosity was organic for Merrill. She had possessed it or it had possessed her from childhood on. Eventually, it led her to library school and to a long and satisfying career. But for Kate's sake, she must push the nagging questions away and try to take this Lily Dale experience seriously. Besides, although Merrill was definitely a skeptic, the hope was that this visit might give her some material for her *Deeper Dive* podcast.

Merrill was surprised that the Beamer could actually slow down to 5 MPH, but Kate kept it in first gear as she crawled down Cleveland Avenue. They passed the Mystic Bookstore and the Crystal Cove Gift Shop, the Southern Comfort Inn ("Does the ghost of Janice Joplin live there?" Merrill asked an annoyed Kate), and a dining hall with the day's menu posted on a large white board standing beside the entrance. Beyond the few commercial establishments were the neighborhoods. Lining the village streets were modest 19th and 20th century houses, many with white picket fences outlining their small lots. Humble only in architectural style, every one of the places seemed to have a vibrantly blooming garden. There were statues of angels on most of the properties who shared their domains with an impressive menagerie of ceramic animals. From exotic cats to mundane rabbits, they were everywhere. "Animal spirit guides," Kate answered when Merrill asked about their significance. Signposts advertising the mediums' names and hours of availability stood in front of almost every little house, many of which were painted in a full range of purples.

"Ooo, that one is purple *AND* lavender," she said to Kate, who gave her friend a warning glance.

"I'm going to park so I can read the directory and see if I can locate the woman I've been to several times in the past. I heard she's moved since I was last here. I really like her," Kate said. "After Greg left, she encouraged me to be bold. I'm sure I got my first record contract because of her."

Well, at least there's that, Merrill thought. She was so proud of her friends. Each of them had struggled but eventually found the courage to begin a second chapter in her life. As for Kate, newly divorced with a nest recently emptied, she had summoned her nerve and taken a huge risk. She could have stayed safely cloistered in her high school music classroom until retirement. Instead, she submitted a recording of three of her piano compositions to an agent in New York who agreed to manage her. Merrill didn't know that Lily Dale had had anything to do with her decision to start over, but when Kate was offered a record contract, she didn't hesitate to take it.

She pulled into a spot in the parking lot of a small lakeside park. Merrill watched a gull land on the grass in front of them as Kate studied the pamphlet. "Oh, here she is!" she squealed with delight and pointed to something in the guide book.

"Who?" Merrill asked.

"Victoria Erikson! She's definitely the one. Second Street is right around the corner." She raised the convertible top and practically hopped out of the car. "Let's go!"

Merrill followed a few steps behind her friend but she could plainly hear her humming as she charged up the hill to Second Street. "What's that tune?" Merrill asked her when she caught up.

"Something I've been working on for a week. I want to run it by Victoria!"

"Oy vey," Merrill muttered.

"What's that?" Kate asked.

"Nothing. What address are we looking for?"

"Thirty-two Second Street. We're almost there," she told Merrill.

Birdsong, yapping dogs, and boat motors were the background sounds of the place. It could have been any lakeside community in this part of New York State, except that it was bustling with dozens of spiritual seekers, mostly women, who they passed on their way to find Victoria. "This place must rake it in," Merrill commented. Kate totally ignored the remark.

"This is it!" she said.

Victoria Erikson's home was a turn of the century cottage painted, what else, Merrill thought, the deepest of purples. Angel sculptures were planted amidst the thick ivy that substituted for a lawn. The two women stood and stared at the vibrantly yellow front door. "Can you read that from here?" Kate asked her friend.

Merrill had to squint to make out the words on the metal placard that hung on the door. "Come inside and ring the doorbell. I'll be right with you," she read aloud. Kate pushed past her and led the way, and before Merrill could say anything, her friend was turning the ornate brass doorknob.

Two very large orange cats lounged on a sofa in what turned out to be the sunroom of Victoria Erikson's cottage. The bright yellow shades on each window prevented the medium's clients from being seen by passersby, and in this September sunlight, the room seemed to glow. Kate looked from one end to the other. "Yes, this has to be her place. I recognize the tabby cats." She pointed to a small table near the entrance to the house. "Sign us in, please." Without waiting for Merrill's response, she reached out and turned the crank of the old-fashioned doorbell.

Merrill picked up a clipboard from a table covered in Irish lace. She was suddenly nervous. "Cats. Typical," she said, as one of the two orange tabbies brushed up against her leg. Sarcasm always seemed to settle her nerves for some reason. "Where's the black one?"

"Shh! I hear footsteps," Kate warned.

The door opened and Merrill's expectations were shattered. This tall, elegant woman was not the crone she had imagined. Her blond hair was in the kind of classy French bun that girls used to wear on prom night. She wore a paisley sarong, purples outnumbering the other colors. Smiling warmly she said, "Hello, ladies. What can I do for you today?"

"We'd like readings," Kate said.

"I'm not sure..."Merrill stammered.

"She's sure," Kate told the woman.

"You're in luck. I've just had a couple of cancellations. Who wants to go first?"

"She does," Kate said, firmly nudging Merrill over the threshold.

As the woman led her into her home, Merrill's eyes struggled to adjust to the dark space that was Victoria Erikson's parlor. Thinking about the lawsuit she would file if she tripped and fell, she suddenly realized that she still had her sunglasses on. She slid them onto the top of her head and as she followed Victoria, she gazed around the small room at what must have been hundreds of knick-knacks on every table and doilies on the back of every chair. There appeared to be no wall space that was not covered in paintings of cats and dogs and framed cross-stitched renderings of Jesus.

"We'll be sitting in here," the woman said, indicating an open door. Merrill entered a small room that was devoid of any of the fussy décor she had seen in Victoria's parlor. A picture window was covered with plain linen drapes that blocked any trace of sunlight. A desk lamp on a table in the corner was the only light source. "Please. Make yourself comfortable," the woman said, indicating the upholstered chair positioned in front of a small table. Victoria glided to the other side of the table, her sarong swirling around her ankles as she passed Merrill. "Have you ever had a reading before?" she asked as she seated herself.

"No, and I've lived in the area for decades!" Oh great, Merrill thought, I've already spilled the beans about something essential. I'll be the easiest mark she's had all day.

"Well, that's fine," Victoria assured her. She put on a pair of readers and looked at the info she had copied from the clipboard. "*Mrs.* Connor?" Merrill paused. She wasn't going to provide her with any more information than she had already.

"Merrill," she said, returning the woman's cordial smile.

"Merrill! That's a beautiful name from Middle English. Did you know that it means, "sparkling sea?" she added.

"I didn't," Merrill answered, and left it at that. She wasn't going to explain that Merrill was her maternal grandmother's maiden name and that she had been named after her. As far as she knew, her parents had been totally unaware of the name's etymology.

Obviously undaunted by her new client's terse responses, the medium continued in her cheerful tone. "Let me explain my approach, Merrill. I'll try to keep it simple and I'll answer any questions or concerns you might have before your reading begins."

"That sounds fine," Merrill lied. Nothing about this felt fine.

"I'll open our session with a prayer. As you may know, Spiritualists do follow the traditions of Christian doctrine. We believe in an Infinite Intelligence and the teachings of Jesus Christ. We believe that the precepts of healing and prophecy that you find in the Bible are proven through Mediumship."

"*You are getting very sleepy...*" Merrill said to herself, picturing Victoria swinging a huge gold pocket-watch in front of Merrill's face. Why was she being such a wiseass? For the sake of doing a good investigation for a potential podcast, she needed to be more open-minded. She was very nervous, she had to admit. Maybe that was why she had plagued Kate with sarcasm all day. She sat up straighter and vowed to take this more seriously.

"Mediums have a gift imparted by God," Victoria continued. "We act as a channel for information between the Spirit and Earth Planes. We pray, train, and practice so that we can become expert at communicating with Spirit through various forms of phenomenon. Some mediums use cards or objects owned by a departed loved one. I like to use a piece of jewelry from a client if it's possible. Is that something you'd be comfortable with?"

Merrill felt a thud of panic in her chest. With her thumb, she began to twirl the ring she had moved to her right hand shortly after Richard's death. As was typical of her, it was the only piece of jewelry she wore today. The thick gold band was inset with six medium-sized garnets. Her young husband-to-be had designed the bands which had been worn by each of them for decades beyond their wedding day. Richard's was buried with him. Merrill thought the ring was extraordinary and when Richard said he wanted to give her a diamond for their twenty-fifth anniversary, she had turned the idea down. "No. I love my garnets, thank you," she had told him.

Victoria held out her hand and Merrill reluctantly took it. Bowing her head and closing her eyes, the medium said a short prayer, not a word of which Merrill could recount after. Victoria let go of her hand and extended hers, palms up. "A piece of your jewelry, please?"

"I only have this," Merrill said, twisting the ring from her finger and handing it to the medium.

"Garnets!" Victoria exclaimed. "Perfect!"

"What do you mean?" Merrill asked.

"In the Torah, it is written that Noah needed a source of light in the Ark."

"Wait," Merrill said, "the Torah?"

"Yes, Spiritualists are interested and open to all religious traditions beyond Christianity. The Torah says that the Sun and Moon didn't shine during the time of the Flood, so Noah brought a garnet on the Ark that shone more brilliantly by night than by day. The gem helped him to distinguish between day and night. Its significance as a source of light is prescient as we begin to try to understand the messages of Spirit today. Please feel free to take notes," Victoria said, sliding a piece of paper and a pen across the table. "Some clients even record their readings."

When Merrill didn't respond, the medium continued. "Merrill, I'd like to welcome Spirit to come into our session now, if that's okay with you."

Prickles erupted on Merrill's scalp the same way they did when she was a kid. Any time she challenged herself to try something she was afraid of, like riding the Comet at Crystal Beach, or ice skating on the semi-frozen pond in their backyard, it happened. She tried to breathe more deeply so she could answer Victoria Erikson, but she couldn't seem to inhale fully. She finally got the words out. "I'm not sure what that means, but okay."

Victoria's right elbow rested on the table as she held the ring in the grasp of her three fingers. Her eyes were closed as she spoke. "Someone is coming in. A woman. Helen or Helene? She's walking with a cane. Do you know anyone who has passed on that would fit that description?"

"No," Merrill said, and almost immediately her anxiety subsided. She willed herself to relax and enjoy the sideshow that was about to take place in this tiny room.

"She may be a deceased relation that you never knew personally, but she wants to be here," the medium said. "She has a message for you." Several seconds later she added. "She's telling me that you need to eat more leafy greens. And now she's walking away."

Merrill didn't blame Helen/Helene. She was ready to bolt from this room, too. How was Victoria keeping a straight face through this routine of hers, she wondered. Merrill pursed her lips to keep from giggling.

"Wait. She's still here. She says you've been given a wonderful gift. You have some powerful psychic powers yourself, if only you'll open yourself up to that blessing, she says."

Oh, brother, Merrill thought to herself. Why didn't I hit the record button on my phone? This was too good not to share with her friends.

"Ah. Helen has left," Victoria said. Her eyes remained closed and she was rubbing her thumb over Merrill's wedding band. It seemed like several minutes had gone by before she spoke again.

"I see a man." She paused for a few seconds. "He is in a museum or gallery. There are sculptures, paintings all around him."

Merrill's heart stood still. She pressed her fingernails into her palms and told herself to breathe.

"He's a loved one who has passed over to Spirit. Am I right?" she asked Merrill.

"Yes. Richard," was all she could manage to say.

"Richard. He says he's very proud of you."

Merrill felt like her ears were filling with water. Had she heard her right? She leaned forward as far as she could. Suddenly, she wanted to hear every word this woman had to say.

"He says, you're very brave. And very inquisitive. Curious." Another interminable pause. "Yes, he's proud of your curious nature. Always has been, he says."

The room felt like it was closing in on the two of them. Merrill couldn't prove that the walls weren't actually moving. She could hear the medium's every inhalation and exhalation. The smell of her Jasmine cologne was suddenly overwhelming.

"Have you been swimming recently?" she asked. "Or diving? He says… yes, he says you're diving deeper."

Christ, what was happening here?

"You will help people with this diving, he says."

"What!?" Merrill felt like she might pass out.

"Someone is missing, he says. A girl or a woman, perhaps. You can find her, he says."

"Stop!" Merrill shouted.

Victoria's eyes flew open. "What is it, Merrill?"

"Give me my ring, now! PLEASE," she heard herself beg.

Victoria handed her the wedding band and stood. She hurried to a wall switch, and a second later, the overhead fixture lit up the room. She turned and saw her client, ashen-faced, staring closely at her garnet ring.

Merrill's hand was trembling. What was happening to her? A split second before the light came on, she saw an inner glow coming from the garnets. Inside each radiant gemstone was a girl. Sarah Ingham.

She understood why the girl's hand was raised. It was clear now, thanks to Richard. The girl was waving at Merrill.

Chapter Eleven

THEY ARE OUR NEIGHBORS

"They are our neighbors. Some of them are our friends. A great many of them have shared their labors and their skills, made beautiful pieces of furniture for us, created masterful quilts for us, built us barns and sheds, satisfied our hunger with delicious baked goods and home-grown produce. And a month ago, after attending a prayer meeting a half a mile from her home, one of their beloved children disappeared."

Merrill paused and Kate's original theme song swelled as it did after each of the podcast lead-ins. The piece lasted just long enough for Kate to pour herself a glass of wine. She was at home, a listening party of one tonight. Sherry was in South Carolina scouting out a couple of potential Airbnb rentals for her clients and Jenna was taking a week-long class from a silversmith at an artists' alliance in Buffalo. Kate suspected that her two friends were listening to *A Deeper Dive* from wherever they were.

She picked up her phone and the glass of rose' and walked out to her deck. The sound of Merrill's voice coming out of the quickening darkness from her outside speaker made her feel anxious somehow. Maybe it was because Kate knew first-hand what a harrowing episode this would be.

"My guest tonight on *A Deeper Dive* is Sheriff John Lovallo who was instrumental in finding Sarah Ingham and safely returning her to her family after she had been missing for three harrowing days. Welcome to the podcast, Sheriff."

"Yes, Merrill. That's true," Kate said aloud. "The sheriff did help. But how about giving credit where credit is due? A certain Lily Dale medium deserves a shout-out, too."

Kate would never forget the look on her friend's face that day as she burst through the screen door and into Victoria Erikson's sunroom. "We need to go. I'm not feeling well," Merrill said.

"I'll call you and make an appointment soon, Victoria. So sorry," Kate said, setting down one of the tabbies who had found a comfortable spot on her lap.

She didn't catch up to Merrill until she reached the parking lot. She was leaning against the car in a way that made Kate think she might faint without the support. She unlocked the doors and once her friend had slid into her seat she spoke. "What's wrong, Merrill?" she asked as each of them adjusted their seat belts. Merrill turned her face toward the car window and said nothing. Kate was stunned by her friend's behavior, and she felt responsible for whatever had happened to her inside Victoria Erikson's reading room. In spite of an urgent need to ascertain what had taken place, Kate held her tongue. The silence between the two women on the first ten minutes of the ride was deafening,

When Kate could no longer stand it, she asked again. "What did Victoria say that was so upsetting? Was it something about Richard?" she asked.

"I don't want to talk about it. Just get me home, please," Merrill said. She sounded so desperate, Kate gunned it and flew over the hills and around the curves. She reached the Westfield village limits in record time.

"Merrill, I'm sorry you're upset," Kate said.

"Not your fault," Merrill answered, practically leaping out of her seat as Kate pulled into her driveway. Merrill grabbed her bags full of produce. "Call you tomorrow."

Kate was shocked when she did call at 6 AM the next morning. Merrill had skipped "hello" and gotten right to the point. "Are you doing anything today?"

Kate was two steps beyond groggy. "What day is it?"

"Sunday. Let's go see Corinne," Merrill said, matter-of-factly.

"Corrine?" Kate said, trying to open her eyes to read the time on her phone.

"Yes. Your former cleaning lady."

"Merrill! What's going on?" Kate asked, more mystified than annoyed.

"When can you get here?"

"Give me an hour," Kate answered.

"How about a half an hour?" It was more of a directive than a question.

"Jesus, Merrill, not even the Amish are up before seven!" Kate said.

"Not true. I've been awake half the night reading about them. I'd be willing to bet a lot of money that Corrine is on her way to a prayer service as we speak," Merrill said.

Forty-five minutes later, Kate pulled the Z4 in front of the Bylers' farmhouse and the two women scanned the driveway. "No buggy," Merrill observed. "Let's cruise down the road. Wherever we see more than one or two buggies, that may be where we'll find Corrine," she said with authority.

As the Beamer crawled along Open Fields Road, Merrill stared at each house and barn, telling Kate to slow down whenever she saw more than one vehicle and horses tied up to a fence or tree nearby. A mile or so beyond the Bylers' place, Merrill counted ten vehicles in the driveway of a home with a huge red barn in back of it. "Stop!" she said, and Kate pulled over onto the shoulder of the road under a large pine stand.

"Can you please tell me what's going on, Merrill? Does this have anything to do with your reading yesterday?"

Merrill ignored the second part of Kate's question. "I can't get the Ingham girl out of my head. From the minute I saw that poster, I've had a feeling that I just can't shake. I feel like she's close by...that's she's waiting to be found. It dawned on me at about 4 AM that Corrine may have some information."

Kate avoided saying out loud what she was thinking. For a librarian and a skeptic, Merrill certainly seemed to believe in hunches. A loud, metallic screech interrupted her thoughts, and the two of them watched as dozens of men, women, and children filed out of the barn.

"Do you see Corrine?" Merrill asked.

"No," Kate answered, but a moment later, she watched as her former employee herded her children out of the barn and followed her husband Jacob to their buggy. "Yes! There she is," she told Merrill.

"Let's turn around and follow them," Merrill said.

"Perfect timing," Kate said as she performed a U-turn and pulled behind the Bylers' vehicle. In the middle of the slow parade of Amish, Kate kept a safe distance. Two of Corrine's little boys, black hats on their heads, sat backwards on the buggy's narrow back board and smiled broadly at the sports car. "Those guys were toddlers when I last had Corrine cleaning for me."

"They're adorable," Merrill commented.

The horses were unnerved when the powerful Beamer pulled into the Bylers' driveway. Jacob calmed the animals and then waved at Kate. "Hello, friend," he called to her. Corrine was busy gathering her children out of the buggy, but when she looked up, a smile spread across her face.

"Kate!" she said. "How nice to see you!"

The two women exchanged a warm embrace. Kate was a habitual hugger, one of the qualities Merrill admired in her. Her own residual shyness seemed to surface when she was in the company of strangers. She hung back for a few minutes while Corrine filled Kate in on her children's advancing ages. "Yes, Abigail turned thirteen in June. She's not home yet. She stayed at the prayer service."

"Thirteen! Unbelievable!" Kate said. "Corrine, this is my friend, Merrill Connor." That seemed to be all the explanation Corrine needed about the stranger's presence.

"Hello! Come inside, ladies. Jacob has coffee going and I baked yesterday. I hid a dozen or so donuts from the children." Merrill followed Kate's lead as Corrine walked them into her home.

The white clapboard walls and ceilings were washed over with the sunlight coming through the bare windows. Merrill was surprised to see a refrigerator in the corner of the spacious kitchen. Then she recalled that her research had informed her that natural gas, rather than electricity, powered the few appliances that the Amish relied upon. Corrine opened a pantry and reached to the highest shelf and took down a Tupperware container that held the donuts that people traveled miles to find.

"Sit down, please ladies," she said, indicating two hand-crafted wooden rocking chairs and a love seat in the main living room. Merrill watched from the parlor as their hostess poured three cups of steaming coffee. She was charmed and heartened by Corrine's welcoming attitude, but she was anxious to find out what the woman knew about Sarah Ingham's disappearance. As soon as she joined them in the main living area of the farmhouse carrying the mugs on a tray, Merrill began.

"Corrine, you mentioned that you have a thirteen-year-old daughter. Does your girl know Sarah Ingham?"

The seconds of silence that fell over the room were palpable. Merrill wasn't sure what she had said to turn Corrine's face beet red, but her hospitable tone changed to mistrust in that moment. "Why, yes. She does, of course. Why do you ask?"

"I'm wondering what you can tell me about Sarah. You see, I have a podcast, a program on the internet, and I'd like to use it to help Sarah, perhaps help the community to find Sarah." The autumn sun had slid behind a bank of clouds and the bright room darkened. How could Merrill explain to this woman what she couldn't clarify for herself? That she had received a message from her dead husband? That she had a vision of Sarah in her garnet ring? That she *must* try to find Sarah Ingham?

"But our minister told us this morning that the Sheriff may be called in soon," Corrine said. Merrill could hear a tinge of resentment in her tone. "We always handle the few crimes we have in our own court system. But a child gone missing....it's something I can never remember happening in our community. And so the Bishop has suggested turning it over to the English, er...to the Sheriff. But no one has come to see us. And our Abigail was...is...Sarah's closest friend." The distinct sound of cartwheels on the stone driveway interrupted Corrine's explanation. "Oh, that's Abigail now."

The young teen walked into the kitchen and stopped abruptly when she saw the two women in her parlor. "Come here, girl," her mother called. "Do you remember Miss Kate from town?"

"Yes. Hello." Kate was on her feet before the girl could say another word, arms extended, rushing in for the hug.

"Abigail, you're so grown and so beautiful!" Kate said.

"This is her friend, Mrs. Connor," her mother said, gesturing toward Merrill.

"Please, Abigail, call me Merrill...or Miss Merrill, if that's okay with you."

"Miss Merrill is looking for Sarah," her mother said.

"Oh."

Merrill's interview expertise was needed here. But she wasn't sure that her talent was a match for the recalcitrance of a teen. She would try her best. "Your mom tells me that you and Sarah are close friends."

"Yes."

Okay, Merrill, she told herself, Richard or whomever or whatever had said that she should dive deeper. That she could help people. So dive in she did. "When was the last time you saw her, Abigail?"

Abigail was silent, staring down at the floor. Finally, she spoke. "Three days ago at prayer meeting. She left early. That was the last time anyone saw her."

"Was it unusual that she would leave early?"

"Her mudder was sick and she needed to check on her, she told me. Her fater had her little sisters and her cousin in the cart, so she was going to walk." Merrill noticed that Abigail became a bit more animated as she told the story.

"How far is her house from the prayer service?" she asked the girl.

"A mile. Maybe less."

"Would you be willing to take me to the prayer service location? And show me the way Sarah had to walk to get home?"

Abigail looked at her mother. "Yes, you may," Corrine said. "But I'll drive the cart. We'll not all fit in Miss Kate's fancy car. John," Corrine called up the stairs to her son. "Come and hitch up the buggy." Abigail's older brother appeared seconds later and hurried out the door without a word to the assembled group. Kate climbed in beside Corrine, and Abigail and Merrill sat on the cushioned back seat.

Within a few moments she discovered she had to shout to be heard over the wheels and the horses' hoofs. And Kate's chatting in the front seat. "Do you mind if I close these?" Merrill asked the girl, pointing to the heavy curtain between the two seats.

"No," the girl said.

Merrill pulled on the black fabric. "Abigail, what can you tell me about Sarah and her family? Does she have any brothers or sisters?"

"Three sisters only. She's the oldest," the girl answered.

"What about her parents? What do they do?" Merrill asked.

"Her mother is very sickly. She's expecting another baby this winter. That's why Sarah had to take over as bookkeeper for her father's business."

"Oh? What kind of business does he have?"

"He's a builder."

"What does he build?"

"All kinds of things," the girl answered, "barns and sheds and other kinds of storage buildings."

Merrill felt the carriage slowing down. She parted the curtains and leaned forward to hear what Corrine was saying. "This is the Weinheimers' where the prayer service was held. The last place Sarah was seen was walking off their front porch." She pointed to a large gray farmhouse. Merrill felt her heartbeat quicken.

"Was her family not with her?"

"They were, but their carriage was crowded, like I said. They had a cousin visiting from Ohio and the three little girls. Sarah told her father that she would walk and meet them at home," Corrine answered.

"Corrine, can you take us to the Ingham residence?"

"Yes, indeed. Mr. Ingham and Sarah's sisters were at the service this morning, so they may not be home just yet. But I'll take you there." Kate lifted the curtain and gave Merrill a questioning glance at the same time that Corrine uttered something in German to the horses.

Merrill nodded at her friend. Yes, she wanted to keep going. She couldn't stop thinking about her garnet ring and Sarah Ingham's frightened eyes. The horses started again, and as they jolted along, Merrill calculated how long it would take a healthy young girl to walk a half mile. No time at all. But someone that morning had stopped Sarah from reaching her home.

Merrill looked out the isinglass window at the beautiful countryside. They passed a little shanty in front of a sprawling farmhouse that was obviously not an Amish residence. There were several cars and motorcycles in the driveway, and the little children playing soccer on the lawn were not dressed in customary Amish attire.

"What's that little building there, Abigail?" she asked.

"It's a phone booth mainly for business calls or emergencies. Some of the English farmers had it built." Before Merrill could ask the girl any more questions, the horses came to a halt.

Through the black fabric, Merrill heard Corrine say something to Kate, and then the curtains parted. "Merrill," Kate said, "it looks like the family is here. Corrine wants to know if you want to meet Mr. Ingham."

"Yes!" Merrill's voice was pitched to be heard over the road noise. "Yes, I would," she said in a more suitable volume.

As she climbed out of the cart, Merrill saw the iron-framed sign: *Samuel Ingham: Builder.* An etching of a barn on a mahogany panel was a work of art in and of itself. A tall man in his late thirties opened the front door and strode off his porch. Samuel Ingham's jacket was off and his suspenders lay against an expansive chest. As he came closer, Merrill saw an expression of what she imagined to be chronic worry on his face.

"Hello again, Samuel," Corrine said before introducing the two English strangers to him. "Mrs. Connor has a radio show. She thinks she may be able to help find Sarah."

Merrill saw the look of incredulity come over Samuel Ingham's face, and she blushed with embarrassment. "Fake it 'til you make it," Richard had said to her whenever she confessed to a lack of confidence in a research assignment. But this was no arrogant professor she was face-to-face with. This was a man whose life had been turned upside down. A father who couldn't find his child.

"Mr. Ingham, I'm so sorry for what your family is going through. I wanted to talk with you because I'm very good at finding facts that are hidden. And because of my program, I have people who might be able to help find Sarah," she said, reaching out to shake his hand. There was no way she would admit to this serious man that she had been talking with spirits twenty-four hours ago. "Is there somewhere we can go to talk?" she asked.

Kate and the Bylers walked over to the horse pasture and stood at the fence watching a newborn foal and its mother while Samuel led Merrill to his front porch. He gestured to the wooden swing and took a seat opposite her. "So I understand that Sarah does bookkeeping for your business?" she said.

"Yes, she's very good with numbers, like her mudder," he said with obvious pride. "She does the billing and banking. For the past few months she's even been going out with me on job estimates."

"Oh. How does that work?" Merrill asked.

"After measurements are taken, Sarah will take notes on the dimensions and whatever details the customer has in mind, such as material choices and the expected time frame for the job. Then she will write it all up so that I can submit it to the customer."

"Quite a responsibility for a fourteen-year-old. You must really be proud of her, Mr. Ingham."

The man did not respond. Merrill prayed he wasn't feeling patronized. She really did marvel at the work ethic of the young teen who had lived inside her head these past twenty-four hours. "Would you be willing to share your list of customers from the past few months?" His silent stoicism made every word that came out of her mouth sound more and more foolish.

"No. I won't do that," Samuel Ingham said.

Merrill summoned up her nerve and said, "I understand the bishop is considering notifying the Sheriff about Sarah's disappearance. I imagine he'll be a lot more persistent and disrupting to your family and the community than I, Mr. Ingham." Had she gone too far? The answer was written all over Ingham's face.

"No," he repeated as he stood up. And with that, her "interview" with Samuel Ingham was over. She followed him to the pasture fence and then without another word he headed to the barn.

"Time to go?" Kate asked.

"Yes," she said.

The women climbed into the Byler buggy and Corrine drove the horses toward her farm.

"Mr. Ingham is usually very nice," Abigail said. "I think he's missing Sarah very much."

"Of course," Merrill answered. "Abigail, did you and Sarah ever talk about her father's building company?"

"Not really. All she ever told me about it was that the office work was boring. She was happier going to her father's job sites for the estimates."

"Did she tell you the names of any of the customers?" Merrill asked the girl.

"No." Abigail lowered her eyes and stared at her folded hands.

"Think hard, Abigail. It could be very important."

The girl was silent and remained that way until the horses reached their destination. As Abigail and the women jumped down from the cart, the two little Byler boys they had seen that morning greeted their mother and sister. "Fater is taking us fishing, Abby. Please come along!" they begged, as each took a hand and began dragging their sister toward the creek behind the farmhouse.

"Thank you, Abigail." Merrill called. "If you think of anything else…" She was reaching into her bag for her business card as she followed the three Byler children. When she caught up to them she asked, "Have you ever used the phone in the little hut?"

"No."

"Well, if you ever want to get in touch with me, here's my number." The little boys continued to pull their sister in the opposite direction. "Thank you, Abigail," she said again.

As Corrine walked them to the Beamer, Kate drew the woman in for another hug. "Thank you so much, friend," she said.

"You're welcome, Kate. Mrs. Connor, will you keep looking for our lost girl?" she asked Merrill.

"I will," Merrill said. She tried to sound confident, in spite of how she felt.

As Corrine walked toward her house, Kate did a modified three point turn to maneuver over the large river rocks that lined the Bylers' driveway. Merrill's disappointment was obvious. She hardly had a word to say to her friend the whole thirty minutes it took to get back to Westfield.

"Call me," Kate shouted at her friend's back, and Merrill heard her shift the Beamer into second gear as she pulled away.

"Uh huh," she said to herself.

An hour later, her nerves were still jangled from the disappointment of not being able to help with Sarah's disappearance. Merrill lay in the hammock on her deck, hands behind her head, and had a heart-to-heart with herself. Was she losing her mind? She had no right to impose on Corrine and her family, and certainly it had been an imposition to go to the Ingham's house and disrupt Mr. Ingham's life beyond what it already had been. Why did she suppose she could find the missing little girl? She didn't believe in the nonsense that mediums sold their clients. So why had she, a skeptic, believed that Richard had been in that room yesterday, with a message from the Great Beyond?

As she replayed her Lily Dale experience, she decided there were very rational explanations for what she had experienced. The "spirit" who had visited Victoria Erikson's reading room, the man in the museum surrounded by art work, could definitely be explained. Richard Connor was renown in their area, not only as a great professor, but as an accomplished artist as well. Victoria Erikson could have read about him in the local papers, or perhaps she was a Fredonia alum herself and had seen an article in the college newsletter. When she asked Merrill about her last name and marital status, she more than likely made an educated guess. Merrill was likely Richard's widow. And Merrill had herself validated that Richard was the man the medium had called forth.

As she followed this path of reason, Merrill grew calmer. Victoria Erikson was one clever lady. Before the "reading" began, the medium had already set her up with the power of suggestion. All that stuff about garnets being the "truth gem" had caught Merrill off guard. When the flash of light in the dark room illuminated the stones, Merrill was a sitting duck. Her imagination had been primed to see that little girl's desperate expression within the gems. Of course, none of Merrill's rationalizations explained all the diving references "Richard" had made. Perhaps the medium had heard of her podcast and knew the title.

Breathing normally at last, Merrill started to gently rock the hammock. Soon the motion and the warm September sun worked their magic. She had so few hours of sleep the night before and so she closed her eyes, giving in.

The sun was just a little lower when her phone interrupted her nap. She glanced at the 716 number on her screen, but Merrill didn't recognize it. She was about to decline the call, but she thought better of it and answered.

"Miss Merrill," the young voice said, "It's me, Abigail."

Merrill's fogginess immediately lifted. "Yes, what is it, Abigail?"

The girl was out of breath, but she persisted. "I thought of something Sarah said to me recently."

"What did she say?" Merrill stood up and listened intently.

"She said she and her fater had a customer on Barnes road. An English customer. She said she didn't like going there because of the weird boy who lived there. But I think she did like going there. I could tell by the look on her face when she said it. Do you know what I mean?"

"I think so," Merrill answered. "Do you remember the name of the customer?"

"I'm not sure. Gibson…Gibbs, something like that," Abigail answered. "Is that helpful?"

"I think so, honey. You're a very brave friend. Thank you!"

Minutes later, as Kate pulled out of Merrill's driveway she said, "Remind me to never again take you to Lily Dale!"

"Okay," Merrill said.

"I hope you have gas money," she said, pointing the Z4 back up the hill to Amish country.

CHAPTER 12

FINDING SARAH

"THANKS FOR HAVING me, Merrill," Sheriff Lovallo said. Merrill didn't want to make her guest uncomfortable, but he was far too close to the microphone. She put her hand over her own mic and sat back in her chair, hoping he would do the same. He did not. "Yes, we are very happy that we found the young Ingham girl as soon as we did. Three days is a long time for a child to be missing, of course, but the outcome could have been tragic. As you may know, the Amish community is an autonomous organization, especially when it comes to legal matters, and although we had heard rumors, they had not contacted us officially about the girl's disappearance. So if it weren't for two local women who helped us locate her, Ms. Kate Sterns and you, Merrill, we may have never found Sarah."

Embarrassment always made her flush crimson, and the sheriff's flattering words had that effect. She was glad for the hundredth time that this was a podcast and not a video production. "Thanks, Officer Lovallo, but Kate and I just happened to be in the right place at the right time." That wasn't exactly true. She wouldn't have been there if it hadn't been for Victoria Erikson and what happened in her little back room. But she wasn't going to attempt an explanation of her Lily Dale experience, not for her listeners and not for this policeman.

A month ago she had lied to Johnny Lovallo about how she and Kate had ended up at Gibb Farm. "We have a friend in the travel industry, and she thought perhaps the owner, who she heard is a summer resident only, might be interested in having short-term renters on his property the rest of the year," she told him that day. "So we took a ride to look at the leaves and pay a visit to the owner."

The truth was that the late afternoon drive a month ago had an entirely different genesis. After Kate picked her up and as soon as the 55 MPH signs began to appear, she shifted into fifth and stepped on it. "Can't you go any faster?" Merrill demanded of her friend. "We've only got a couple more hours of daylight, and there are no streetlights way the hell out here!"

"You're in a fifty-thousand-dollar BMW Z4 that can hold its own on any racetrack, Merrill! Yes, I can go faster," Kate said, accelerating to prove her point.

Merrill held her phone close to her face and squinted. In her hurry, she had forgotten her glasses. "Okay. According to Google Maps, the intersection of Plank and Barnes is a half mile away."

"Here we are," Kate said moments later, downshifting into second as she turned onto the gravel road.

Amish farms were easily distinguished from English places by the types of vehicles parked in the driveways. "Slow down, Kate! I'm trying to read the names on the mailboxes."

"Speed up, slow down," Kate muttered.

Soon they were crawling by the ever more expansive lots and houses with magnificent barns erected on the properties. There were security gates in front of most of them. Merrill craned her neck to see as the women traveled the country road that seemed several miles long.

"Back up, Kate! That one said Gibb!" Merrill shouted as they passed an oversized mailbox that was shaped like a barn. Kate did as she was told and in seconds the women were staring at a sprawling brick structure with a matching wall extending the width of the expansive lot. Behind the massive house was the largest barn Merrill had ever seen. "Thank goodness there's no security gate. Let's see if anyone's home," Merrill said. Kate pulled into the driveway and up to the house. The women unhooked their seatbelts and got out.

As they climbed the many steps that led to the mansion's front door Kate said, "I hope these are *friendly*, filthy-rich people."

Merrill pressed the doorbell and from inside the women heard the familiar "Ode to Joy" as it chimed and echoed throughout the first floor. They waited a few seconds and Merrill pressed it again. This time Kate nervously hummed along.

When no one appeared at the door, they stood on the massive porch for a few more seconds. "It would appear that no one's home. Let's take a walk out back, shall we?" Merrill said.

Kate and Merrill followed a red brick walk to the barn. Looking up, Merrill observed the huge iron weather vane in the shape of a horse that topped the structure. "I wouldn't call this a shed, would you?" she asked Kate.

"Definitely not a shed," Kate responded. "I could fit three of my houses inside it."

From the barn's interior came the sounds of horses. Peering into a window, Merrill counted a dozen stalls with feeding buckets in front of each one. "Yup, horses eating, but no people. Some human had to have been here recently."

The women continued to follow the brick path past a several stories high silo. "Those two could be defined as sheds, I guess," Kate said, pointing to two substantial outbuildings that stood in front of a pine forest.

The two friends headed in lockstep toward the buildings. "Which one looks newest?" Merrill asked.

"No idea," Kate answered, circling the building that was closest to the stand of pines while Merrill walked from the front to the back of the other structure. Moments later she shouted, "Hey, Merrill, this one actually has a date carved into the concrete pad!"

Merrill hurried to the back of the building where Kate stood pointing down at the engraved words. "June, 2017," she read. "This past summer! This has to be Samuel Ingham's work!"

"So what do we do now?" Kate asked.

"Now, we sit on that beautiful porch and wait for Mr. Gibb to return home."

The women started back on the path toward the house. Suddenly, Kate grabbed her friend's arm. "Did you hear that noise?"

"What noise?"

"A knocking. I think it came from that furthest storage building!" They stood still and listened. "That! Did you hear that?"

"No," Merrill answered. "I don't hear anything! It must be your musician's supersonic hearing. I trust it! Let's go back!"

The closer they came to the building, the harder Merrill strained to make out any sound coming from it. And then she did hear something. A muffled voice. A girl's voice. "Help me! Please help me!"

"Oh, my God," Merrill said, running toward the double door of the building. A large padlock stopped her.

"Help me!" again the voice called from what seemed like miles away.

"I can't see anyone," Kate said as she returned from her run around the radius of the building. "I looked in every window. Nothing but farm equipment and a couple of four- wheeled…"

Faint knocking and the pleading voice interrupted her. Merrill pulled on the chained padlock in desperation. "Damn it! I'm calling the Sheriff!" she said.

"Hello? Are you there?" Kate stood by the door and screamed at the top of her lungs. "Stay with us! Help is on the way!"

Within minutes of Merrill's 911 call, Sheriff Lovallo and another officer pulled into the Gibb Farm. The two women waved frantically as the squad car raced toward them on the brick pathway. Jumping out of the car with a black tool bag, the sheriff ran toward the women. The second officer pulled a huge bolt cutter out of the bag and went to work on the padlock. Minutes later, the cops stepped into the large space, Merrill and Kate following closely behind. Each of the four headed in a different direction, on the hunt for the little girl.

"Hello?" they each shouted and then waited for the girl to answer. Merrill heard the voice coming from the direction of the closed door she stood in front of.

"Help! I'm down here!" the girl shouted.

Merrill turned and pulled the door open. Sunshine from a skylight flooded the stairway that seconds before had been pitch black. At the bottom sat a young girl with her left arm and ankle handcuffed to a chair.

Sarah Ingham raised her free hand in front of her face and waved at Merrill Connor. Just as she had in the poster. Just as she had from inside Merrill's garnets.

CHAPTER 13

THE JOHNNY EPISODE

To Merrill's relief, the sheriff had finally moved the proper distance from the microphone. "After three days of terror," he said, "I delivered Sarah Ingham, safe and sound, to her parents."

"And how would you describe her condition when you found her?" Merrill asked.

"The young lady was examined that night by a physician at Westfield Memorial. The doctor found her to be in a remarkably healthy condition. Apparently, her abductor made sure she had plenty of water, and until that last day of her captivity, he had been feeding her, too," Lovallo told Merrill's audience.

"Sheriff," she asked, "what can you tell us about the person who took Sarah?"

"Well, first let me say that he was a minor at the time of the abduction, so he has not been charged as an adult," the sheriff began. "And because Sarah knew him, she was not taken under duress."

"So, she went willingly?"

"Yes. He was an acquaintance. They had met that summer. When he pulled up and offered her a ride that day it had just started to rain, so she accepted. She was in a hurry to get home to look in on her sick mother," the Sheriff answered.

"But this boy was English, not Amish," Merrill said. "How did she know this person?"

"They met at his uncle's place, where Sarah's father, Samuel, had worked. Sarah went with her father several times to that horse farm. Merrill, as I told you when you invited me to participate in your podcast, I won't be using the boy's name because he is a juvenile."

And neither would Merrill. "Understood," she said. "Can you tell us more about what led up to Sarah's abduction?"

"Yes. Apparently, each time she went out to the uncle's farm with her father, she and the boy had brief, but pleasant conversations. Sarah is very shy. I'm not sure if you know that, Merrill. But she in no way played any role in her disappearance," Lovallo said.

"Okay, Sheriff, but what do the police know about this boy?"

"We questioned his uncle for hours, and he was very cooperative, very forthcoming with us," he said.

"And what did he tell you?"

"He said that his nephew had been with him since late May. His parents had brought him to the farm after the kid had been expelled from school for fighting."

"So he had a troubled history," Merrill said.

"Well, I don't know if I would say that. He had a history of being picked on and bullied. He stood out with his peers. He was, how can I say this, unique. And with adolescents, I'm sure you know that being recognized as different can put a target on a kid's back. His uncle believes he is on the autism spectrum, but of course, he's not qualified to give a diagnosis."

"Did any expert diagnose the perpetrator with this brain disorder?" she asked.

"Well, no. He attended a private school and as I understand it, his parents did not agree to have him assessed."

"I see," Merrill said. "Go on, please, Sheriff."

"Well, according to the uncle, his brother and his wife were at their wits' ends. He had always gotten along with his nephew, so he offered to let him stay with him for the summer."

"And how did that go?" Merrill asked.

"Better than expected. His uncle told us that it had been a good summer for his nephew. From the start, the kid seemed to love everything about the farm, especially the horses. He worked very hard, according to the uncle. He even hayed with the crew that his uncle had hired, and that is brutally tough physical labor. When the uncle contracted Samuel Ingham's outfit to build a storage building, the kid actually worked alongside the men."

"Remarkable," Merrill said.

"Although the boy mostly kept his feelings to himself, the uncle believed that he was doing much better emotionally. Until, that is, his parents came out to the farm for a visit that last week in August. They told the boy that they had enrolled him in another private school, this one a boarding school. That news is probably what freaked him out. His uncle said for the week leading up to the abduction, he noticed that his nephew was very anxious. He described him as a nervous wreck."

"But Sheriff, kids can become distraught without committing crimes, without kidnapping another human being," Merrill said.

"This is true, Merrill, but apparently this kid was convinced that Sarah Ingham was his true love."

"How do you know that, Sheriff?"

"From Sarah herself. She said his plan was to come back for her. He was going to steal a car and come back to Mayville and then they would run away together. Of course, he didn't tell her this until he had handcuffed her in the storage shed basement."

"How did he convince her to go to his uncle's home? How did Sarah end up in that shed?" Merrill asked.

"He told her he needed to stop and feed the horses and he convinced her that he had to get some feed from the storage building," Johnny explained.

"How frightening this must have been for her. How did she react to this plan?" Merrill asked.

"She's a smart girl. She played along with him. He brought her food and water for that day-and-a-half. He told her he would go back to his parents' home and gather the equipment they would need. Camping stuff. Some of his sister's clothes for her so that her Amish garb wouldn't give them away. And he was true to his word. He was actually five miles from the uncle's farm when we apprehended him," Lovallo said.

"And where is he now?"

"He's in a non-secure residential treatment center. It's way up north, almost to the Canadian border. He'll be there until his 18ᵗʰ birthday. I talked with his case manager a couple of days ago. She says he's being assessed and has been seeing a therapist daily."

"And what about Sarah? How is she doing?" Merrill asked.

"She seems to be doing well. She has a strong family and a very supportive community. She's actually going back out again with Samuel to do job estimates,"

"The amazing resilience of youth, right Sheriff?" Merrill said.

"Yes, that's right." The sheriff smiled at her and said, "She told me to give you a message, Merrill."

"Really? What is it?" Merrill held her breath as the sheriff spoke.

"She said, 'Tell Miss Merrill thanks for being in the right place, at the right time and finding me. Thank her for looking deeper.'"

Chapter Fourteen

CELEBRITY

MERRILL HEADED DOWN the last aisle toward the produce section of the Top Spot, or Bottom Spot, as the locals called their only grocery store. The nickname was very fitting, given the establishment's inadequate selection of fresh meats and produce. This early in the morning Merrill hoped she might have her choice of unbruised strawberries and wrinkle-free grapes.

Her mission was interrupted by a shout coming from somewhere behind her. "Hey, Merrill! Congratulations!" She turned and saw Mel Dodds, her neighbor and fellow library board member pushing his cart in walk-race speed in her direction. "Great work finding that little girl!" he yelled. He was standing a yard away from her.

"Thanks, Mel. But I didn't do it by myself." Merrill blushed crimson, her usual response to a compliment. Her whole life, she had been a supporter, and the spotlight did not agree with her. Her husband's art, her children's and her friends' accomplishments, the students and professors she had served, they were the ones deserving of accolades. Richard had told her again and again that she was too modest. He wanted her to take compliments to heart, and she could hardly avoid them these days.

Since her *Deeper Dive* segment with Sheriff Lovallo, she had become Westfield's own version of a celebrity. She couldn't go to the post office or the Y or run her usual two miles around the high school track without an admirer lavishing her with praise. Even in her sacrosanct place, the library basement where she did much of her research and the recording of the podcast, several of her "fans" found her and congratulated her for finding Sarah Ingham.

Merrill was flabbergasted when Sheriff Lovallo, or "Johnny" as he insisted she call him, had stopped by the library yesterday on his day off to invite her to have a cup of coffee with him. She had told a white lie and said that her son was making lunch for her and that she had to get home, but she didn't sound convincing, even to herself.

"How about tomorrow?" he asked, apparently unabashed by her reluctant demeanor. Out of uniform, he looked like most men in her age group. A little worse for wear physically, but his confidence overshadowed the slight limp a bum knee produced. He really was fairly pleasant to look at. She wasn't at all bothered by the receding hairline or the smile lines around his mouth. But his chutzpah was a force to be reckoned with. In her professional role at the college Merrill had come off as competent and confident, but she could be very shy, almost demure, with people she had just met.

"Okay," she said, trying not to sound hesitant. "Meet you at the Diner at 10 tomorrow?"

"Terrific!" he said. Was he beaming at her? Whatever his expression was meant to convey, it made Merrill uneasy.

On her drive home from the grocery store, she tried to analyze her discomfort in the sheriff's presence yesterday. Was it his brashness? His eagerness to explore what more life had to offer, even in this late chapter of life? But, she argued with herself, hadn't that been exactly what she had reveled in since she started the podcast? Why did Johnny's enthusiasm scare her? She would talk it over with Richard when she…It had been three years since his death, but from time to time she would forget that her husband would not be in his studio when she came in from the garage.

As soon as she put her groceries down on the counter, she called Jenna. "What do you think Johnny Lovallo wants from me?"

"What do you mean?" Jenna asked.

"Why is he asking me out for coffee?" Merrill demanded.

Jenna turned off whatever piece of equipment buzzed in the background. Merrill remembered that her friend had a deadline coming up. She was finishing the collection she was taking to a jewelry show in Michigan this weekend, but Merrill's question had obviously grabbed all of her attention. "Um, because you're a super star all over the county these days. Because you're an interesting person with a rocking bod…"

"Stop!" Merrill begged. "I mean, really. Why does he want to spend time with me?"

Jenna knew she had to think fast and come up with a viable reason that had nothing to do with Johnny Lovallo being in any way attracted to her friend. "Maybe he wants to ask you about podcasting."

"Yeah. Right, okay. Maybe," Merrill said, wanting to believe her friend.

"Don't sweat it, lady! Have coffee with him and find out." Jenna heard Merrill's doorbell and tried to muffle her sigh of relief.

"Someone's at the door. Gotta run. Good luck this weekend," Merrill said and headed to the front of the house. She peered out from the side lite at a woman she did not recognize standing on her front porch. Merrill unlocked the door and opened it.

"Hello," the woman said. "Merrill Connor?"

"I am. What can I do for you?" Standing this close to her, Merrill could see that this woman wasn't as young as she had thought at first glance. She was shorter than Merrill by a half a foot or so, and her small stature had fooled her into assuming she was young. Her face was furrowed and drawn and her eyes drooped, giving her an exhausted countenance. Merrill was immediately curious. What had prematurely aged this woman?

"I'm a fan of your podcast. I've been listening since week one, and I think you're great."

"Well, thanks," Merrill said, once again nonplussed by a stranger's admiration. "Have a seat, won't you?" she said, directing her to the oversized porch swing. "What did you say your name was?"

"Joanna."

Merrill sat down in a wicker chair across from the woman. "So, Joanna. How did you know where I live?"

"I went to the library looking for you and the woman at the desk said she didn't know when you'd be in your basement studio. She gave me your address."

Merrill made a mental note to give Doris Breonski a piece of her mind. It was not okay to tell strangers where she lived. "Do you live in Westfield, Joanna?" she asked.

"No, not presently, but I did grow up here," the woman said. "I live in Brooklyn now." She seemed to be doing an intense inventory of Merrill's face. "My mother, Grace Phillips, vanished from the Mill Springs Mall twenty years ago. She's been missing ever since."

Merrill's jaw dropped. She stared at the woman so hard she felt a little wave of vertigo sweep over her. She closed her eyes for a second. When she opened them she saw that Joanna had stepped off the swing and was standing in front of her.

"I want you to take a deeper dive, Merrill," the stranger said. "I want you to find out what happened to my mother."

CHAPTER FIFTEEN

THE MAIN DINER

SITTING IN A corner booth of the Main Diner, Merrill tried very hard not to stare at Johnny Lovallo. Had he had that little mustache when he made his surprise stop at her library workspace? Or before that, on the first day she saw him at the Gibb Farm? She couldn't remember. So much for my great powers of observation, she thought to herself.

"Is something wrong, Merrill?" he asked. "Is the pie not what you expected?"

"What? Oh, no," she answered. She obliged him by eating a fork full of strawberry rhubarb filling. In spite of the dire circumstances of their first meeting, she hardly knew this man. It wouldn't be right to pull out her arsenal of sarcasm and say, "No, it's your face I didn't expect." That would not do. He wouldn't be interested in knowing that she hated facial hair, no matter how fast it had grown.

"Oh, good. Thanks for agreeing to get together," he said, picking up his coffee mug. "How have you been?"

Did he really care how she had been for a whole day since they had last seen one another? Merrill hated small talk, but it looked like that was the direction they were headed. "I've been fine," she answered. She attempted to smile back at the Sheriff, whose grin, she was sure, was genuine.

"Have you gotten used to being the Westfield area's hero yet?"

This would have been the perfect segue to tell him about one particular fan and Joanna Phillips's appearance at her house yesterday, but instead she said, "Not really. But I'm sure you must be used to unsolicited praise in your line of work, er, line of duty." His staring at her in between gulps of the Diner's Special Dark Brew was making her nervous. "When I worked as a librarian, I didn't get many, or any, high fives in the grocery store. These days, it's becoming a common occurrence," she told him.

"Well, you deserve it, Merrill. All of the high fives and kudos that are coming your way, you've earned them. Sarah Ingham may not have been found if it hadn't been for your attention to detail and unselfish..." Lovallo paused in the middle of his praise as a tall man with a cane approached their table.

"Hey, Merrill, great podcast! You're a regular 21st century Angela Lansbury, aren't you?" he said.

"Thanks?" Merrill said, but the stranger moved toward the front door without responding.

Johnny Lovallo widened his grin. "See that? You're famous!"

She saw the crimson color of her face reflected back at her from the napkin holder. This was so painful. She hardly knew this guy, but his expression said it all. He wanted something from her.

"Merrill?" Here it was.

She looked up from her pie. "Yes, Sheriff Lovallo?"

"Johnny. Please," he said. She held her breath as she awaited his next words. "What if I asked you..." He seemed to be having trouble breathing, too. "What if I offered you a job with our department?"

She was stunned and relieved all at the same time. "A job?"

"Yes. It would be part-time. As a matter of fact, you could make your own hours," he said. "You could still do your podcast, of course. And you wouldn't need to come to the station on a regular basis."

Was that a snort she heard coming out of her own body? She was so relieved that 'Johnny' had not had anything else of a personal nature to ask, she heard the sound before she could stifle it. "What in the world am I qualified to do for the Sheriff's department?" she asked him.

"What you do best," he said. Obviously, hope had been restored in the

Sheriff. He was smiling from ear to ear. He took a breath and said, "Research. You'd do that. Or maybe we would call it searching. Like you did for Sarah Ingham. You'd search for the hidden details and clues," he said. "And of course your library science training is ideal…"

"But surely you already have criminal investigators in your department," Merrill said.

"As a matter of fact we do have one, but she's about to start a maternity leave in a week, and the guy we hired to replace her just took a better paying job with the Erie County Sheriff's Department. As soon as he called to tell me, I thought of you," he said.

She wiped her mouth on the wadded up napkin she had nervously destroyed while the sheriff spoke. "I'm flattered, Johnny," she said. "I truly am, but I'm not sure if that would be the right decision for me." The guy looked so disappointed, she felt a little sorry for him. He cast his eyes down and stared into his empty coffee mug. Merrill tried to sound consoling when she said, "I hope you can understand."

"Sure," he said half-heartedly as he reached into his jeans pocket for his wallet. "But if you change your mind…"

"Wait, please" she said as he stood to leave. "I have something I'd like to ask you, Sherriff."

"Sure. What is it?" His face brightened as he lowered himself back down into the booth.

"Do you remember the Grace Phillips case from 1997? The Westfield woman who disappeared from the Mill Springs Mall?"

He paused for what seemed so long, she was sure he didn't know what she was talking about. She was surprised when he said, "Of course, I remember it. I joined the department in 2000, so I was still in the Academy when it happened." His usual booming voice was almost a whisper and his congeniality seemed to have evaporated. He was obviously rattled by her question. When he finally spoke again he said, "Grace Phillips's disappearance was the first cold case I was assigned to when I joined the department. And the mystery surrounding her vanishing, the official status of the case is that it remains unsolved. Why do you ask?"

"Joanna Phillips came to see me yesterday."

The sheriff was making eye contact again. And the volume of his voice was back up to a nine. "The daughter?"

She glanced around the room, but none of the other diners seemed to have heard Lovallo's question. "Yes," Merrill answered.

"Yes, I know her. Joanna was the last family member to see Grace. I had to go to New York City to interview her on her college campus my first month on the job."

"She's apparently a fan of *A Deeper Dive*," Merrill said. "She's asked me to look into her mother's disappearance."

Lovallo scratched his head and looked away. She couldn't tell if he was pissed or just deep in thought. "I'll be honest," he said. "After five years of actively pursuing dead ends, I put Grace Phillips's file on the bottom of my very slim stack of cold cases."

Merrill held her breath as she waited for him to continue. They sat in silence so long, she was startled when he spoke again. "But I'd be willing to share that file with my new research assistant. Now *that* would be totally appropriate," he said, the grin once again spreading across his face.

PART THREE

CHAPTER SIXTEEN

YEARBOOK

"THAT'S HER," JOANNA said, pointing to a picture in the 1997 West-field Golden Eagles yearbook that Merrill had retrieved from the library's archives. "That's my mother."

At the conclusion of the stranger's unexpected visit to her home last week, Merrill had agreed to meet with Grace Phillips's daughter again, this time in her library "office." On the opposite end of the table from where the two women sat, Merrill's podcast equipment, including a couple of laptops, a camera, two microphones, and two pairs of headphones took up most of the table's surface. Seated side by side with the yearbook opened in front of them, Merrill bent closer to the picture of a smiling brunette standing in front of a bulletin board with red letters that spelled out, "Welcome to the Resource Room."

Merrill was struck by the way that Grace Phillips held her shoulders back with a kind of confidence that beautiful women seem to be born with. Her presence was so much bolder than that of her rather plain daughter, whose slumped posture was the first thing Merrill had noticed the day that she appeared at her door. The outfit the teacher's assistant wore, a red cardigan sweater with a short kilt and tall leather boots, could have been worn by any high school girl in 1997. As a matter of fact, Merrill thought to herself, the Grace Phillips pictured here could have easily passed for a teenager.

"So your mom was a teaching assistant at the high school, right?" she asked. The woman in the yearbook seemed to be looking back into Merrill's eyes.

"Yes. She was in the process of getting her bachelor's degree in special education. She wanted more than anything to be a teacher," she said. It suddenly occurred to Merrill that Joanna was close to the age her mother had been when she disappeared.

"Your family must have been very proud of her," Merrill said.

"No, not really," she answered. Merrill couldn't help but notice that Joanna had begun to frantically tear apart the tissue in her hand. Pieces of it were falling on the table. "My mother's return to college was a bone of contention for my father. I remember a lot of shouting in the house when she announced that she was going beyond the teacher assistant's certificate to get her bachelor's degree. I was as upset as my father when she told my brothers and I about her decision."

"Oh? Why was that?" Merrill asked.

"I was furious to think she might actually be on the faculty of my high school, in my space. Every day," Joanna said. "I don't think the twins cared one way or the other. They were in middle school when she disappeared."

"But you made it clear that you were angry with her when she made that decision to get her degree?" Merrill asked.

"I wasn't the kind of kid that veiled her emotions. I was angry with my mother for as far back as I can remember for all kinds of things, real or imagined. Angry and resentful, those were my default modes with her from the time I was about twelve." The woman looked down at the shredded tissue in her hand, and stood up. "Wastebasket?"

"Over in the corner," Merrill said, pointing to it. "That is probably a very hard thing for you to admit, especially since you were only sixteen when she...she was taken from you."

Joanna sat down again and began paging through the yearbook. "Chalk up my mature attitude to years of therapy," she answered. "Of course, I think my hate for my mother back then, and it *was* pure hate, was warranted. She totally deserved it. All of my shrinks have agreed that it made sense that I would wish her dead on a daily basis. But to tell the total truth, Merrill, I really wanted to kill her myself."

A thrill of anticipation and then a nameless dread washed over Merrill. It took all of her nerve and concentration to ask the question. "Why would you want to kill your mother, Joanna?"

"Because of *him*," she said, pointing to the yearbook. At the top of the page Joanna had turned to was the word FOOTBALL. Merrill followed Joanna's finger to the picture of a tall kid holding his helmet under his arm and smirking at the photographer like he had been told a private joke. "My mother's boyfriend," Joanna said.

"Wait," Merrill said, and she sounded as flustered as she felt. "You're saying your mother was having an affair with a high school boy?"

"Yes. And not just any boy, but the boy I was in love with." Suddenly, the thirty-something woman sitting next to Merrill seemed to travel back to that time. Her tone was one of a young teen who was devastated. She turned to another page, this one displaying Brad Child's senior portrait.

Merrill hesitated before she asked the woman her next question. "But how do you know that your mother was having an affair with…"Merrill looked down at the yearbook again. "Brad Childs?"

"Everybody who saw them together could see it. First of all, he was a Special Ed student. She was the teaching assistant in that classroom, so they were together a lot during the day for legitimate reasons. But he would hang around her classroom every chance he got. And she would go out of her way to help him after school. She never missed a football game that fall either. The way they looked at each other. It was disgusting." Joanna's tone matched her words.

"Did the administration, the principal or any adult know about this?" Merrill asked. "It would definitely have been against the law for her to have been…" Merrill struggled to find a term that was not sexually explicit. "Involved with a minor."

"No, not that I know of," Joanna answered. "But it was common knowledge with the kids. The two of them would walk down the hall together, and she would stand at his locker with him between classes. The students knew. They knew and it made my life a living hell. That and the fact that I had a mad crush on the boy who was obviously in love with my mother."

Merrill felt like she was listening to the plot summary of a Greek myth. "Oh, Joanna, how awful for you," she said.

"At the time, I thought no one could possibly be more furious than I was with my mother. And then she vanished, so I guess I was wrong." The woman pulled another tissue from her purse and dabbed at her eyes. "The tremendous guilt I felt and still feel for having my wish come true, that she would disappear from my life, it's kept me in a state of paralysis for decades. In spite of my expensive shrinks, it still affects every aspect of my life. My career, and of course, my relationships. I still hate her for what she did, but at the same time, someone robbed me of the chance to repair the damage." The woman broke down and sobbed. "They robbed me of a mother!"

Merrill felt helpless as she witnessed Joanna Phillips's misery. She brought the box of tissues to her. The woman wiped her face and asked, "Will you help me, Merrill?"

"What is it that you think I can do, Joanna?"

"The same thing you did for that Amish family. You found their daughter. Please find my mother, Merrill," she said.

CHAPTER SEVENTEEN

COLD

MERRILL CLOSED THE last of the three-ring binders that Johnny Lovallo's intern had delivered to her library office two weeks before. She sighed deeply, opened the new notebook she was dedicating to the project, and wrote her final observation. "The solvability factors of this cold case are next to zero."

Johnny had been right to discourage her from taking on the disappearance of Grace Phillips. There were just too many roadblocks to discovering what had happened to the woman twenty years before, and the passing of all that time was not the least of them. The community's initial shock at the news of the woman's disappearance had dissipated over the decades. And Johnny had told her that no eyewitnesses to the alleged abduction had ever come forward. The memories of the few people who had been questioned in 1997 were certainly dulled by now. But Merrill felt such sympathy for Grace Phillips's daughter that, for her sake, she had agreed that she would at least look over what evidence there was in the cold case file that Sheriff Johnny Lovallo had inherited.

"Merrill, when I asked you to do some research for the department, I intended to assign you to some current investigations that we're working on. Ones that demand a more technical and a more academic approach to the research than our guys have the time or expertise to do," Johnny told her in their latest phone conversation.

"Okay, I hear you, Johnny." She had finally relented to his insistence that she call him by his first name. "But just give me some time to see what I can find inside these boxes, okay?" she asked.

"Fine," he said. "Like I told you, 2,000 pieces of paper, a teenager's diary, and a broken high heel, that's all there is in those evidence boxes, and without a body, that's all there will ever be, in my humble opinion."

Remembering this comment, she rose and walked to the corner of the crowded room. Digging down to the bottom of one of the evidence boxes, she pulled out a plastic bag. Inside was a woman's shoe. It was covered in what was once a shiny blue fabric, but time had worn most of the sheen off. Of the spiked heel variety, it was the type that Merrill herself had never worn in the college library or anywhere else, for that matter. A couple of hours after Grace Phillips's disappearance, a security guard found it in the main thoroughfare of the Mill Springs Mall. It lay on its side near the fountain. A fountain into which every kid in the county, including Merrill's, had thrown pennies at some time or other while their parents shopped. When the police showed her the shoe, sixteen-year-old Joanna had identified it as one of the pair her mother wore that day. Its mate had never been found. Merrill turned the bag over and over and examined every surface of the shoe for the hundredth time. "What do *you* know?" she asked it aloud.

Merrill put the shoe back in the evidence box and stared down at the cartons on her office floor. Before she had rolled up her sleeves and dug into what had been compiled on this case over the course of twenty years, Merrill had done some general research on cold cases. She found that the label is an accurate one only if no arrest has been made within five years of the crime. And in terms of the nature of Grace Phillips's vanishing, Merrill discovered that the woman was one of 600,000 individuals who go missing every year. "What complicates this thing even further is that a body was never discovered," Johnny had explained.

Merrill pulled Joanna's diary out of the carton and reread a bookmarked page for what must have been the tenth time. A wide-tipped red marker scrawled the words that filled two spaces of the lined page. It was as if the girl wanted the words to scream her message. As had been the case each time she read it, Merrill could clearly imagine the seething rage that the teenaged Joanna harbored toward her mother.

She is a total SLUT!!!

Everyone in school sees it!!!

She is a LIAR!!!

I need to get the nerve up to tell my father. How can she do this to us? To him? She is a SELFISH BITCH!!!

It's my time to have a life. Her time is OVER.

How many kids my age have to watch their mother make a FOOL of herself and her family in the halls of their school?

And of all the boys who drool all over her, she chooses HIM!!!!!"

A shiver crawled up Merrill's neck, and she placed the diary back in the bin. She pulled on the sweater she kept on the hook behind the door. The converted storage room that was now her office and podcast studio was cold no matter what the season. She turned on the small space heater she had brought from home. The noisy fan was the white noise she needed to go deeper into her thought process.

From her research on unsolved disappearances, Merrill knew the lack of a corpse, indeed, was a major stumbling block in these investigations. An article that defined the term "solvability factors" in cold cases became her guidepost. As she combed through the police files, she checked off each category as it applied to this mystery. The first one was new testing of old evidence. The physical evidence, in this case, the shoe, had been tested back in 1997 and again ten years later when DNA testing was more sophisticated. It matched no one in the database and so proved nothing.

Another potential break in a case like this would be a witness coming forward years later, and according to the files, no one had been directly questioned since 1997. In terms of motive, only one unproven theory was assigned at the beginning of the investigation all those years ago: the shocking love triangle involving a teenager and his married teacher. But after hours of questioning at the time of Grace's disappearance, Dan Phillips, who was the ostensibly spurned husband in this case, had a rock-solid alibi. He had been at a meeting with another contractor and a couple of businessmen that day until seven at night, and all three of them had verified it. Phillips insisted to the police that he didn't believe that his wife was capable of having sex with a minor, so why would he be jealous? Why would he want her to disappear? He loved his wife. Because a body was never recovered, he did not collect a cent of the $50,000 insurance policy for years after his wife went missing. That and the fact that he was a wealthy man took money as a possible motive off the table, too.

The seventeen-year-old who was the subject of much gossip during his senior year, Brad Childs, had been called into the sheriff's office twice, accompanied by his father. The kid had been a mess during the first round of interviews. According to the lead investigator's notes, the kid sobbed so hard he could barely be understood. But he was much more composed the second time they brought him in. He sat next to his father as he denied having had an affair with his teacher. And apparently, Grace's husband, at least, believed him.

Heaving a sigh, Merrill walked to her desk and collapsed into the chair whose casters always sent her on an unintended ride. She reached for her phone and checked the time. Joanna Phillips was due here any minute. The woman was returning to her New York City home later this afternoon, and Merrill's forage through the binders had yielded more questions for Grace's daughter than answers. Merrill had written these down in her notebook. She turned to the page and began to highlight the ones that were a priority. The sound of someone coming down the stairs toward her underground space stopped her and she looked up.

Joanna did not offer a polite greeting. She was a woman who spared no words. But Merrill did not take offense at her abruptness. The woman was damaged goods. And how ironic, that more than anything, she wanted to find the mother who had broken her. "Whoa! It's cold in here! And...kind of creepy, too," Joanna said, glancing around from one corner to the other of the small space. Merrill thought the woman looked pale, almost sickly under the unforgiving fluorescent light. "Have you found anything yet?"

"Hello, Joanna," Merrill said. She stood and turned off the wall switch and turned on the floor lamp she had brought from home to cut down on the eye strain she had dealt with all her years as a librarian. "No, I haven't. I'm just familiarizing myself with the available facts, and I've made a list of people I'd like to talk to. Starting with you."

"Me? I didn't have anything to do with my mother's disappearing into thin air! Jesus, I'm the victim here, Merrill!" she shouted.

The woman could certainly have her feathers ruffled easily, Merrill thought. "I understand that, Joanna, but you were the last one to see her before she went missing, as far as we know. I'd like to hear your account of what happened that day. And a little bit more about your relationship with your mom. Would that be okay?" Merrill's calm tone seemed to work. Joanna sat down in the chair across from her.

"Yes. Okay," she said.

"Would it be alright if I recorded your interview?"

"Are you going to use it on *A Deeper Dive*?" Joanna asked.

"I'm not sure. But if I do, I will definitely ask your permission before the podcast airs," she said. Merrill knew that she would have to get Johnny Lovallo's approval, too, but she decided not to bring this up to Joanna just yet. "Would you like a cup of coffee or a Coke?"

"Coffee, please."

Merrill turned the power button on the Keurig she had brought from home and placed a pod in the machine. As the coffee brewed, she turned on the voice recorder on her laptop. "I'd like to have you tell me about that afternoon when you and your mom went to the mall." Merrill brought the mug of coffee to the woman and sat down across from her. She listened to the rather mundane details of that fateful day as told by Grace's child. She nodded as Joanna described the place where she had parked, her growing impatience with her mother as the fifteen minute errand turned into something else.

"Can we back up to what happened before the two of you got in the car that day?" Merrill didn't wait for an answer. "According to the phone records in the police file, a call made to your home from the phone booth outside of the school came in shortly before you and your mom left for the mall. It lasted for less than a minute. Do you remember her being on the phone?"

"No."

"Do you think that phone call could have had anything to do with your mother's sudden decision to go to the mall?"

"No idea. All I cared about at the time was that I was going to get to drive the van before I had to be at musical practice." The woman blew gently on her coffee and was silent for several seconds. "I do remember being surprised that she suddenly wanted to leave earlier than we needed to. I was in the middle of doing my homework when she started knocking on my door, telling me to hurry up if I wanted to drive."

"What was your mother's mission that day?" Merrill asked.

"She never said and I didn't ask." Merrill didn't miss the resentful tone. "I was a pretty selfish brat in those days," the woman added. Joanna described her anger at having to go inside to look for her mother, followed by her panicky run through the mall as she searched for her.

"And you called your dad when you couldn't find her, right?"

"Yes. I think I blanked out in the car until he finally came for me," Joanna said.

"He must have been very upset himself," Merrill said.

"I think he was, but he was probably trying to hold it together for me. When we got home, he showed the same calm attitude, most likely for the sake of my brothers." Joanna took a sip of the coffee. "He was, he is, a tough guy, my dad. My mother was the weak one in that marriage."

"What do you mean, Joanna?" Merrill asked delicately.

"She's the one who cheated! With a teenager! It doesn't get much weaker, more irresponsible than that, does it?" Joanna's usual pallor changed as her face turned red with anger.

Merrill didn't respond to the question. Instead, she said, "I'm so sorry that you and your family had to go through this, Joanna." The sixteen-year-old's diary in the case file was an extreme example of teenage angst. But Merrill found the hate for her mother almost justifiable. The girl had been in love with a boy who seemed to be in love with her mother. "Joanna, from what I gleaned from your diary, you felt it was becoming common knowledge around your school that Brad Childs and your mother..."

"Oh, yes! Everyone, kids, teachers, coaches, some parents...everyone knew they were sleeping together. At least that's what I thought at the time."

"How hard that must have been for you," Merrill said, asserting her sympathy once again.

"Harder for my dad, I guess. He refused to believe it. He still doesn't believe she was capable of it," she said, her hostility obvious.

Merrill had read the three interviews that Dan Phillips had given the police. What Joanna told her now was true; he had not believed that his wife had been unfaithful. The only possible proof to the contrary, his young daughter's diary, he had discounted as the product of a teenager's "overactive imagination." "Do you think your dad would talk with me?" Merrill asked.

Joanna was shaking her head before Merrill completed her query. "No. He refuses to talk about it with anyone, not even the twins or me."

After Joanna handed Merrill her business card and left to catch her plane, Merrill turned off the voice recorder. She mustered up her nerve and dialed the number she had copied from the police files. On the third ring, a woman answered. "Phillips Contracting."

"May I please speak with Mr. Phillips?"

"Please hold," the receptionist said.

Moments later, a raspy voice said, "Hello. This is Dan."

"Mr. Phillips, my name is Merrill Connor. I'm a research assistant for the Westfield Sheriff's office and I'm currently investigating the 1997 case of your wife's ..." The abrupt click told her that Joanna had been right. Dan Phillips would definitely not speak with her.

She rubbed her cold hands together, trying to recover from the stranger's outright rebuff. She could hear Richard's voice in her head. "Keep going. Don't wimp out!"

Richard. He was always with her. She took a moment to let the tears come, but she wiped them away before they fell.

CHAPTER EIGHTEEN

STUDIO

Merrill ladled yesterday's chicken soup into a bowl and placed it in the microwave. Westfield was having a good old-fashioned Western New York winter and it was soup weather, for sure. While she waited for it to warm up, she looked out the kitchen window and watched as gusts of wind blew the early December snow around her backyard. The view did not distract her from the question that nagged at her since her meeting a few hours ago with Joanna Phillips.

There were still two minutes left on the microwave timer. She picked her phone up from the counter and didn't bother with hello when Johnny Lovallo answered. "How come Brad Childs has only been questioned twice in twenty years?"

"Not sure," he answered. Merrill thought he might as well add, 'Don't care.' She was getting the definite feeling that Johnny thought of this cold case as *her* investigation. Of the two of them, in the last fifteen years she was the only one who had met and interviewed anyone who had been in Grace Phillips's life.

After Joanna's exit from her library studio, Merrill spent two hours digging through the case binders looking for a conversation between Childs and the cops, and although the boy had been brought in twice, she found only one time when he actually spoke. It was in the April 1997 file, one month after Grace had disappeared.

"Say that again," Lovallo practically shouted.

Merrill raised her voice to match his volume. "I said, how come the minor who was ostensibly Grace Phillips's victim has never been questioned except for those two times twenty years ago?" Her beeping microwave was the only sound she heard. The silence from her phone meant she had caught Johnny Lovallo unprepared or unable to answer her.

Finally, he uttered a barely audible, "Hmmm. I'm not sure. Let me get back to you on that." The abruptness of the hang-up click made her chuckle. Merrill had to concede that it was one more sign that they were becoming, if not friendly, at least comfortable with their roles in this investigation.

She stirred the steaming soup and carried it back to her place at the window that framed four of Richard's snow-covered sculptures. Installed in the garden over the course of a couple of decades, they were abstract and elegant, the marble reflecting the beauty of each changing season. Her husband had mounted spotlights so that even at night the statues could be seen. Merrill never left her kitchen without gazing out at them for a few minutes. "Richard," she said aloud, "how the hell did I get myself into this?"

She put her phone, notebook, the bowl of soup and a spoon on a tray and walked out to Richard's studio. Just three years into widowhood, Merrill was beginning to find comfort, rather than anguish, within this room. Gigi and Bob, their elderly dogs, had both died within the past year, and Merrill missed their company, especially when she entered the Shed. Thankfully, a portion of Richard's photography consisted of several black and whites of the two border collies. He had made frames for each of them and they hung in the studio. It was her habit to stop in front of each picture before heading to the comfortable side chair that she had claimed as her own when they had converted the original shed into a studio space.

Merrill finished eating and put her reading glasses on. Pulling her notebook closer, she reread the notes she had taken this morning on the 1997 police interviews of Brad Childs. With his father present at the two meetings that were held at the Westfield precinct, the kid had been so broken up at the first one, he was barely able to speak. A month later the boy seemed to have pulled it together, and he and his father sat down again with the investigators. In tandem, both Childs denied the rumors that Grace Phillips had stolen Brad's innocence.

Her phone rang and she picked up. "You're right," Johnny Lovallo said when she answered the phone. Were they ever going to say hello or good-bye to one another like civilized people, Merrill wondered. "And his old man was with him, too. He was a minor at the time, so that was necessary. He admitted that he was in love with Grace, but he swore that there was no sexual relationship. His father was quick to put in his two cents on that subject."

"Yes. The transcript shows that he did more talking than the kid," Merrill said.

"And Brad Childs' alibi was substantiated by *both* of his parents," Johnny said.

"Yes, I read that. He couldn't have been the one who called Grace from the school phone booth. Brad was salmon fishing up north with his father that day."

"Yup. Grace disappeared the day after he and his father arrived at Salmon River. Rock solid alibi, complete with Pizza Hut and bait shop receipts," Johnny said.

She bit her tongue before the sarcasm slipped out. *Tell me something I don't know* is what she wanted to say, *I've read the files too!* Instead, she said, "I'd like to talk with Brad Childs, Johnny," and waited several seconds for his response. Yelling or silence seemed to be the cop's go-to responses. "Can you give me some contact information?" She waited a few seconds and added, "Please?" It was her small attempt at showing some civility.

"As of now, I have nothing. But I'll see what I can find." Click.

"So much for the effectiveness of modeling common courtesy," Merrill said to the empty room.

She took a deep breath. Merrill needed to separate herself from the Grace Phillips case for a while. Picking up her notebook from the table, she stood up. Her plan for the next episode of the podcast was going to be a tribute to the Art Department at Fredonia State, and a portion of it would pay homage to the works and brilliance of her husband, Richard Connor. Merrill knew she was strong enough to do it now that she had entered the third year of grieving the only man she had ever loved. She would do it for Richard, yes, but to broach the subject of her widowhood in such a public way she thought might be healing for her, as well.

She began to circle the room where her husband had spent so many hours. He had designed the addition himself, incorporating the existing shed into the plan. He was delighted to have a creative outlet and a space within the walls of their home, so much more convenient than driving to his Fredonia State studio, especially once the disease began to debilitate him.

As she walked, Merrill admired each piece. A small bronze sculpture placed on top of a carved oak stand, a watercolor of the woods on campus that Richard could see from his classroom, a glass etching of her profile he had been experimenting with while he still possessed the small motor control to work on it. Every piece in this space brought him back to her. As she circled the room, she stopped to make notes, jotting down details and memories of his work process before and after the disease that eventually killed him. Now she stood in front of his last artistic effort.

How far she had come, she thought, staring at the painting of the free diver. In her initial stage of grief, the piece had terrified Merrill. But now it was clear to her that the woman in the picture wasn't falling. She was an athlete, determined and intentional in her quest to go as far as she could into the ocean's depths. She was deep diving, yes, with no equipment. She was free.

Merrill's phone vibrated and she crossed the room to get it. "I couldn't get an address for Brad Childs, but I've got a phone number," Johnny Lovallo said.

"Okay. Great! Text it to me," she said, and hung up before he could.

CHAPTER NINETEEN

WINTER SPIRITS

Merrill cautiously maneuvered her Nissan through the un-
plowed streets of Lily Dale. "Don't Spiritualists have to pay taxes?" she
asked. Jenna knew this wiseass remark was typical when her friend's nerves
were getting the better of her, so she ignored the question.

After Merrill's bizarre encounter with Victoria Erikson last fall, she
vowed to all of her friends that she would never return to this place. In spite
of the "vision" that led to finding Sarah Ingham, Merrill remained skeptical
about the paranormal. Long after the young teen was returned safely to
her home, she argued with Kate about exactly what it was that happened
in Victoria's back room. Kate was insistent in her defense of the medium.
For years she had been an ardent believer in the practice and perceptions
gained through Spiritualism, and she believed wholeheartedly that Richard
had come through from another realm with a message for his widow. Merrill countered with her own more logical explanation. That day, she told her
friends, she had been so disturbed about Sarah's disappearance, she had
hallucinated. Victoria's religious interpretation of the prescience of garnets,
her own anxiety about having a reading, and the sudden flash of light in the
room had triggered the apparition of the young girl, she insisted. Everything else, Richard's supposed "visit," and all that had followed, including
Sarah's rescue, were part of a string of fortunate coincidences.

And yet, here she was again, and this time without Kate urging her to
return. Desperate times call for desperate measures, she told herself, and

she was indeed feeling at a loss. After several unanswered calls to the number Johnny had given her for Brad Childs, someone finally picked up on the tenth ring. Whoever it was dropped the phone twice before uttering a husky, "Hello?"

"Yes, hello. Mr. Childs?" she asked.

"Who's this?" Merrill couldn't miss the slur in his voice. The man had either suffered a stroke or he was very drunk.

"My name is Merrill Connor. I'm a research assistant for the Westfield Sheriff's Department..." Click. Since meeting Johnny Lovallo she was getting used to people hanging up without saying goodbye. She hit redial several times at various hours during the following days and nights. But there had been no answer.

When she reached out to the cop again to tell him about her futile attempts to reach Childs, Johnny told her that he had dropped in on Brad's mother the day before, unannounced.

"What did she say?" Merrill asked.

"His dad passed away last year. The old lady wasn't much more forthcoming than the father had been years ago. She did say that her son was recently let go from his job as a waiter in a Rochester restaurant. He abandoned his apartment three months ago without paying the rent and she has no idea where he's been living since. I got the clear impression that she gave me Child's cell number just so I would go away."

"Can't you ding or ping his cell phone, or whatever you call it, to find out where he is?" she asked Lovallo.

"Not without just cause backed up by a subpoena," he answered.

"Damn," she said and hung up. Merrill did not like this feeling of inadequacy. Whenever she came up against an obstacle in her job as a researcher or in her new efforts as a podcaster, she rooted out every possible resource, turned over every rock and stone, no matter how outside the traditional boundaries they were. She stared out her kitchen window now at Richard's sculptures. Suddenly, it hit her. A medium in Lily Dale who claimed she could communicate with the dead was the ultimate definition of an outside source.

"Sorry, Merrill, but I'm in Nashville this week," Kate said when Merrill called and invited her to go with her on this unlikely journey to the place she had sworn off. "But of course, I'd be glad to give you Victoria's number."

As soon as she hung up with Kate and before she could change her mind, Merrill dialed the medium's number. Victoria Erikson did not sound the least bit surprised to hear from the woman who had fled her home months before. Merrill tried to imitate the calm tone of the medium as she made an appointment for the next day.

Thankfully, Jenna agreed to come along on this mission, just to keep Merrill company. The usual twenty minute ride had taken longer because of the snow, but, except for a couple of terrorist deer who had run out in front of the SUV as they drove over the hilly backroads, it was uneventful. "Are you nervous?" Jenna asked her friend.

"About the deer?"

"About Lily Dale." She was used to Merrill's dodging with sarcasm, and unlike Kate, she didn't take it personally. But Jenna couldn't help but notice that her friend twirled her garnet ring over and over throughout the trip, and she stopped doing it only when they arrived at the iron gate.

"No. I just can't believe I'm actually doing this again, but here we are," Merrill said as they pulled in front of the little house on Cleveland Avenue. Lily Dale was deserted on this December day, so different from that afternoon last fall. Most of the mediums were seasonal residents, but Victoria, as Kate had told her, was here year round.

The two women walked up the snow-covered steps and opened the door to the sunporch. Merrill twisted the doorbell crank and within seconds they heard footsteps. The door opened and there stood Victoria, towering over them. She was dressed in jeans, tall leather boots, and a coat-length sweater of multi-colored, mostly purple patches. She was even more striking than Merrill remembered, and her perfect skin and glossy hair made guessing her age next to impossible.

"Please come in, ladies. There's no heat on the sunporch but your friend can wait for you in the living room." She led them inside and invited Jenna to have a seat by the fireplace. "How have you been, Merrill?" she asked warmly.

Again Merrill answered in her head, "*You tell me!*" but she held back and instead told Victoria, "Very well, thanks."

"Make yourself comfortable, please," she said to Jenna and led Merrill down the narrow hallway to the medium's inner sanctum.

Before she was invited, Merrill sat down in the seat across from Victoria's chair and began to tug on her ring. She was anxious to get started. Victoria turned off the overhead light and turned on the lamp, as she had done the last time. As Victoria seated herself, Merrill tried to hand her wedding band to the medium. "Hold on, Merrill!" There was a note of annoyance in her voice. "First, a prayer asking for guidance from Spirit." As the woman prayed, Merrill tried not to squirm in her seat. She didn't have all day. She had to find Brad Childs.

In her second session with a psychic, all manner of dead people from Merrill's past came parading through Victoria's little room: her first grade teacher, a grad school classmate, her neighbor from the apartment building in Buffalo that she and Richard had lived in years ago. In spite of the crowd size, not one of them offered any insight into Brad Childs' whereabouts.

"Where's Richard?" she asked the psychic. Merrill felt like an idiot for asking. But Victoria bowed her head and twisted the ring between her fingers, as she had done a few months ago when Sarah Ingham had gone missing.

"Richard. Yes, the man in the art gallery...he's coming in, very hazily though. Oh, yes. He's here. He's smiling," Victoria said.

"Great!" Merrill said. "Ask him where I can find Brad Childs."

"Oh, my. He's turned away. Oh! He's leaving."

"What??" Merrill was pissed. "Don't go, Richard. Tell me where to find him!"

"Shhh, Merrill, please!" the medium admonished her. She seemed to be putting a lot of energy into closing her eyes as tightly as she could. Seconds passed. "Cross the street," Victoria said so softly Merrill could barely make out the words. "He's gone, Merrill," she said.

"What did he say? Cross the street??!! What the hell, Richard! Brad Childs is in Lily Dale?" she shouted.

"Calm down, Merrill, please," Victoria urged.

Merrill for the second time in three months stood up and flicked on the overhead light without being asked. She dug through her purse for her wallet and handed Victoria her credit card. "Ring, please," she said and reached across the desk to take it. "Thanks for seeing me on such short notice."

Jenna pulled on her jacket and had to run to keep up with Merrill as she charged down the front steps. "Walk with me, please. I'm so mad I need to blow off some steam," Merrill said. The power walk took them around the block and into the little park where she and Kate had parked on that beautiful fall day.

"What happened in there?" Jenna asked.

"Pretty much nothing. I guess I'll have to go back to earthly sources to find this guy." The two women walked through the thickening snow for another ten minutes.

"Merrill, the sun is going to set soon. Let's go back to the car," Jenna said with as much patience as she could muster. Merrill nodded. Jenna was a good friend and didn't deserve to have to deal with her temper tantrum.

As they turned down Cleveland Avenue, Merrill suddenly stopped. She pushed the Nissan's remote start on her key fob and said to her friend, "You get in the car and get warm. Just give me a minute."

"No. I'm going with you, Merrill," Jenna answered and followed her as she ran across the street to the shoreline of Cassadaga Lake. The wind was blowing from the north and the women stood on the rise above the small fresh water lake and shivered.

"What do you see?" Merrill asked, scanning the shoreline.

"Pine trees, a frozen lake. Two guys ice fishing," Jenna answered, her teeth chattering.

"'Cross the street,' Richard said. That's it! That's what he meant! Fishing!!!" Merrill was jumping up and down, and Jenna was afraid that her friend had lost her mind. She was relieved when Merrill said, "Jenna, we're done here. Let's go." As soon as the women reached the car, they climbed in. Immediately, the heat began to thaw their frozen fingers and toes.

Merrill pulled her cellphone from her coat pocket. She held up her index finger so that Jenna would know this would be a short call. "I think I found him…Yeah… I'm in Lily Dale. No, he's not in Lily Dale…He's fishing… Probably on that river his father took him to when Grace vanished… No, I don't know for certain! It's a hunch, okay? Salmon River… Okay… Okay…Yes. Okay. Call me back."

As she hung up, Merrill had a sudden realization that she wouldn't share the details of her reading with Jenna, or anyone else, for that matter. At her first session with Victoria the message that Helen/Helene had given her was that Merrill herself had psychic powers. She had discounted it at the time, but maybe she shouldn't have been so quick to dismiss the idea. Perhaps it explained why her hunch about Brad Child's possible location resonated so strongly.

As Merrill pulled slowly away from the curb, she glanced over at the psychic's house. There was movement at one of the sunporch windows. Victoria Erikson smiled and waved as the Nissan slowly headed toward the gate.

When the cop called her back a few minutes later, Merrill's Bluetooth transmitted Johnny's conversation so that Jenna could hear it too. "I have the address of the Childs' fishing camp on Salmon River. I'll text it to you. It's four hours away in Bumfu…er the middle of nowhere, Merrill. Way up north. No hotel for miles, so I'm not sure where you'll stay. The department will pay for it, of course, if you find some kind of lodging," he said. "Preferably cheap lodging."

"Thanks, I guess," Merrill said.

"Stay in touch," Lovallo said, and Jenna would swear that they both hung up at the exact same moment.

CHAPTER TWENTY

EAST ON 90

W HAT WOULD MERRILL do without her friends, she wondered as she headed east on the Thruway. This time Sherry had come to her rescue. One of her clients owned a cabin on Kasoag Lake. According to Google Maps, it was minutes away from the Childs' fishing camp.

There was no guarantee, of course, that Merrill would find Brad there, but what was the alternative? And Johnny Lovallo seemed to have faith in her. He hadn't grilled her about Lily Dale or how it was connected to her hunch about Brad Childs' whereabouts. He just showed up at her door yesterday and dropped off a county credit card. "Don't spend it all in one place and be safe," were his last words as he left her porch.

As soon as his car pulled out of her driveway, she headed to the library. In her basement office she spent a few hours reading Joanna's diary cover to cover. She made copies of the pages containing anything about school, including the sections where the girl mooned over Brad and the ones where she railed against her mother, "the BITCH." The teen's venomous characterization of just about everyone who was in her life at that time truly rattled Merrill. As far as she could recall, her own high school days and those of her daughters and son had been mainly carefree times, but perhaps she had burnished those memories from decades ago. As she highlighted the names and the wrongdoings of each of these people as far as Joanna was concerned, she formulated questions for Brad Childs.

Two hours into her drive on the Thruway through the stark winter landscape of New York, Merrill felt herself being lulled into a kind of stupor. Jenna had offered to come with her, but she preferred to be alone when she was in this "hunting" mode. There would not be time for relaxation, for a glass of wine, or dinner out. As much as she enjoyed her friends, she knew that their presence, though congenial, would wreck Merrill's focus. But as her eyelids grew heavy, she wished that Jenna was sitting next to her. She glanced at the navigation screen. Two hours and ten minutes to go. She pulled off 90 to the Ontario rest stop. She needed to stretch and use the restroom.

Feeling energized after she relieved her bladder, she ordered a large black coffee at Tim Horton's. Finding a booth away from the weekend travelers, she sat down and pulled out her notebook. She read over Joanna's inventory of "Assholes" and "Freaks." Most of these "scumbags" were high school kids, but a few teachers were targets of her wrath, too. Reserved for the worst of her vitriol, however, was Grace Phillips. The girl had recorded all the dates and instances when Brad and her mother were seen together. If her accounts could be believed, the two had certainly given the impression that they were involved in an intimate relationship. "Yuck," Merrill said, barely under her breath.

She climbed back into her car, fully awakened by the caffeine and roiled with disgust that the rereading of Joanna's diary had caused. She turned on the radio, switching the channel three times before turning it off. "Nothing but politics!" she complained out loud.

Finally, the navigational system's dignified British voice spoke once again. "Exit onto Route 81 North on the right." A few minutes later she took the Pulaski exit onto State Route 30 until she reached Altmar. "You have reached your destination on the left," the miscellaneous navigator said. Merrill pulled into the wide driveway of a cedar-shingled cabin with a bright blue metal roof. She gazed at the wraparound porch and something about the structure after the long drive comforted her.

"How cute is this?" she asked out loud. Opening the tailgate, she grabbed her duffel and work bags and a small cooler containing her food essentials for the next couple of days. Setting them down in front of the entry door, she walked to the side of the porch that fronted the lake. "Wow, how beautiful," she said, and wondered if she was talking to herself more than was usual. She had lived alone for three years, so she supposed this could be the norm for the rest of her life.

Kasoag Lake was partially frozen in spite of the fact that there had been an unusual warm-up over the past week. A small pine-covered island was close enough so that, had it been summer, Merrill could have swum to it. Suddenly she felt an ache in the middle of her chest. Merrill wished Richard could be here with her. He would definitely have set up an easel, or a camera tripod, or both, and captured the lovely vista.

Merrill walked to the side door where the security keypad was located and punched in the code Sherry had sent her. The cabin's kitchen was warm and bright, and after she emptied the contents of the cooler into the refrigerator, she studied a framed map of the area that hung next to it. With her index finger, she traced Route 22 past the Salmon River Fish Hatchery, to Bennett's Bridge, and on north to Salmon River Falls. She wasn't exactly sure where the Childs' fishing camp was, but it couldn't be more than a few minutes from this cozy place. She felt her "hunter" mode kick in. She would have a quick sandwich and head out to find Brad Childs.

The back wall of the cabin was made up of four floor-to-ceiling windows. Merrill carried her plate to a small table in the great room and ate her roast beef sandwich while she stared out at the winter beauty of Kasoag Lake. She took a last swallow of coffee and tidied up quickly. She wanted to find the Childs' hunting camp before the sun set.

She had driven only five miles when she heard the navigator's voice. "Your destination is on the left." Merrill's heartbeat quickened as she pulled into a driveway behind a beat-up Ford Falcon. She hoped it belonged to the man she had come all this way to talk with. She turned off the engine and stared at an A-framed cabin that reached up two stories into the overgrown pine forest. The building held none of the charm of her lakeside Airbnb. Instead, she observed its rotting logs and missing roof shingles. She grabbed her bag from the passenger seat and stepped out into the cooling afternoon air.

Merrill's sneakers crunched the pine cones and leaves that lay on the cracked driveway, remnants of last autumn. The top step to the porch was missing and Merrill had to jump the gap. She walked to the front door and knocked, first politely, and when no one came, she started pounding. After five minutes of this, she began peering into the windows on the porch. They were so filthy from forest sediment and other miscellaneous smears, she could see nothing.

Pulling out her phone, she quick-dialed Brad Child's number. After ten rings, a man said, "What the hell do you want?"

"Brad. It's Merrill Connor. I'm standing on the porch of your cabin."

"What? Why? What do you want from me?" he shouted.

"I'd like to talk to you." She took a deep breath. "About what happened to you when you were in high school." When he hung up on her, she was disappointed but not surprised. She walked the length of the porch again, determined perhaps beyond reason, to have a conversation with this stranger.

She heard a muffled shout as she retraced her steps to his front door. "You're with the cops, right?" There was no doubt in Merrill's mind that this was not a question, but an accusation.

"I'm a librarian. I do research for the Sheriff's Department on a part-time basis. But my main concern is for Joanna Phillips," she shouted. "I want to help her find her mother." Nothing but silence from behind the door. It lasted several minutes and Merrill decided she might have to give up for now. She jumped off the cabin porch and was walking back to her car when he spoke again.

"Come back in the morning," he yelled. "Around ten. Wear boots or hikers."

Well, at least he had agreed to meet with her, she thought as she started the Nissan. That in and of itself was amazing. What would she do with the hours until then? She back-tracked into the little village of Altmar. "Live Bait" flashed in blue neon in the window of the little general store. Merrill parked in front and entered the store. She walked past a huge cooler full of fish bait as varied as the most diverse sushi bar. In the back, Merrill found a selection of hiking boots, but only one pair in her size. She carried them to the counter and handed the clerk her Chautauqua County Sheriff's credit card. "Going to do some hiking, huh?" the young man asked. She avoided direct eye contact with him, but tried to sound cordial.

"That's the plan," she said.

"Lots of places around here to do that," he said, as though trying to reassure her, "but the Gorge at Salmon River Falls is the most beautiful."

Returning to her Airbnb cabin, Merrill spent the rest of the daylight hours reading over Joanna's diary entries regarding Brad. Typical teenage girl mooning over a boy, she thought. So incredibly different from the hateful tone she used as she observed him in her mother's company. "Saw the bitch at his locker after 7th period," she read. "So did a hundred other kids. She's ruining his life. And mine...Looked into the Resource Room after Social Studies. Could she sit any closer to him?!? He's never in the cafeteria anymore...he takes a tray to her classroom. Heard one of the football players say, 'You've been late to practice three days in a row. Coach Harding and Coach Woodhall are pissed! Get your shit together, Childs!' "She is so selfish! Doesn't she see what she's doing to him???!!! I'm sure other teachers are starting to notice. I hope she gets fired!"

Merrill sighed. She couldn't tell if it was the four hour drive or Joanna's angst-ridden journal that had tired her out. She poured a glass of wine and bundled up into her parka, which she had thankfully brought. The Adirondack chair on the porch was the perfect spot to watch the early winter sunset. She tried to meditate, to gather some strength and focus for whatever her meeting with Brad Childs might bring.

Deep in thought, she suddenly realized that her pocket was vibrating. "It's Lovallo," was the brusque greeting. "Are you okay, Merrill? Have you seen Brad Childs yet?"

"I'm fine, and no I haven't exactly seen him, but I did find him. He shouted at me through the cabin door. I'm going for a hike with him tomorrow morning."

"Hiking! Where?"

"I'm not sure, but I bought some boots for the occasion, on the department's dime, of course."

He ignored her wiseass remark. "You need to check in with me when you know the location of this hike!" He sounded worried. "Merrill, did you hear me?"

"Yes, I heard you, boss. I'll be sure to drop a pin on Maps when we get to wherever we're going."

"Okay. Good."

Back inside the warm cabin, Merrill decided there was no reason not to go to bed before 8 PM. She pulled her pajamas on, brushed her teeth, and grabbed the novel she had started weeks ago. Outside, the wind began to howl and tree branches smacked against the bedroom window. Merrill decided that sleep was preferable to reading and she turned off the small bedside lamp. Closing her eyes, she thought about how much she had changed since Richard's death. Not much scared her anymore.

CHAPTER TWENTY-ONE

THE GORGE

THE FIRST WORD that came to Merrill's mind as Brad Childs walked onto the porch of his cabin was *hunched.* She knew that he was thirty-eight years old, in the prime of life, but his posture belied it. He cautiously maneuvered the broken steps, and at the same time waved in the direction of the Nissan, never making eye contact with her. She rolled down the window as he opened his car door. "Follow me," he said.

Johnny Lovallo's angry stare flashed in her head. She knew he would be anxious until he heard from her this morning. "Where are we going?" she asked Brad Childs.

"Salmon River Falls, the Gorge Trail," he said. "Don't you read your text messages, lady?"

She slid into her car and grabbed her phone. Sure enough, the man had messaged her early this morning. "Gorge Trail parking lot."

Merrill punched in the destination on the navigation screen and did her best to follow closely behind his Ford on the narrow two-lane road, but two delivery trucks and four Amish buggies got in the way. She felt mildly irritated, but not anxious about getting lost. According to Google Earth, Salmon River Falls was ten miles north from her Airbnb. She had seen it on the map in the kitchen and after the general store clerk had suggested that was the hiker's ideal destination, she did some cursory research on the place when she returned from Altmar. Like so many beautiful locales in New York State, it originally belonged to the Five Nations of the Iroquois Indians. For the native people, the river had been a prolific fishing ground. But European occupation began in the early 1800's, and by the 1900's the white occupiers had created and harnessed hydroelectric power at the Falls.

For ten miles, Merrill followed the navigator's instructions and the many signs for Salmon River. Turning down a tree-lined lane, she spotted Child's vacated car in the parking lot of the Falls and pulled next to it. Lifting her backpack off the passenger seat, she pulled out her phone, and as she had promised, dropped a pin on her Maps program so that Johnny Lovallo would know her whereabouts. According to the posted map, the entrance to the Gorge Trail was a half-mile from the parking area. As she followed the signage to the designated meeting point, she was anxious to learn what kind of man Childs had become. As a boy, he may very well have been a victim of sexual assault, although he never admitted that to the police. It didn't take Merrill very long in his company to discover that his life had been in ruins from the time Grace Phillips disappeared.

"Gorge Trail Closed, November 15th to May 1st," Merrill read. She had never been a rule- breaker, and yet here she stood, surrounded by massive hemlocks and white pines and the sound of a roaring waterfall somewhere in the distance. She stared in awe at the steep cliffs and slopes that ringed hundreds of feet above the cavernous gorge.

"Mrs. Connor?" The deep voice startled her and she turned to face Brad Childs.

"Yes, but call me Merrill, please," she said.

Up close this stubble-faced man looked nothing like the clean-cut jock in the 1997 Westfield High School yearbook. He desperately needed a haircut and some serious sleep. Slumped and disheveled, he seemed much older than his years. He looked down at her new boots and seemed satisfied with what he saw. "Let's walk," he said.

"Wait. It says the trail is closed," Merrill said, but she followed him in spite of the sign.

For forty-five minutes the two negotiated the sheer slopes that rose above the gorge and exchanged not a word. "Brad, can we stop for a bit, please?" she asked at last, trying not to sound out of breath. She was a yoga loyalist, a part-time runner, and her walk to the library and back each day was a total of four miles, but this hike was a much more demanding work-out.

He stopped and pulled a bottle of water out of his pack, and she did the same. "So what did you want to ask me?" Was that a tone of hostility or insecurity she heard in his voice? She couldn't tell.

Recalling the list of questions she had made in her notebook last night, she took a deep breath and began. "I'd like to talk about the nature of your relationship with Grace Phillips," she said. "You told the police in 1997 that the two of you were very close. You were a senior in high school at the time and she was an adult with a husband and children. Is that the way you would characterize your connection with her all these years later?"

"She was my teacher. And she was the only person I could trust in those days. Even though I was a very messed-up kid, she had faith in me. Every-one except Grace...my parents, my friends, my teammates, my coaches... they didn't really care what I thought or felt. They just generally viewed me as a loser. And that's the way I thought of myself until Grace came into my life."

His agitation was visible in the furious white puffs he breathed into the winter air, so Merrill decided to shift gears. "So what happened to you after Grace's...disappearance? That must have been a very difficult time for you."

"I was pretty much a zombie, so I just did the bare minimum of what I was told to do. I graduated from high school that June, but barely. I went to college at my father's insistence. It took four weeks of not showing up for football practice and six weeks of not going to classes for me to flunk out. School had always been hard for me and without Grace...I was lost. I came home, took a job on the production line at Welch's, and married a high school classmate. That lasted three years." He put the empty water bottle into his backpack and retrieved a silver flask from his pocket. He chugged from it while he walked. "I was fired shortly after the divorce, so I left and moved up north for a while."

They were drawing nearer to the roaring falls and Merrill had to speed up so that she would be able to hear him. She increased her pace and soon they were side-by-side. "Did you know anyone around here in the Salmon River area when you came back?" she asked.

"Not really. My family mainly hunted and fished when they spent time at my grandpa's cabin. We didn't make any friends. I managed to find a maintenance job here at the park, but it was seasonal." He stopped and took another hit from the flask. "And I didn't get hired back the next year."

"You were still a young man. Did you have a roommate or any friends from work?" Merrill was practically shouting to be heard over the roar of the water.

"I made one friend. I married her, but that was annulled three months later, so I was alone again." A bald eagle screeched as it left its hemlock perch, and the two of them stopped and watched it fly away.

"This is such a beautiful area. I can see why you and your family loved it," Merrill said. "But it must have been very lonely for you after your marriage failed. Did you go back to Westfield then?"

"No. My parents, especially my old man, weren't fans of my lifestyle choices. They made that very clear. I moved to Rochester. Spent some time in jail there in 2005," he said.

"What for?" Merrill asked.

"I had a couple of assault charges and no funds for a good lawyer," Brad said.

"Assault charges?"

"Yeah. I had a run-in with my landlord, and then a couple of bar fights after that sealed the deal," he said taking another hit from the flask. "I spent six miserable months getting sober in jail. I mainly drink alone these days. Keeps the odds of me ending up in jail again pretty low." They walked for a few minutes more and then he spoke again. This time, Merrill heard the child inside the man. "If Grace had lived…had not disappeared, she would have never let me fall so low."

Merrill felt real compassion for Brad Childs. It seemed like half of his life had been spent in a kind of drunken anguish. He hadn't admitted to there having been a sexual component in his association with Grace Phillips, but Merrill's strong hunch told her there had been. She had researched the plight of adolescent boys who were victims of sexual abuse by adults in positions of power. Brad's was a story all too often told by others who had fallen prey to these types of relationships. Twenty years after it had taken place, Brad was still defending the woman.

"Are you hungry?" she asked him. "Yelp says the Altmar Diner is great for breakfast." He started to shake his head and she added, "I'm buying."

"Okay. Why not?" he said and turned in the direction they had come.

The diner was crowded and noisy. As Merrill passed several tables of late season doe hunters, she began to doubt that this was the fitting venue for a meaningful conversation with Brad Childs regarding his teenage love affair with a woman twice his age. She was relieved to find a booth close to the kitchen and away from the throng of lunch time customers. As she pulled off her jacket, she looked up and watched Brad Childs through the window as he walked past, casting furtive glances to his left and right, as if he was being hunted. He looked straight ahead as he approached the booth she had chosen. He hadn't sat down before asking, "So what exactly do you want to know about me and Grace?"

A waitress approached the table with a carafe of coffee. "Shall we order first?" Merrill asked him. He didn't reply, but she was relieved to see him pulling off his jacket. "Yes, please," she said to the waitress, sliding the coffee mugs to her.

After Brad ordered, he began looking around the diner like a man planning an escape route. Merrill decided that she would need to ask him the right questions and soon. She swallowed hard and said, "Were you in love with Grace Phillips, Brad?"

"I told you. She was the best thing that ever happened to me," he said defensively.

She inhaled deeply and persevered. "Did you have sex with Grace Phillips?"

He sipped his coffee and looked past her. "We were in love. That was more important than the sex."

It seemed to Merrill that she had just garnered some crucial information that couldn't be found in the original case file. Grace Phillips had been a predator, and her victim had just admitted it. Encouraged, she pushed on. "I'm sure that's what it felt like to you as a seventeen-year-old, Brad, but in looking back, does it seem like that was a wise choice for either of you? Especially for Grace, who had a husband and children? Did you think that you had a chance of becoming a real couple, given her situation?"

"You don't understand!" His face was flushed and for the first time today, he was looking directly at her. "Grace was really unhappy with her husband. He had all kinds of issues, but a really bad temper was the worst of them. She never knew when he might blow up about the smallest things. He had started pushing her around when they argued, she told me. Going to college and teaching were her ways to escape him. But her interests and passions only made it worse. The creep was jealous of her happiness!"

Merrill took a sip of her coffee. She wanted to frame this question so that he would answer it. "When Dan Phillips was questioned by the police about the affair between you and his wife, he said he didn't believe it. Do you think he had something to do with her disappearance, in spite of that?"

Brad Childs ran his hand through his hair. Merrill noticed the tiny beads of sweat that were forming on his forehead. "He might have. The guy was evil and capable of that. But there were *so many* people who hated the fact that we were together."

Merrill tried to gather her thoughts. There had been no other names of potential witnesses to this illicit affair in the original case file. Joanna's diary was filled with vague references to "all the kids" and "a few teachers." And Dan Phillips claimed to the investigators that he knew of no one who may have wanted to harm his wife. "Who were these *other* people, Brad?"

He leaned back into the booth and hunched his shoulders. "Lots of the kids thought they knew something. Some teachers, too."

"They knew the two of you were a couple?" Merrill lowered her voice, intending to elicit more from him.

"They *thought* they knew. In some of my classes, I noticed that I was getting the stare down from my teachers. The Resource Room teacher, Mrs. Niche, seemed suspicious. It was during her lunch period when Grace worked with me. From time to time, she would come into her classroom, supposedly to get a book or some papers, which were always in the back of the room behind the portable wall where Grace and I were. Mrs. Niche's student teacher, who was also an assistant coach on the football team, started barging in for no reason during my Resource period, too. Grace took classes with him at the college."

"What was his name?" Merrill asked.

"The guys called him Woodie. His name was Jack Wood, Woods… Wood something."

Merrill took out her notebook and wrote: *Mrs. Niche, Jack Wood (Woods)*. She was sure that Mrs. Niche had been interviewed in 1997, but she was the only school staff member who the police had talked to. Jack Wood had not appeared in the file. When she had first read over that part of the record, she guessed that because both Brad's father and Dan Phillips had denied that there was anything sexual about Grace's relationship with the kid, the cops had found no reason to pursue it with adults who Grace worked with. Merrill knew that a cold case could be activated by new information given by eyewitnesses, so she would definitely follow up with both Mrs. Niche and this Coach Wood.

Brad was watching as she wrote. "You're from Westfield, right?"

"Yes, I am," Merrill said.

"So you know what small town schools are like. The rumor mill was really fired up by that spring. I think one of my teammates may have said something to my coaches. Maybe that's why Woodie kept barging in on us. To check on me. The guy was gay. Grace always teased me about his having a crush on me."

She felt a flash of revulsion at this newly discovered side of the missing woman. So Grace was a pedophile and a homophobe! Merrill's own son was gay, and she was sensitive to any hateful stereotypes ascribed to homosexuality. And of course that comment made by an adult to a straight teenage boy in 1997 was almost certainly charged with bias. The anger pushed her to ask the question that had haunted her from the moment she had read the case file. "Brad. Why didn't you tell the police about your love affair with Grace?"

Brad Childs' eyes began to fill. Her change in tone seemed to push him to answer. "All the way home from Salmon River that day my father shouted at me, warning me for my own good, he said. He said it would kill my mother if I told. It would destroy our family's reputation. It would ruin my chances to go to college. To have a good life."

She leaned across the table and asked the man, "Do you think it was a coincidence that you were out of town the day Grace disappeared? Do you think your father had something to do with her vanishing?"

"I don't know. I've thought about that possibility for years. A month before my release date from jail, I was sober enough to get up the nerve to ask him. But he dropped dead of a heart attack before I got the chance."

"Here we go, sweeties," the waitress said as she placed platters with eggs and pancakes before them. "Enjoy."

Brad Childs pulled on his jacket and slid out of the booth. "I changed my mind. I'm not hungry. Sorry if you didn't get what you needed from me to help Joanna. She should probably be asking her father if she wants to know what happened to her mother."

"Wait, Brad! Who do you think called Grace from the school phone booth that day?"

"No idea," he said over his shoulder.

"Shit," Merrill said under her breath as she watched him walk away. She cut into a blueberry pancake with her fork, but she was too anxious to eat. "Can I have the check, please?" she asked the waitress.

CHAPTER TWENTY-TWO

AFTER THE FALLS

Hall and Oates were singing "Sarah Smile." It was Richard's and Merrill's favorite love song of all time, and she knew all of the lyrics and riffs and typically would be singing at top volume in the empty car. But she was so deep in thought, she didn't sing along. Instead, she stared at the curves and dips of the lakeside road and robotically navigated the Nissan as she mulled over what she had learned during these past few hours.

There was a real possibility that she had screwed up her chance to learn more about Grace Phillips's disappearance from her lover. Brad Child's abrupt departure from the diner was a pretty certain indication that he was through talking to her.

The song was silenced by her phone. "How was your lunch?" Johnny Lovallo asked.

"Are you tracking me?" she asked.

"Of course," he said. "I can't afford to let anything happen to our star researcher. Did you get anything out of him?"

"Maybe. I'll send you some notes when I get home. I think I'll pack up a day early and head west. I'm pretty sure that Brad Childs is done talking to me."

After Johnny hung up, Merrill thought over Brad's admittance that he had had a sexual relationship with Grace Phillips. And that there were other adults who suspected it at the time. That was astonishing in and of itself, but it didn't answer any questions about the woman's vanishing into thin air.

Merrill was so deep in thought, she missed the driveway to the Airbnb. She pulled over on the shoulder and backed up before realizing that there was a familiar car parked in front of the rental. She got out of the Nissan and hurried toward the BMW.

"What are you doing here?" Merrill asked before Kate had a chance to say hello. The two women hugged and Merrill added, "I thought you never took the Z out until May!"

"I checked the forecast. Dry and sunny for the rest of the week, so I decided to take her out for a ride," Kate said.

"Four hours across the state? That's a road trip, not a ride," Merrill said, hearing the joy in her own voice. Her encounter with Brad Childs had left her feeling lonely, almost bereft. It was a familiar emptiness, one that she had experienced many times since Richard's death. And here was one of her best friends to the rescue. She watched as Kate walked to the trunk of the Beamer and pulled out her Vera Bradley bag. She slung it over her shoulder before answering.

"Yup. I had to, once I learned that you had the nerve to go to Lily Dale again without me," she said with faux resentment. "Sherry gave me the address and the code. I decided you and I needed some catch-up time." She pulled from the trunk two Wegman's bags and passed one to Merrill. "I brought dinner. And wine," she added reaching into the passenger seat. "Get the other one, please," she instructed Merrill. "White for me, red for you."

Two hours later the women had eaten their steaks and salads and were sitting in front of the fireplace, sipping wine and gazing out at the last moments of the sun setting over Kasoag Lake. "So tell me how you ended up in this neck of the woods, Merrill. I have to believe Victoria Erikson had something to do with it."

Merrill hesitated. She wasn't sure how to explain this to herself, never mind someone else. "I suppose you could say that. Don't get me wrong, Kate. I'll never be a believer like you, but something about those two weird visits to Lily Dale…"

"Yes?" Kate, leaning in, looked into her friend's eyes.

"I guess the only way to explain it is that I've felt Richard's presence dozens of times since his death. But it's only when I summon him. When I'm trying to make a decision, or if one of the kids is in a predicament, I actively reach out to him, or to his spirit, whatever you and Victoria would call it," she said.

Kate reached for the bottles on the long table in front of the couch and topped off each of their wine glasses. "Go on," she said. "How do you *actively* reach out to Richard?"

"Well, most of the time, I walk into his studio and concentrate on one of his pieces. It can be a painting, a photograph, a sculpture, and I just...*feel* his presence. He doesn't *say* a thing, unlike the chatty Richard who Victoria seems to have summoned forth in Lily Dale."

"Did he actually tell you to try to find this guy at Salmon River?"

"No. Not directly. But after that first session with Victoria, I decided to try to be as open-minded as possible. It's all smoke screens and coincidence, I'm sure. But I'll give credit where credit is due. She made it possible for me to connect some dots...and I did find Brad Childs."

"What's he like?" Kate asked.

"Broken. Like many victims of sexual exploitation, Brad Childs either doesn't understand or refuses to believe that he was Grace Phillips's prey. He's still defending the woman who "loved" him. And from my research, I don't think he's had the therapy he needs. He drinks, can't hold a job or keep a relationship. On top of that sexual trauma, the only person, at least in *his* mind, who loved him, suddenly disappeared."

"So did you get anything from him that wasn't in the file?" Kate asked.

"Yes. I'm not sure it's very pertinent, though."

"So why not go back to Lily Dale to solve the Grace Phillips disappearance? Ask for Victoria's help one more time."

"I don't think so. Victoria Erikson is only one person."

Kate corrected her. "You mean one medium."

"Yes, one medium," she said. "I've been thinking. I may have a way to get many more people involved in helping me solve this case," she said and drained the last of her wine.

"What do you mean?" Kate asked.

"Let's open another bottle first," Merrill said.

CHAPTER TWENTY-THREE

WHY ARE YOU DOING THIS?

WITH JASON'S HELP, Merrill installed Zoom and sent emails to each
of the participants for this episode of the podcast, and she was about to invite each of the three of them in. Thanks to her talented son, her audience
could now watch this and any future video episodes of A Deeper Dive from
the website he had built. She asked Jason to stay during this segment, for
technical, and perhaps moral support. From his place behind the laptop, he
listened and watched as Leah Winslow, who had been his father's student,
paid tribute to her teacher.

"Professor Connor was definitely a major influence in my life and work,"
the artist said. "Was and is still," she added. "I had wonderful teachers in all
of my undergraduate studio art courses, but he was inspirational in a very
unique way."

Merrill felt her face flush, as it always did when she was excited. She had
worked on the planning of this episode for days, ever since she had left
the cabin on Kasoag Lake. The logistics were the most complicated ones
she had undertaken since she started the podcast, but the preparation for
it had given her a short reprieve from the Grace Phillips case. Although
she was elated to hear this praise for her husband, she took a deep breath
and concentrated on maintaining an objective tone. "Unique in what way,
Leah?"

"He gave me something that I would probably have to spend years to
discover on my own. Dr. Connor taught me to value the *process* of making

art. To appreciate it as much as the final product," she said. Leah had joined Merrill's podcast from her studio in New York. Behind the young woman stood several easels displaying her work, some still in progress. Merrill immediately recognized the painting that had been chosen for a *New Yorker* cover.

"When I got to New York," Leah continued, "I was competing with people who had graduated from some of the best and most expensive art schools in the world. But what Fredonia, a state university, and especially Dr. Connor gave me, was the confidence to believe I was their equal. I'll be forever grateful for that."

"Thank you so much, Leah, for participating in this honorarium for Richard. And all the best to you. Richard always said your future was bright."

"You're so welcome, Merrill, and I couldn't have done it without his encouragement," she said. "I'm looking forward to hearing from the other guests and to watching your tour of Dr. Connor's home studio."

The next tribute to him would have blown Richard away, Merrill knew. Her husband had spoken often and fondly about this student, Kyle Marsh. "The professor was such a talented artist himself. That could have been very intimidating for a young person. But from day one in his classes, Dr. Connor taught us to believe in our own uniqueness," he said.

The camera captured the man's classroom at Jamestown Community College, and behind him were representations of his own students' work. Merrill's heart swelled as she looked at them. Here were creations that were a testament to Richard's influence on young artists in spite of the fact that he had passed on. They were his current students, nonetheless. Through Kyle and other teachers he had inspired, Richard lived still.

"His one rule was *Make No Dull Art.* He actually had the print-making classes design different versions of the saying, and they were posted in almost every student's studio space. The man was funny and passionate. He stirred something in us and at the same time, challenged us. Richard Connor made thinking outside of the box a thing before it became a global concept. He was just…so cool!" Before Merrill could speak he added, "I feel sorry for the kids who never knew him."

"Thank you, Kyle. But I think, through you, your students *are* coming to know him and his philosophy. Please thank them for me, too," Merrill said. Jason gave her a signal and she invited another participant in.

"My final guest is another former student of Richard's who wants to pay tribute. Douglas Penning was enrolled in the last photography class that Richard taught before his health forced him to retire." A man appeared on the screen who looked to Merrill like life had laden him with some significant burdens. She noted the deep lines that ran from his cheeks to his jaw, the wrinkles around his mouth and eyes, and his vanishing hairline seemed premature for a man his age.

"Hello, Mrs. Connor, and thanks for doing this." Penning paused and slid his glasses onto the top of his head.

Merrill suspected that he was nervous, so she said nothing about the several black and white photographs behind him. The one that had caught her eye from the beginning was a picture of her late husband, seated in the detested wheelchair. Obviously unaware that he was being photographed, Merrill suspected Penning had caught him during one of his teaching moments. The camera had captured his hands in the characteristic gesture of a teacher. Those same hands that had been cruelly handicapped as the disease progressed. "You're welcome, Douglas," she said. "I know Richard would appreciate your doing this."

"My story is a little different from Leah and Kyle's. I grew up in Brocton and really had no desire to be an artist, or to be anything else, for that matter. I got a factory job in Dunkirk right out of high school. I was lucky, but I was bored, so bored I got into some trouble with the law. My probation officer, at our last meeting, handed me Fredonia's Community course schedule, the ones they offer while the college kids are on winter break. He told me there were a couple of scholarships still available that would cover the tuition. So it was either Intro to Mandarin or the professor's Intro to Photography class. I enrolled in the photography course."

"And how did that go?" Merrill asked.

"Well, I found out on Day One of that class what Kyle means about Dr. Connor challenging his students. As a matter of fact, in my case anyway, he delivered an ass-kicking to me pretty much every day that I attended." A smile broke through Penning's dour demeanor and Merrill thought it erased several years from his face. "In spite of that, it took all of five minutes in his presence for me to decide that I didn't want to miss a moment of his class. I was intrigued with the professor's brief, but illuminating, "chats." That's what he called his lectures."

Merrill interrupted him. "I believe you captured a moment of one of those in that wonderful photograph of him behind you. Am I right?"

"Yes, you are. His short bursts of brilliance would rev me up for the actual taking of pictures. And I loved the hands-on portion of the course!" As Doug Penning spoke, he was doing a Benjamin Button transformation, shedding years. "I hadn't been that excited about anything in my life at that point. I would come out of the darkroom and be hanging some of my prints up to dry. I felt pretty proud of those first tries. But there would be Connor, er, Dr. Connor looking over my shoulder. He'd say, 'That's pretty good, Doug. Now what can you do next time to make it better?' I would think about it and the next time, I was sure they were better. And there he would be behind me again, asking the same thing. Before I met your husband, I would have quit whatever it was that people urged me to do better. But for the first time in my life, the chip on my shoulder was shrinking."

God, Merrill thought to herself, how I miss my husband. "So his words were motivating, not debilitating?"

"For sure," Doug said. "With six classes left in the course, he was spending more time in the wheelchair. He would roll up behind me as I worked, and this time he asked a different question. 'Penning, why exactly are you doing this?'

'What do you mean?' I asked him.

'What is your reason for making art?' he asked.

'I don't know. To keep the streets safe from thugs like me?' That cracked him up, but he kept pushing me.

'Who's your audience?' he asked.

'I have to have an audience?'

I could see that the remark pissed him off. 'You need to dig deeper, Penning. Until you do, you're just using up precious time.'

In that moment, lightning struck. Here was a man, a teacher and an artist, who knew about time, who knew what a limited commodity it was."

"And did you dig deeper?" Merrill asked.

"I did. I realized that until I reached out to others and tried to communicate with my photographs, I was just taking up space. Art for art's sake is bullshit. My life was better because I was making art and reaching out to an audience that could appreciate it. That's what I found when Dr. Connor made me dive deeper."

Merrill thanked Doug Penning and encouraged her listeners to check out the links to each of the artists and their works on the podcast website. She signaled to Jason and he ended the Zoom meeting.

"That went great, Mom. I'd say there's more video in your future," Jason said.

The last five minutes of this episode would be a tour of Richard's home studio with Merrill as guide. Jason would tape and post it for *A Deeper Dive* fans. She would showcase a piece from each genre: photography, sculpture, and his final painting, which Merrill had left on the easel where he had painstakingly worked for the last few weeks of his life.

As the tour drew to a close Merrill spoke to the camera. "Mr. Penning told you about my husband's advice that changed his own art career, and perhaps his whole life. This painting of Richard's is called, *A Deeper Dive.*" She balled her fist and dug her nails into her palms so that she would not break down during this last part of the tour. "He completed it in spite of the fact that the disease had rendered his hands useless. It's not only an example of his artistry, but his guiding principle of life. For me, the painting is a message from my husband that continues to encourage me." She paused and took a breath. "It's a reminder to not give up, even when the challenge, when life itself, seems impossible. It inspired this podcast, as a matter of fact." As she spoke, Jason panned in on the central figure of the painting, the free diver, while his mother continued.

"I want you, my listeners, to know that thanks to Richard's inspiration, this podcast will be moving in a new direction. For the past month, I've been working with the Westfield Sheriff's Department as a research assistant. In particular, I've been looking into a twenty-year-old cold case." Merrill tried to ignore her son's shocked expression as he stood behind the camera. "Some of you who are local residents may remember the disappearance from the Mill Springs Mall of Grace Phillips, a teacher's assistant at Westfield High School. Neither she, nor her remains, have ever been found."

Merrill paused and took a deep breath. "Lately, I've been researching and listening to other podcasts, especially those with a true crime theme. I've been particularly interested in the ones where listeners participate in trying to solve a mystery. With the permission of Deputy Lovallo of the Westfield Sheriff's Department, I'm going to post the details of the Grace Phillips case on my website. I'm inviting you, my audience, to take a deeper dive with me. If you have any information that would aid in leading us to a resolution in this unsolved crime, I'd like you to send me an email. You'll find the address on the *Deeper Dive* website. Until next time, this is Merrill Connor, signing off."

As Kate's theme song played, Jason panned in on his father's painting once again and then turned the camera off. "A murder investigation? Mom, what's going on? I'm not sure this is something I want you to be involved in! Do the girls know about this?"

"No, your sisters don't know about my working on an unsolved crime. Why should they? First of all, it's not a murder investigation without a body. It's a missing person case, like Sarah Ingham. That's why the police contacted me in the first place."

"Mom, Sarah Ingham is alive and well! Safe at home with her parents. This Phillips woman was more than likely murdered! I don't want my mother to endanger her life for the sake of a hobby! Why are you doing this?"

The irony of her son asking her the same question his father had asked Doug Penning was not lost on her, but she decided not to point it out. Jason was her youngest and the most protective of her kids. When he was in nursery school, and she was in graduate school, he would frequently tell his teacher that he had to leave early to check on his mom.

"Are you hungry, honey?" she asked him now. "I made some pretty tasty chili yesterday. Want some?"

After her son left, Merrill watched the recording of today's podcast. She was pleased, and she had Jason to thank for it. The Doug Penning segment especially moved her. She sat down at her desk and pulled out her notebook and attempted to answer the question Richard had asked his student.

At the top of the page she wrote: "Why are you doing this?" and underlined the question. Below the heading, she wrote the answer.

For Joanna
For Brad Childs
For Grace

CHAPTER TWENTY-FOUR

WHAT IN THE HELL IS A MURDERINO?

"Wᴀᴛ ɪɴ ᴛʜᴇ hell is a murderino?" Johnny Lovallo shouted at her. When they were together, she seemed to bring out the youngest child of seven in the detective, a period in his life when his simplest needs, he had told her, had to be expressed at the top of his lungs if they were ever to be heeded. And he, at the same time, brought out Merrill's sarcastic streak.

"Quiet! You realize you're in a public library, don't you?" she asked him. "A murderino is…haven't you ever heard of *My Favorite Murder,* or *Up and Vanished, S- Town,* or *Bear Brook?*"

He lowered his voice, maybe in deference to her, but more likely so that she would go easier on him. "I listen to a lot of music, but I don't know any of those bands."

"They're not bands, Sheriff; they're true crime podcasts."

"On the radio?" he asked as he followed her down the stairs to her office.

He seemed so clueless, she almost felt sorry for him. "Sometimes. But mostly on the internet," she said, trying to take the edge out of her tone. "The ones I named typically deal with unsolved murders, and sometimes the fan base does more than listen. That's what murderinos are. They're listeners who actually become involved, and sometimes they are instrumental in solving cold cases. Concerning the vanishing of Grace Phillips, I believe *A Deeper Dive* can cast a wider net for potential witnesses than *one* researcher working for *one* police department can."

"How so?" Lovallo asked, settling into the chair across from her.

She hoped he wouldn't get too comfortable. She was expecting someone who had responded to her podcast plea regarding Grace's disappearance, and she really didn't want to involve Lovallo. Not yet, anyway. "Well, isn't the goal of all cold case investigators to find evidence that went undiscovered the first time, to have more potential witnesses come forward than did originally?"

"The initial investigators questioned plenty of people in 1997, and then every five years after that." Merrill could hear the familiar defensiveness Lovallo had whenever they discussed the original investigation.

"A total of twenty that first year, and then fifteen in 2002, and those were all repeats. No one after that. I've studied the files, you know." She was trying not to be a smartass so that he would answer a question that had plagued her since her trip to the Salmon River. "Johnny, why was Brad Childs left off the follow-up witness list after his first time as a seventeen-year-old?"

He pulled out his phone and made a note. "That's a question for a much older man than me. I'll reach out to Rog Foretti who headed the team back then. He retired in 2000. Hopefully I'll find him in between his pickle ball games."

Merrill was relieved when the sheriff stood to leave. She hadn't told him that after her meeting with Brad Childs, she believed there was a possibility that a motive for Grace's disappearance could finally be established. One of Merrill's theories was that perhaps to protect his wounded pride and public reputation, Dan Phillips had not told the police everything he knew about his wife's behavior up until the day she went missing. Maybe he didn't want to open the door to speculation that he was a jealous husband, that he could therefore be involved in her vanishing. So he told the police that he did not believe his wife was carrying on with one of her students.

Another theory of Merrill's was that Brad's father had something to do with Grace's disappearance. Brad had told her that Mr. Childs had not been honest about everything he knew regarding his son's romance with his teacher. And she had already discovered that Brad, because of his father's insistence, had not been forthcoming when he was interviewed as a teen. He had denied then that he and Grace had been lovers, and so the official case files did not establish that fact.

Before she shared her speculations with Lovallo, Merrill wanted an opportunity to verify Grace and Brad's affair with other potential witnesses who had been overlooked or summarily dismissed as viable during the 1997 investigation. This included the person who would be heading down the library stairs soon. "Great. Thanks for reaching out to Foretti, Johnny," she said.

"Keep in touch, Merrill," the sheriff said as he turned and walked out of her studio. That was *almost* a goodbye, Merrill thought. She listened to his echoing footsteps as he climbed to the main floor of the Prenderson Library.

She opened her laptop and read Marlene Niche's email again. The special education teacher, retired now, had been interviewed in 1997. But the cops' questions concerned her opinion about Grace as a colleague. Before Johnny had shown up this morning, Merrill had read over the notes on Mrs. Niche's meeting with the police. She told them she admired Grace. Her work ethic, especially, had impressed the whole Special Education staff. Mrs. Niche, who worked most closely with her, respected the fact that the mother of three teens was working full time and going back to school to get her BA and her teaching certificate. The veteran educator had told the police that Grace was an "invaluable" teaching assistant. But nowhere in the notes could Merrill find that Niche had been asked any questions about her student Brad Childs.

Marlene Niche was a tall, broad-shouldered blond, and for a woman who was probably ten years older than Merrill, she exuded the kind of confidence that good teachers possess. She looked as though she would still be a force to be reckoned with, inside or outside of a classroom. Merrill stood and extended her hand. "Please have a seat, Mrs. Niche. Thanks for reaching out to me and for coming today."

"Call me Marlene, and you're very welcome, Mrs. Connor. I've been a fan of your podcast from the beginning," she said, slipping her jacket off and sitting down in the chair Lovallo had vacated. "I'm not sure I can tell you anything I didn't tell the police twenty years ago, but I'm happy to answer any of your questions."

"I'm going to record our conversation. Is that okay?" Merrill asked. "Just for the sake of keeping track of the details. I won't use it on the podcast without your permission."

"I have no problem with that," the woman said, and Merrill turned on her voice recorder.

"Marlene, I've read over your interview with the police in 1997, and I know you were fond of Grace Phillips. I'd like to know how your students felt about her."

The retired teacher didn't hesitate. "Oh, they loved her. She was always eager to help above and beyond their school assignments. I had juniors and seniors, and they were kids who often struggled with academics. As my assistant, Grace often worked with them one-on-one, giving them strategies to use when they were frustrated or lost. She built a trust with them. They were likely to seek her out for personal advice, too."

"I see. Can you tell me about the logistics of your classroom? How was the space set up and shared with Mrs. Phillips?"

"Well, as a special education teacher, each student on any given day would guide us in terms of the arrangement. There were ten or twelve desks in the classroom. I would typically do the whole class instruction, and Grace would help with the individual Resource Room teaching. We had a portable cubicle set up so that she was able to work with students behind the wall while I was teaching, if that was necessary."

"Were you in the room when Grace provided this individual help?" Merrill asked.

"Most of the time. But because of scheduling… teachers do have to eat and use the restroom, you know…Grace would occasionally be alone with a student." Merrill saw that Mrs. Niche was either uncomfortable in the wooden library chair, or perhaps it was Merrill's question that had made her squirm a bit.

"I see," Merrill said. "And Grace often worked with Brad Childs when you were at lunch, is that right?"

The retired teacher looked somewhat taken aback at hearing his name. "Yes. That's true." She paused and stared at the books on the shelf behind

Merrill before continuing. "I think Brad had a crush on Grace, in spite of the age difference."

"Marlene, do you think Grace was having an affair with a student, with Brad?" Merrill asked.

"I really couldn't say, Merrill. I never witnessed anything specific. But to be perfectly frank, I did worry about it. Kids talk. Teachers talk. Sometimes it's bullshit, but sometimes there's a kernel of truth in the midst of the gossip. That's why from time to time, during my lunch periods, I'd send my student teacher to run inter...to my classroom during that time. He and Grace were friends. They were both attending classes that semester at Fredonia, so they often commuted together."

"Were you going to say that this guy...what's his name?" Merrill asked.

"Jack Woodhall," Marlene Niche answered.

"Were you going to say that you sent your student teacher to run interference? To make sure nothing inappropriate happened between a teacher and her student?" Merrill asked.

"Oh, no. It wasn't that. It was more about keeping Grace's name out of the faculty room, or Gossip Central, as I liked to call it. You know what they say about small towns and small minds, right?"

Merrill nodded and Marlene continued. "Well, you can add small schools to that epigram. I thought Grace was too fine a teacher to have her career ruined before it started. So sometimes I sent Jack to my classroom to make sure everything was copacetic. He often ate his lunch in there, which I appreciated. For Grace's sake, I mean," she added.

"What became of your student teacher?" Merrill asked. "I think I'd like to talk with him about Grace."

Marlene Niche lowered her eyes and spoke just above a whisper. "Well, it certainly wasn't what I would have expected of Jack. He was supposed to graduate with his BA in Special Education from Fredonia that spring. But I came in on a Monday morning and there was a letter from the college in my mailbox. It said that my student teacher had withdrawn from the program and would not be returning to school that semester."

"But why?" Merrill asked.

"I'm not sure. No one seemed to know, but there were plenty of ignorant people in the faculty room who opined their own theories. All I know is that he dropped out of the teaching program and off my radar," Marlene Niche said. "He never even contacted me so that I could gather the books and other things he had left. That was a tough time at school, especially in my classroom with the two of them gone. The kids, especially the athletes that he had coached, liked Jack and they missed him. But they were all in mourning for Grace."

As soon as Mrs. Niche left, Merrill looked over the 1997 Westfield Police Department's witness list for the hundredth time. Jack Woodhall did not appear among the names. She picked up her phone, and before she could say hello to Johnny Lovallo, he recited, "'A murderino is a person who is interested in, especially obsessed with, murders. Including serial murderers, spree killers and rage/thrill killers. Dubbed murderinos by a member of the *My Favorite Murder* podcast fan page on Facebook.'"

"Okay, Detective, congratulations. You've done your homework," she said, but he wasn't done.

"'Murderinos gather there to discuss the podcast and interesting murders.' Ha, more like Freakarinos, I'd say," he scoffed.

"Now that you've shared your enlightenment, I need you to get me whatever information you can on a Jack Woodhall. He was a student teacher at Westfield High at the same time Grace Phillips worked there in '97. And they commuted to college classes together. I would think he might have first-hand information on who exactly Grace Phillips was and what was going on in her life at the time. He was arrested in late spring following her disappearance. I want to know what the charges were and where he is now."

"Wait a minute! Who's the researcher here?" he asked.

"You have much easier access to things like drivers' licenses and arrest records than I do. Besides, you don't pay me enough for me to take on any more responsibility than I have already," she said.

"Okay, okay, no need to get sarcastic. I'll get back to you with whatever I find," he said. She knew the click was coming, and there it was.

CHAPTER TWENTY-FIVE

MALL WALKERS

SITTING AT THE oak library table that took up most of the space in the tiny room, Merrill scrolled through the recent emails in her Deeper Dive account. She had already read the eleven that were sent shortly after her tribute to Richard. Eight of them were from fans of that episode. They were messages of appreciation and encouragement. Marlene Niche was one of these devotees. Three were from ardent admirers of her late husband's work. One of those ended with a question: would Merrill be interested in selling any of her husband's sculptures that she had featured on the episode?

The twelfth one had been posted very early this morning. The bolded subject line sent a chill down Merrill's spine: **I was at the mall that day.**

"Hello Ms. Connor. A friend told me about A Deeper Dive and I have been listening to the last few episodes. I decided to get in touch because I was at the Mill Springs Mall on the day that Grace Phillips disappeared. I saw her. She was with a man. Here's my phone number if you'd like to get in touch with me. Cory Brooks."

Merrill knew that, except for Joanna Phillips, the mall manager, several store managers, and a security cop who had been on duty that day, the police had not interviewed anyone else who had been present at the shopping center on March 25th, 1997. But after listening to her podcast for forty minutes, here was someone who had come forward claiming to have seen Grace that day. Merrill could feel her heart pounding. She wondered if Cory Brooks was a woman or a man? No matter the person's gender, Merrill prayed this was not a sick joke. She added the name to her contacts, and as she did, her phone vibrated.

"Hi, Mrs. Connor," Joanna Phillips said. Merrill didn't recognize her voice so much as the familiar tone of sadness in it.

"Hello, Joanna. Please call me Merrill."

"Merrill. I'm just calling to touch base with you. Have there been any new developments since your podcast?"

Merrill was distracted by the sound of footsteps on the stairway. She rarely saw anyone here in "the catacombs," as the staff called this section of the basement, unless they had come to see her. A man, obviously bundled up against the cruel December cold, lumbered down the last few steps. He began to pull the scarf away from his face, but when Merrill tried to make eye contact with him, he pulled it back over his mouth and turned away. She watched as he disappeared into the microfiche area and the local history stacks.

"Joanna, I'm just leaving the library. Can I give you a call in a bit?" she asked, closing her laptop and pulling on her coat.

At home two hours later, Merrill called Joanna with a startling invitation. "What are you doing tomorrow afternoon at three-thirty? Can you be available to have a Skype session from the Mill Springs Mall?"

It turned out that Cory Brooks was a woman who had lived in the area all of her thirty-nine years. Her first job, she informed Merrill over the phone that afternoon, was at the Orange Julius kiosk at the mall. Her first day there, which would turn out to be her last, was the day Grace disappeared.

"I was so nervous," the woman explained. "I had never had a job before. My mother and I were fighting all the time back then. I was desperate to get out of the house and get my own apartment,"

Merrill was struck by her rapid style of speaking. "Cory, would it be okay if I recorded our conversation, just so I don't forget any details?" she asked.

"I guess that wouldn't be a problem."

Merrill turned on her phone voice recorder. "Go ahead, Cory."

"That day I started my shift at noon, which I quickly found out was a very busy period for smoothie sales. I felt like time was just flying by. I was glad they had trained me early in the morning a week before with no customers in the mall, but it was different with real people ordering all kinds of stuff. I remember I was very nervous and my head was spinning. I had to redo a couple of orders, and I gave the wrong change once, but because it was a weekday, by three-thirty, things had slowed down. Fewer people wanted an Orange Julius at that time of day, thank goodness. A guy was supposed to be there at three to relieve the other worker, but he called in sick, so there I was alone on my first day of work." The woman paused and took a deep breath. "Did I mention that I'm on the spectrum?"

"The spectrum?" Merrill was confused.

"Yes. I wasn't tested or diagnosed until I applied to community college five years ago. Autism wasn't understood or even recognized when I was a kid. People just thought I was weird. They told me so a few times a day once I started school. But yeah. I'm mildly autistic. Highly functional, I am. But the Orange Julius job was a very big challenge for me."

Merrill was taken aback by Cory Brook's candid words, but she tried not to show it for fear that the woman would decide not to go any further with her recollection. "I see. What else can you tell me about that day at the mall?"

"Well, finally, there were no customers so I started cleaning the smoothie machinery. I had my back to the counter. I heard someone clearing his throat. When I turned around the guy, the guy who turned out to be with Grace, said, 'Two small ones, please.'"

As Cory Brooks spoke, Merrill asked herself for the umpteenth time why the Westfield Sheriff's Department had not rounded up every person who worked in the mall that day. Like Cory. "Do you remember what this man looked like? What age he might have been?"

"Honestly, he was a pretty basic guy. He didn't stand out at all. He was youngish. Thirty or so? He wore wire-rimmed glasses and some kind of a wool hat, like a ski cap. That seemed weird because it was a kind of warm spring day. I don't have any clear memory of his face. But I did notice the woman at the fountain. The one he brought the drink to, and I'm almost one hundred percent certain that it was Mrs. Phillips."

"Did you know Grace Phillips, Cory?"

"No, I didn't, but the pictures of her in the newspaper the next day... that was the woman I saw at the fountain. She was very pretty. And stylish. I remember thinking that her shoes matched her blue raincoat perfectly."

Merrill's face was red hot. She tried to sound calm as she asked Cory Brooks her next question. "Would you be willing to meet me at the mall tomorrow afternoon, Cory?"

Merrill pulled into a parking spot a half-hour before she was to meet Cory Brooks in front of the mall fountain. According to the case files, this was the space that Joanna and her mother had parked in that day. Her intention was to traverse the length of the mall before the woman joined her. As she walked through the main entrance, Merrill felt a shiver travel up her spine with the realization that Grace Phillips, too, had gone through this door. And never come back out.

Throughout the eighties and nineties, the mall was the busiest shopping center under one roof in the county. Merrill had been here hundreds of times, until online shopping became the best way to purchase pretty much anything. Besides, Walden Books had closed up years ago, so since the kids had grown up and left home, she had little reason to shop here. Today, she started out at the J.C. Penney's end and walked the entire length of the mall to the Sear's store. According to the police file, Joanna had stopped at the Nike store that day to ask if her mother had been there, but it had closed years ago. It was a video game store now.

Walking back toward the entrance, Merrill slowed down as she approached the green concrete fountain, still functioning and apparently still a popular vessel for bored kids to toss their pennies. Under the splashing waterfall stood two children made of stone, a boy and a girl who shared an umbrella to protect them from the always rainy weather of the fountain. The two child-sized statues were favorites of Merrill's own little kids way back when. As she walked back toward the Orange Julius booth, she pulled her phone from her purse and Skyped Joanna Phillips.

"Did you know Cory Brooks by any chance? I believe she graduated a few years before you, but she is from Westfield," Merrill asked her.

"I don't think so. Don't forget, I was pretty much a loner throughout my childhood years and my teens. Is that the fountain behind you?"

"It is. I'm going to ask Cory to explain what and who she saw that afternoon. And I thought it made sense to reenact it here," Merrill explained.

"I never went back to that mall after Mom disappeared," Joanna said. Merrill could see her eyes were welling up with tears. She knew how suddenly and thoroughly grief could vanquish and overtake every part of you. Sometimes it snuck up on you for no apparent reason. But even though twenty years had passed, Merrill realized that the return to the place she had last been with her mother would be especially painful for Joanna. Her need to ultimately bring some comfort to this woman was what propelled Merrill forward on this mission.

"I know how hard this must be for you, Joanna…" Before she could complete her sentence, she was distracted by a petite redhead emerging from a small crowd of shoppers. She began waving wildly and when Merrill waved back, the woman made a beeline for her.

"Merrill Connor," she said, and reached out her hand. "I recognized you from the picture on the *Deeper Dive* site. I'm Cory." Besides her childish stature, Merrill was struck again by the woman's staccato speaking style.

"Thanks so much for meeting with me, Cory. I have Joanna Phillips, Grace's daughter, on the phone. She'll be watching and listening to us today. She may have some questions for you, too."

On Merrill's phone screen, the two women acknowledged one another. Cory added, "I'm sorry for your loss." Joanna said nothing, but she nodded uncertainly. She didn't seem to know what to make of this woman.

"Let's go over to the Orange Julius booth, where you were that afternoon," Merrill said. When they reached the kiosk which was a few dozen yards from the fountain, Merrill said, "Cory, tell us about your experience here that day, starting with what happened when the man came to the counter."

"Well, I had my back to the counter, but when he got my attention, he said, 'two small ones, please,' and I said, 'Small what's?' and he said. 'Two small Julius.' I noticed that he kept turning to look back behind him, in that direction." Cory pointed at the fountain. There were several people sitting on the edge today, very clearly visible from the Orange Julius kiosk. She turned her phone camera toward it so that Joanna could see what Merrill saw.

"After he ordered, I noticed that he turned and gave a little wave to the lady who sat on the ledge of the fountain," Cory continued. "I went to work making the drinks, and when I turned around, he had his back to me. I could see that he was still looking at the woman. A couple of other customers were there by then, reading the menu boards. I set his drinks on the counter in front of him. The man threw a twenty dollar bill down and mumbled something. I was pretty sure he said, 'No change.' Then he picked up the drinks and took off toward the fountain," Cory said.

"Let's walk," Merrill said to Cory. When they reached the fountain, the two women sat down on the ledge. "Go ahead, Cory. What happened next?"

"While I waited on the two other customers, I tried to keep my eyes on him because I was going to bring his change to him. I knew I would get in trouble with the manager when he tried to balance the day's receipts if I didn't. The guy was sitting close to the woman, to Grace Phillips. They were both sipping their drinks and their heads were kind of bowed together, like they were talking about something private."

"Were there any other people sitting here?" Merrill asked.

"No. Not on the side I could see, anyway," Cory answered.

"Did my mother look like she was stressed, like the man was forcing her to be there?" Joanna asked.

"I wasn't close enough to see the look on her face, but no. She seemed, I don't know…not exactly comfortable, but I don't think he was a stranger to her. When my customers left, I got the change I owed him from the register, and I was going to go over and give it to him. But by the time I turned around, they were gone."

"Did you see where they went?" Joanna asked.

"No. I hadn't seen them get up to leave. The strangest thing was, the woman, Grace, left one of those pretty blue shoes on the floor in front of where she'd been sitting. Right about here," Cory said, pointing down at the floor. "Her left shoe. The police picked it up when they came. I saw them put it in a bag." Cory took a breath, at last.

Merrill asked, "Cory. Did the police talk to you that day?"

"No. I called the station the next day after I read the article in the paper. The one about Grace Phillips disappearing. But they said they were interviewing other witnesses and they would call me in a few days. But they never did. My mother said I should mind my own business, that they would never believe someone like me."

Merrill had a suspicion that Cory's quirkiness, as she had perceived it after their two minute phone conversation was the reason the cops had not taken her seriously. Her own mother must have understood that. As Cory and Merrill stood up with their backs to the fountain, Joanna spoke. "So you may have been the last one to see my mom that day, Cory. Except for the person who took her." Merrill could hear the grief in her voice. "It's ironic that she disappeared after you saw her at the fountain. That was the place she always told me and my brothers to go if we got separated from one another. It would be the place we would be sure to meet up, where we would be safe, she told us." Merrill and Cory watched as Joanna slowly shook her head. "But apparently she wasn't safe there," she said.

At Larry's that evening, surrounded by her friends, Merrill was eating her last wing and sharing with them all that she didn't know about the cold case and the woman who had gone missing so many years before.

"So what was Grace's long game do you think? Did she have one?" Sherry asked.

"It seems as if only one person knew or would admit he knew that she was having an affair with a minor," Merrill said.

"Come on, Merrill. I don't think we can call that an affair! Mrs. Phillips was a pedophile!" Kate yelled, loudly enough that the waitress passing by shot the four of them a wary glance.

"Unfortunately, the victim never disclosed that to the police," Merrill said, lowering her voice in hopes that Kate would follow suit.

"Why didn't he, do you think?" Jenna asked.

"It seems like his father had Brad firmly under his thumb and demanded that he not tell the police. Certainly Dan Phillips didn't believe it, so that clears the husband. He didn't believe it, so he had no motive. He claims there was nothing between his wife and Childs, so why would he be jealous?"

Kate said, "So who was Grace close with? I'd like to think that if I disappeared, you all would have the inside scoop on what was happening in my life at the time. That you'd be able to give the cops some information that would help them find me."

Merrill said, "Apparently, Grace wasn't a very social person. It was work, college, and her family. There didn't seem to be much time for anything or anyone else."

"Hm…"Sherry said. Something was on the tip of her tongue, Merrill could tell. "She was a hottie, right? I remember thinking so when those photos of her were published when she disappeared. Not exactly a natural beauty, but very stylish."

"She was very attractive, yes," Merrill answered.

"Well, what about her hair stylist, her manicurist?" Sherry said. "Maybe she talked to one of them. I know I have a debriefing session every couple of weeks with my own glam squad."

Merrill looked around the table as the other three women nodded in agreement. She picked up the last wing on her plate and said, "I guess I could try to find out who did her hair from her daughter." Before she could take a bite, her phone rang.

"What have you got for me?" Johnny Lovallo asked.

Kate and Jenna looked at one another across the table and comically mirrored each other's lovesick look. Simultaneously, each mouthed one word: "Johnny."

Merrill left her friends at the table. She locked the ladies' room door behind her and lowered her voice so that no one on the other side could hear her. She gave Johnny a quick summary of her day at the mall and Cory Brooks' explanation of what she had witnessed twenty years before.

"I don't know, Merrill!" he answered loudly when she asked how the police could have botched this so badly. "I wasn't even in the department at the time, remember?" He was shouting now. "I'll send an investigator to interview the woman and we'll finally have an official record from an eyewitness from that day! At least a self-proclaimed eyewitness." He took a breath and seemed to calm himself. "Good work, Connor," he said. "Keep me informed if you find any other Murderinos with information."

Jenna had driven Merrill to Wing Night that evening. As they pulled up in front of her house, Merrill finished telling her friend about her mall walking with Cory Brooks and Johnny Lovallo's request. "I got notifications of a couple of emails after we arrived at Larry's." She yawned loudly. "Hopefully, they'll make good bedtime reading."

Chapter Twenty-six

ANOTHER MURDERINO

Johnny Lovallo set the cardboard carrier from the Main Diner and a manila folder onto the library table and pulled his jacket off. His ability at all times to do at least two things at once reminded Merrill of a modern dancer, all the moves combining and coordinating into one kinetically charged routine. "So what have you got?" he asked her, bending back the tab on the lid and handing her a cup of coffee.

"This email came last night," she said, pointing to her computer screen. Johnny lifted the lid on his cup and walked behind her so he could see what was on her laptop. Below the blank subject line he read aloud:

"*I listened to your show, A Deeper Dive, about Grace Phillips. I have some information to share. R. Luiz*" A 716 number was written in parentheses next to the message.

"Another Murderino, huh?" the detective asked, sitting down beside her. "Did you call this person?"

"As soon as I finished reading it. And I recorded our conversation."

Johnny's untrimmed eyebrows raised in a way that Merrill was coming to understand signaled that he was impressed. "With her permission, of course. I've skipped over our introductions at the beginning of our discussion for you. This is Mrs. Roberta Luiz," she said. She leaned closer to her keyboard and pressed play.

"I was about to end my shift that day. I was pushing my supply

cart down the hall after I finished cleaning the restrooms. When I turned the corner into the corridor, I noticed a lady and a man coming toward me. The lady was stumbling. I thought maybe she was drunk. She almost ran into the cart. I stopped so that I wouldn't run into her, and the man put his arm around her. Like he was protecting her. She was looking down and mumbling. I'm pretty sure she said, 'shoe.' I looked down then and saw that she was only wearing only one. A bright blue shoe."

"Was the couple heading toward the restrooms?"

"No. I watched him guide her in the opposite direction, toward the emergency exit door. And then he turned and looked over his shoulder at me. It was a look that said that I better get about my business. So that's what I did. I pushed my cart toward the main corridor."

"What did the man look like, Mrs. Luiz?"

"He wasn't very tall. About the woman's height, I'd say. He wore those aviator glasses. Wire-rimmed. And a ski hat. Red with a tassle on top. I remember thinking that was a little weird because it was spring time. Not that cold out."

"When did you realize that the woman was Grace Phillips?"

"The next day. You couldn't watch WKBW News for a couple of weeks without seeing pictures of her."

"The police had a list of all the employees that worked that day. What did you tell them when they called you?"

"I wasn't on their list. My daughter Rosemary was. They called her."

"But..."

"I got that job at the mall for my daughter. She's the one who played your podcast for me. The one where you asked for your listeners' help. Rosemary insisted that I should get in touch with you. She'd been in jail six months before Grace Phillips disappeared, and she was on parole at the time. That morning I tried to get her up, but she was awful sick from whatever she had done the

*night before. It could have been booze, meth, heroin, or some other
kind of poison she was putting into her body in those days. So I
went into work and punched her time card and covered her shift so
she wouldn't get in trouble. When the police finally called, she told
them she hadn't seen Grace Phillips that day."*

"So you never did go to the police?"

"No."

"Why not, Mrs. Luiz?"

"Do you have kids, Mrs. Connor?

"Yes, I do. Three."

"Any of them ever been in trouble? I had to keep that girl out of
jail. If I had called the police, I would have had to tell them that she
violated parole and wasn't at work that day. It would have ruined
her. She was doing enough to destroy herself. So no, I never told the
police what I saw that day."

"Would you talk with them now?"

"Twenty years too late?"

"I can assure you that in 1997 no one else came forward with
information about a man being in the mall with Mrs. Phillips that
day. If you would tell them what you saw, they might be able to
identify this man. Which could lead to discovering what happened
to Grace."

During what seemed like a very long silence, Merrill turned to study
Johnny Lovallo's face. There was nothing in his expression that told her that
he was impressed with Roberta Luiz's story.

"Rosemary is doing well now. She finally got her life together
soon after this happened. I'll send you my address. Yes, I will talk
to them."

Merrill turned off the recorder. Johnny slid his chair back and took another sip of his coffee. "I'll get a guy over to Roberta Luiz's house tomorrow,
right after he interviews Cory Brooks." He started to stand, but sat back
down and stared at her, narrowing his eyes in his signature squint. She had

asked him once if he needed glasses but he ignored the question. She had come to realize that the expression meant he was deep in thought, as if he were trying to figure out some kind of puzzle. "You're something, you know that, Connor?"

"What do you mean?"

"You're a very smart woman, obviously, but you've also got a dogged determination, a work ethic like I've never seen before. Most retirees take cruises and buy condos in Southern Florida, but you…well, Florida's loss is Westfield's gain," he said and stood up. As he pulled on his jacket he added, "My gain, too."

Oh, no, Merrill thought. He wasn't going to muck up their relationship with some kind of weird professing of romantic feelings was he? "I brought you a present," he said.

Merrill stifled a gasp. And then he reached across the table for the folder. "Jack Woodhall's employment history and arrest record. We haven't got a current address or phone number, but I've got somebody working on that." The next thing she knew, she was listening to his retreating footsteps on the stairs. It sounded like he was taking them two at a time.

"Stay in touch," she called out to the empty room.

Chapter Twenty-seven

CREEPED OUT

As silence returned to her little podcast studio, Merrill sat and tried not to be creeped out about the over-the-top praise Johnny Lovallo had heaped on her. Instead, she concentrated on the new information she had brought to the detective's attention and to the cold case in general. Because of *A Deeper Dive*, she had discovered not one, but two eyewitnesses who saw Grace Phillips the day she had disappeared. Each woman had seen a man with her and in their independent recountings, their descriptions of him were virtually the same. And it was all due to her podcast audience. Of course Johnny Lovallo was appreciative of her efforts, and grateful too. Why wouldn't he be, she reasoned.

Her musing was interrupted by the sound of an email notification, but before she could check her laptop, her phone rang. Jenna's voice was a welcome relief from the squeamishness Johnny's complimentary words had left her with. "Hi, Merrill. What are you up to this morning?"

"I'm just about to leave the library and head home. I had a meeting with Detective Lovallo."

"Hmm...why doesn't that surprise me?" Jenna said.

"Why *would* that surprise you...he's my boss, remember?" Merrill said, making a minimal effort to keep from sounding defensive. She didn't appreciate her friends' middle school attitude about her relationship with Johnny Lovallo. At Larry's the other night when she took his call, they had come very close to crossing the line. She and Richard shared the deepest love, a one of a kind love, and the women she was closest with knew that. But she was finally at a stage in her grieving where she could welcome a friendship with a man. That's what she wanted and felt that she had with Johnny. The women needed to understand that.

"Okay, okay. I read you loud and clear," Jenna said. "I called because I think I have a contact for you. Someone you might want to talk to. A woman who worked at Vince's Salon in the 90's. She remembers Grace."

"Really? You're amazing, my friend!" Merrill said. She felt a pang of shame for the hostility she expressed seconds before. Her friends were ultimately supportive of her. She couldn't have come this far in this stage of her life without them. "Joanna's recollection of the location of the place was pretty foggy. She had to get on a Westfield Yesterday Facebook page to find a picture of the Main Street storefront she remembered her mother going to at least once a month for a cut and color. But she couldn't recall the name of any stylist that may have worked on her."

"Well, I had a long nail appointment and a conversation with a very talkative lady named Jodie Ames this morning. She's been working there for thirty years, well within the range of time that Grace could have been a customer. She says she thinks she may have done her nails once or twice, but she definitely remembers her as a regular hair customer. Anyway..." Jenna paused dramatically. "*Jodie is still in touch with Vince*!!!" she said.

"Vince? Who's Vince?" Merrill said, totally lost in the details of Jenna's news.

"Vince! Of Vince's Salon! He sold the place in 2005, but he's alive and well and living in Port Charlotte, Florida. Jodie gave me his phone number!"

"That's wonderful, Jenna!" Merrill said. "Text it to me, please. Jason is coming over for lunch, so I've got to get home. Thank you, dear friend!"

She was reheating last night's pasta and sauce when her son came through the kitchen door. "Mom." Jason snapped his fingers in front of his mother's eyes, attempting to bring her back from whatever thoughts she seemed to be lost inside. "Where are you, Mom?"

"Oh. So sorry, honey. I'm trying to organize my ideas for the next *Deeper Dive*." It was a white lie, she told herself, a little fib, maybe a half-truth, since these days the podcast was always on her mind. But she wasn't ready to share the details of her investigation of the cold case with her son. She knew he worried about her involvement in a criminal investigation.

It was too late to turn back now, though, especially in light of the information that Cory Brooks and Roberta Luiz had shared. In fact, she had been organizing her thoughts about where their accounts might take her next. But there was no need to share her plans with her son, or anyone else, for that matter. Not yet, anyway.

As soon as Jason left, Merrill dialed Vince's number. The man himself answered. It took a while for her to get through her introduction and her purpose for calling. It didn't help that Vince Martucci seemed to be a bit more than mildly hearing impaired. By the time she had almost convinced him that she wasn't selling something, that she was a research assistant for the Westfield Sherriff's Department, he had handed the phone over to his wife.

"Yes," the woman said. "Of course we remember Grace Phillips. Her mother, her mother-in-law, and Grace herself were long-time clients. What can I help you with today?" She made it clear that she and Vince wanted to go to the pool before cocktail hour and that Merrill should get to the point.

"Do you happen to remember the stylist who usually worked on Grace?" Merrill asked.

"Just a minute." Mrs. Vince covered the phone, but Merrill could still hear her yell to her husband. "He says it was probably Crystal. She worked on the younger girls and women who came into the salon." Merrill held on as the woman rifled through an address book looking for Crystal's phone number. "Here it is," she said. "She's retired, too. She lives in Phoenix now. You may not find her at home. Retired people are much busier than they were when they worked, you know."

Tell me about it, Merrill thought as she thanked Mrs. Martucci for her help. She dialed the number, but Crystal did not pick up. She left a voice message that she hoped wasn't too off-putting. She needed Crystal to call her back.

In the meantime, she would take a look through Jack Woodhall's arrest record. Marlene Niche's account had convinced her that he could be a valuable asset in unlocking the mystery of Grace, especially, Merrill hoped, the enigma of her relationship with Brad Childs.

Three separate stacks of documents each with paper-clipped pages were what she found when she opened the folder. The first was the slimmest. It included two pages citing Woodhall's employment over the years up to and including 2001. Merrill put it aside, since this would tell her the least about his association with Grace. The second stack contained a hundred or so sheets of paper from the Ontario County Court system. It was his arrest record. The third one was the fattest sheath of papers. It was a record of the trial of Jack Woodhall for third degree stalking and harassment, and second degree assault, also from Ontario County. A record of the sentencing hearing from 1998 was the last page in this pile. Merrill turned back to the arrest record.

Two pages of the file were dedicated to multiple police narratives over the course of six months recorded by officers who had been called to an apartment in Geneseo. Sometimes those complaints came from concerned neighbors, and other times they were called in by George Simpson, Woodhall's roommate. Just as often as Simpson called, the cops were alerted by Woodhall himself; he claimed that it was George Simpson who was endangering *his* life.

All of these minor incidences were resolved with no legal action until the winter of 1997, when George Simpson went to court seeking a temporary restraining order against his now former roommate. At the hearing Simpson said he was tired of being stalked and harassed by Woodhall. The order was granted, but two months after the hearing, Jack Woodhall returned to his former home with a baseball bat. Simpson suffered several broken teeth, a fractured nose, and broken facial bones. Merrill turned the page to an 8X10 black and white photograph. She could barely discern that it was a face, or had been a face, until Jack Woodhall had beaten it so badly that all of the man's features were grotesquely swollen beyond recognition.

Woodhall was sentenced to three years in the Lakeshore Prison, just miles away from Westfield Central where he had once been Marlene Niche's student teacher. Merrill was surprised to see that he was released six months after his incarceration. He might still be on parole. If that was the case, more than likely it wouldn't be hard for Johnny to find Woodhall's most recent contact information.

The photographs of George Simpson's broken face had made Merrill nauseous. She placed the documents into the folder, grabbed her phone and headed for the Shed. It had been a long day already and it wasn't even four o'clock. She needed some time to shake off the anxiety that Mrs. Luiz's story had caused her. She couldn't get the image of the Orange Julius man out of her head. When she closed her eyes, she could see him guiding Grace Phillips down that hallway to her ultimate destiny. Johnny Lovallo entered her thoughts, with his squinty eyes and smart alec ways. That was unsettling too. Lying, well, not exactly lying, but not being candid with her son left her feeling uncomfortably guilty. And the scolding she received from Mrs. Martucci, whose "wisdom" about what retirement should look like was still with her.

She sat down in Richard's recliner, leaned back, and stretched out. Closing her eyes, she quickly felt herself retreating from this messy day. The deeper into sleep she traveled, the more vivid the images that floated like confetti in front of her. Her kids' faces, her dogs who had been gone for a couple of years, Brad Childs standing by the gorge, Cory Brooks, the stone children at the fountain, Joanna Phillips, Grace Phillips. And then the horror of that broken human face, George Simpson's face. Finally, Richard stood before her, tall, and handsome, still untouched by the disease. He was asking a question, but she couldn't make out the words. Before she could ask him what he had said, he turned and walked away from her as she slept into the early evening.

CHAPTER TWENTY-EIGHT

CRYSTAL

The Shed was wrapped in the darkness of the March evening by the time Merrill opened her eyes again. She had been resting deeply until her phone began notifying her of her earthly commitments. Next to the Missed Call icon was an unfamiliar number. Spam of some sort, no doubt. She deleted it. Glancing at the subject lines of several new emails on the *Deeper Dive* account, Merrill decided they were of no real import, at least not to her investigation of Grace Phillips's disappearance. There was also a second request from the art collector who had reached out a couple of days before. She started to read the message, but a call came through before she could finish.

"Is this Merrill Connor?"

She couldn't place the husky-voiced woman. "It is," she answered.

"This is Crystal Karolidis," the stranger said. "You left me a message. About Grace Phillips."

Merrill straightened the recliner to its upright position and reached to turn a lamp on. "Yes, Crystal. Thanks so much for getting back to me. As I explained, I'm doing research on a cold case, Grace's disappearance that is, for the Sheriff's Department. I understand Grace was a client of yours."

"She was. From the time she was a teenager. Grace and I went all the way back to her prom hairdos," she said.

"And you saw her as an adult, as well?" Merrill asked.

"Throughout her 20's I saw her a few times a year for haircuts and special events. When the grays started coming in, throughout her 30's she had a standing five week appointment with me for a cut and color," Crystal said.

"Wow!" Merrill exclaimed, trying to do the math in her head. "Over the years, that must have added up to a lot of time spent together,"

"That's true, it did," the woman agreed.

"So would you say you had more of a friendship than a stylist/client relationship?"

"Yes. Absolutely. Grace was one of a handful of clients who I was very close with."

"I see. Crystal, I don't want to make you uncomfortable, but I'd like to know what Grace might have shared with you, about her personal life, I mean. I think it might help in discovering what happened to her. May I ask you some questions about that?"

"Go ahead," the woman said.

Merrill couldn't get a read on Crystal's attitude. That was the problem with the phone. But she couldn't get to Tucson, so it would have to do. "And may I record our conversation?" she asked tentatively.

"I don't see why that would be a problem," the woman answered and Merrill felt relieved as she pressed record.

"I've read Grace's case file and I was surprised to learn that there were very few witnesses who were interviewed at the time of her disappearance who actually knew her well. I'd like you to tell me what she was like from your point of view, as someone who spent a lot of one-on-one time with her." When Crystal didn't respond, Merrill added, "Maybe starting with when you first met her as a young girl."

"Well, as a teen, when I first met her, Grace was very quiet and shy. Very straight-laced, I'd say, especially for a kid who grew up in the crazy seventies. It became my personal goal to make her laugh when she was in the chair." Crystal chuckled at the memory.

"What do you mean when you say Grace was straight-laced?" Merrill asked.

"Well, she was a very obedient kid. Her mother usually stood behind me when I was cutting or blow-drying her hair, giving me instructions. I thought it was pretty weird for the mother of a girl that old to do that, but she was paying the bill, so..." Crystal took a deep drag on a cigarette or a joint. Merrill couldn't tell which. "Yeah, a few years later, her mother went bonkers when Grace brought in a picture of a super short style she wanted for her wedding. She, of course, sucked it up and went along with her mother's instructions, so I had to do a French braid. That look was pretty much old-fashioned by then."

"What was your impression of Grace after she married? Did she seem different, perhaps more independent, once she was out from under her mother's roof?"

"Well, she was *so* young. I don't think she knew herself well enough to know if she really wanted to get married in the first place. But she did what was expected, so her parents were on board, which I'm sure made life easier for her in some ways. In those days, Grace avoided making waves."

"What do you mean by doing the expected?"

"You know how it was for a lot of small-town girls back then. Grace married her high school sweetheart who came from the "right side" of town and they started a family, all before she turned twenty," Crystal said.

"Do you think she was unhappy with that decision? To marry so young?"

"No, not at first. Her baby Joanna was her pride and joy, even though she was colicky for what seemed like a year. But then, after the twins were born, Grace seemed exhausted. She practically fell asleep in the chair each time I saw her. And she was quieter. I'd joke around like usual, but she hardly seemed to notice. It made me sad to see her that way." Crystal paused and Merrill waited. "And then I actually didn't see her for a couple of years. She stopped coming to the salon. But when she came back, I could see she was a different Grace."

"Different?"

"Well, she'd lost the baby weight and about twenty pounds more. Grace was always beautiful, but at that point in her life, she seemed like she was aging backwards. And she was so much more talkative than she had ever been."

"Why do you think that was?" Merrill asked.

"Well, for one thing she was working on her college degree. She was busier than ever, what with the kids, the house, and her studying. But she just seemed to come alive. I think it was because she felt so good about herself. And a couple of years later when she got the teaching assistant job at the high school, she was a new Grace, so excited about the path she was on."

"How do you think her marriage was during that time, Crystal?"

"Well, she didn't talk about Dan much in those days. She was preoccupied with her kids, especially Joanna, who told her mother on a regular basis that she hated her. I didn't think that was unusual, and I told her so. Almost every mother of a teenage daughter felt that way, at least when they vented in my chair."

"Did she ever talk about Dan? About her marriage?" Merrill asked.

"Eventually, she did talk to me about it. She said I was the only one in her life that she could trust." Crystal paused for a few seconds, long enough to take another hit of whatever she was smoking, "She told me it was terrible. She said that she and Dan barely spoke to one another, unless they were arguing," she said.

"Did she tell you what they argued about?" Merrill asked.

"He didn't like the fact that she was getting a degree. In my opinion, he was jealous of her." Crystal was silent again for a few seconds. "And I wasn't so sure that he wasn't putting his hands on her."

"Did she ever tell you that he was abusive?"

"Not physically, but verbally, yes. She admitted as much. Dan Phillips was a bully in a lot of ways, and not just with Grace," Crystal said.

"What do you mean, a bully? In what other ways?"

"He had a lot of power and influence in our small town," she said.

"How so? What kind of power?" Merrill asked.

"He employed dozens of people in his contracting business, so of course, they were loyal to him. He was on the village board so that he could keep a tight rein on other contractors who might be competition for his company. And I'm pretty sure the Westfield cops were in his pocket. He had a lot of sway over who got hired on the force, who got promoted, who was fired, because of his position on the board."

Merrill felt the goosebumps traveling up and down her arms. She was stunned at the complexity of information Crystal had regarding Grace's husband. Could Dan's influence on the department have kept the investigation into his wife's disappearance limited? "That does seem like a lot of power on several fronts, doesn't it?" Merrill said.

"Yeah. And rumor had it that he was going to run for mayor. Until Grace vanished and he kind of retired from everything. Except his company. Said the kids needed him at home more than ever. Family came first, he said. At least that's what his mother told me. She was a client, too." A dog yapped in the background. "Hush!" Crystal called out.

Merrill shook her head in wonder. She had learned more about Grace and Dan Phillips's marriage dynamic in the last five minutes than those official files could have ever given her. Sherry had been so right to point her in the hair stylist's direction. The chicken wings would be on Merrill's tab this Thursday. "You still there?" Crystal asked her.

"Yes, Crystal, I am." Merrill said. "Can you tell me your most recent memories of Grace, just before she went missing?"

"The last couple of times I saw her that winter before she vanished, she was very quiet. And that last time I saw her, I noticed fingerprint bruises on her wrists. When I asked her about them she tried to avoid my questions. I wouldn't back off though. I had known her too long. She was like family. When I took her in the back room to rinse her, we were alone. So I asked her how things were at home, and I wasn't very surprised when she told me that said she had made up her mind. She was going to leave Dan. She was putting a plan in place, she said."

Merrill held her breath. She felt that the next thing Crystal said would be crucial to the case. On the other end of the line, the woman inhaled deeply and then spoke. "At first, when I heard about her disappearing, I thought it was part of her plan. But I know she wouldn't leave the kids. Not forever, anyway. That's why I held out hope that she would return in those first months." Merrill could hear the pain in the woman's voice all these years later.

"Crystal. Did Grace ever tell you she had someone else in her life? Romantically?"

"No, she didn't," Crystal answered. "But that's not to say there wasn't somebody. She deserved to have someone who loved and supported her. Maybe she had someone. Maybe she ran off with him."

Merrill knew the answer to her next question, but she asked it anyway. "Crystal, did the police ever question you about Grace?"

"No," the woman said.

After she thanked Crystal and hung up, Merrill spent the rest of the night on the phone. First she called Joanna and asked her what she remembered about her mother and father's relationship just before she disappeared. Grace's daughter said she really had no clear recollection of her parents' feelings for one another. She didn't remember a lot of arguing or any kind of disagreements between them, except about her mother going back to college. She was probably right when she summed it up for Merrill.

"I was a very insecure, messed up sixteen-year-old. I don't remember having any thoughts about my parents' relationship. Or about anyone else but myself, for that matter." Joanna's unease with this subject was obvious to Merrill.

"Okay, Joanna. I'm diving back into the old files and adding my new notes this week. I'll get back to you with some kind of summary soon," she said.

"Merrill."

"Yes?"

"I don't think you should reach out to my father," Joanna said.

"Let's talk later this week. Good night, Joanna."

Merrill was heating up her dinner when her phone rang again. "Merrill Connor?" the stranger said.

"Yes. This is she."

"Dan Phillips," he answered. "I understand you've got some questions about my relationship with my wife."

Chapter Twenty-nine

THE HUSBAND

The early morning sun poured through the window, highlighting the veins of rose quartz in the granite island, and its rays reflected off the copper pendant lights hanging above it. The timer buzzed and Merrill grabbed the mitts off the counter and pulled the blueberry muffins out of the oven. Sunshine and the smell of freshly brewed coffee usually made her happy, but the thought that Dan Phillips would be in her kitchen in a few minutes had set her nerves on edge.

Maybe she should have told Johnny that Grace's husband had not only asked to meet with her, but he said he wanted to come here, to her home. But there would be time enough for Merrill to disclose that to the detective. In spite of her nerves, she wanted to scope out this man on her own. Lovallo could be consulted after the meeting. She didn't want to take the risk of Phillips being intimidated by a sheriff's car in her driveway, or for that matter, by the officer himself in her kitchen. Better to have a one-on-one meeting with Phillips. She thought about what Crystal had said about the guy's temper and swallowed hard.

Joanna had obviously been upset when they talked last night, but she was fairly sure she didn't know that her father was meeting with Merrill today. Actually, as Merrill thought about it, she had told no one he was coming. Maybe she should have confided in one of her friends. Or Jason. She shook her head and chided herself for being so paranoid. After all, the police had cleared Dan Phillips of any wrongdoing twenty years before. The man had lost his wife, he was a victim, too, Merrill reminded herself.

Her goal today was simply to find out more about Grace from the person who had probably known her better than anyone else.

Picking the muffins up off the cooling rack, she placed them on a glass tray. They looked and smelled delicious. Merrill's sense of culinary accomplishment was superseded by a sudden foreboding. Someone was watching her. She whirled around and saw a man standing at her back door window, his fist raised. "Oh. Just a second," she called and wiped her hands on a dish towel and opened the back door. "I'm so sorry," she said, "I didn't hear you pull in." She glanced at the clock on the stove and realized he had shown up twenty minutes early.

"No," Dan Phillips said, stepping into her kitchen, "you didn't." The man's brooding expression told Merrill that no introductions or handshakes would be appropriate or necessary. "I parked a couple of blocks away. I'm in my company pick-up, and, well, your podcast seems to have put me back into the middle of the village rumor mill. I didn't want to add fuel to the fire by parking in your driveway."

"I see," was all she could get out. His gruffness had shaken her up.

The stranger standing in the middle of her kitchen was what Jenna would have called 'handsome, but haggard.' He was tall and trim, and although he wore a pale green fisherman style sweater with his leather jacket open, Merrill's second thought was that he was skinny, too thin somehow for a man his age. Looking down, she noticed that his boots looked shiny and expensive, as though they had never been anywhere near a construction site.

"Please, have a seat, Mr. Phillips," she said, not surprised that he didn't ask her to call him Dan. She motioned to a chair at the kitchen table and she was a bit surprised when he sat. "Would you like a cup of coffee?"

"No," he replied.

Merrill pulled out the chair directly across from him and sat down. "Can I take your jacket?" she asked. He was scrutinizing the kitchen, the cabinets, the appliances, even the flooring, like he was there to do a renovation estimate.

A Deeper Dive

"I won't be staying long. I just want to ask you a few questions. I guess that's the opposite of what goes on with a …what is it that you actually do, Mrs. Connor? For the Westfield Sheriff's Office, I mean."

She wasn't sure why this man was managing to register a 100 on her hostility scale. Had Crystal's account of Dan Phillips had that much of an influence on her? He kept his voice just above whisper level, and his tone, well, his tone was dead even at all times. Yet, something about him was giving off a very negative vibe. She felt that if she said one wrong word, he would reach across the table and calmly grab her by the throat. "I'm a research assistant for the department." She swallowed hard and added, "Once I retired from the college, I wasn't looking for a job. I kind of fell into it. It turned out they needed someone with my particular skill set."

"Something to do with your finding that Amish girl, right?" Dan Phillips said.

"Yes. That's how I came to know Detective Lovallo." From across the table she studied the man's face. He had one of those very closely shaved beards, and for a man of his age, a lot of hair on his head, too. All in all, she imagined many women would find him attractive in spite of his aloofness. She wondered why, as Joanna had told her, he had never remarried.

"You're a widow, right?" he asked.

She pondered whether the guy was reading her mind before answering. "Yes. Just over three years." Where was he going with this interrogation?

"Kids?" he asked.

"Three," she replied.

"Same as me," he said. "Your kids were adults when their father died, I assume," he said, and now his eyes were drilling into her. He didn't give her a chance to answer. "Mine were young. Three teenagers when their mother disappeared."

"That must have been terrible," she said. "Difficult for you in so many ways, I would imagine."

"Yes. It was devastating for me and traumatizing for my kids. That's why I'm here today. I want you to stop questioning my daughter, or anyone else for that matter, regarding my relationship with my wife." His voice, with its stage-whisper timbre, was searing into her brain. She knew her face must be crimson red.

"Joanna came to *me*, Mr. Phillips, with questions. About the original investigation..."

Suddenly the man was on his feet, looking down at her. "Grace and I had a good marriage. That's what I told the police in '97, and that's what I'm telling you now." He walked across the room, and with his hand on the doorknob, he turned back to look at her. In spite of his demands he still spoke in that monotone. "I'm warning you, Mrs. Connor. I want you to stop. Stop prying and stop inviting others to pry into my business. I won't have my life or my kids' lives turned upside down again," he said. "Stop, or else..."

Merrill's heart was pounding, but she stood up and looked him in the eyes. "Or else what, Mr. Phillips?"

"Or else you may once again be a retired college librarian, and nothing more."

Looking out the window, Merrill saw the top of his head as he descended the deck stairs. She walked to the middle of the room and stood still for several minutes, trying to grasp what had just happened. Crystal's assessment of the guy may have been right. Maybe he did have an anger problem, but his quietly righteous demeanor and monotone delivery of insults, warnings, and threats confused her. Merrill wasn't sure how she felt about what just happened in her kitchen, but the longer she paced back and forth, the angrier she became.

From the time she was a kid, whenever she was challenged or bullied in any way, she became furious. And Dan Phillips was certainly a bully. She had to get out of here right now, she told herself, or her head would explode.

She went into the study and gathered up her notebook, her laptop, and the two bins containing the cold case files. The April sun had tricked her and she hadn't put on a jacket before heading outside and loading her stuff into her car. She ran back in to the hall tree and slipped her parka on. In the kitchen, she poured herself a large takeout mug of coffee, grabbed a couple of the muffins, and slammed the front door behind her.

As she drove, Merrill replayed Dan Phillips's "visit" in her head. Yes, he was pissed. Yes, he had threatened her, but he hadn't promised to break her legs or make her disappear. What was it that he had actually promised if she didn't drop out of the pursuit for truth regarding his wife's fate? That he would make her a retired librarian. She chuckled out loud as she thought about this. As far as threats went, it seemed pretty ludicrous and empty.

Stevie Nicks was singing her heart out. "*Give to me your leather, take from me your lace...*" Merrill turned the dial up and joined her.

CHAPTER THIRTY

THE COLLECTOR

MERRILL WAS so thrown by Dan Phillips's tirade in her kitchen, she had forgotten that the library wouldn't be open this early on a Saturday morning. Luckily, she had her key in her bag. Her intention was to clear her head by doing what she had done whenever she was midway through a research project. She would write a progress report summarizing the facts she had so far and then she would focus upon what else needed to be investigated in order to come to a logical hypothesis regarding Grace Phillips's disappearance.

Cautiously carrying the evidence bins down the stairs to the Catacombs with this mission in mind, she felt her nerves calming. The bad feeling that Dan Phillips had left her with was subsiding as she thought about the task at hand. She set her laptop on the table, pulled out the first folder from the Westfield Sheriff's files, and focused "like a laser." This was how her former colleagues had described her ability to become totally engaged in a project, in spite of the myriad of distractions in a college library. As she had done for so many years, Merrill concentrated on outlining and writing a report of her findings so far. An hour later she was so deep in thought, she didn't see the man standing directly in front of her until he cleared his throat and stuck his hand out. "Mrs. Connor. I'm Sebastian Crowell."

Merrill stood and shook the extended hand. "Hello," she said. He had startled her, but now she was just annoyed by the interruption. "I'm just a volunteer, Mr. Crowell. You'll find the librarians upstairs." She did a quick study of the middle-aged man's face. There was something familiar about him, but she wasn't sure what.

"Oh, no. I'm here to see *you*. There's no one upstairs yet," he explained. "I pounded a bit on the front door and the janitor let me in. He said he saw your car in the lot, so he thought you'd be here. I apologize if I alarmed you. I've tried to get in touch by email, but I never received a reply."

Merrill saw that the man's eyes, framed by green, wire-rimmed glasses, blinked at an abnormal rate. A nervous tic, perhaps, she thought. He seemed to be cataloguing everything on her table. The laptop, the opened files, her notebook, his eyes tracked back and forth as though he was taking an inventory. Merrill responded to the stranger, although she had no idea what he was talking about. "Email?"

"Yes. You see, I'm a fan of your late husband's work. That's why I was thrilled to watch the video tour you did of your personal collection of his art. Of course, I'm also a listener of *A Deeper Dive*. That's how I happened to see it. Please, sit down, Mrs. Connor." The man pulled out the chair across from her.

"I'm sorry I didn't get back to you Mr..."

"Crowell. Sebastian is fine." He removed his glasses and with his other hand, reached into his pocket. Pulling out a small chamois, he began polishing his glasses.

"Sebastian. I certainly intended to," she said.

"I understand. You're a busy person Mrs....It's Merrill, right?"

"Yes." She watched as he put his glasses back on.

"Merrill," he said again. "It's good to stay busy. I've lost a loved one, too. I know how hard it is."

"I'm sorry," Merrill said. Isn't that what people expected you to say? She had heard it dozens of times since Richard had passed away. It almost always felt empty when she was on the receiving end of the phrase. But she sensed a depth of sadness coming from this guy, and she actually did feel sorry for him.

"Thank you," he said, unzipping his jacket and loosening the woolen scarf that was wrapped around his throat. She noticed beads of sweat on his brow. The dozens of heating zones is this ancient building made comfort impossible.

"What can I do for you, Sebastian?"

"Well, as I told you in my email, I'm very interested in owning a piece of Richard Connor's art work. As I'm sure you know, there are some private owners, but your collection, understandably, is the most inclusive of all the mediums he mastered throughout the years. I love the sculptures, but I'm particularly interested in his paintings, of which I understand there are very few."

"I'm sorry, Mr....Sebastian. I'm not going to sell any of Richard's work. They belong in our home and eventually, after I die, some will be given to the college and the rest will be passed on to our children. That's the way my husband wanted it. I'll honor his wishes." She couldn't tell if her refusal to sell was registering with the man. His mouth was set in a tight pursing of his lips, which Merrill read as determination, or maybe arrogance.

"Well, I am certainly disappointed, but I'll have to accept your answer, I suppose." Behind the glasses, his eyes went back to tracking everything in the studio, as though he were watching a ping pong match. He was silent for several seconds. "I hope you don't mind me asking, Merrill, but have you had Dr. Connor's works appraised and insured? If there were ever a security breach to your home, or a fire..." He stopped talking and let his words sink in.

"I don't mind telling you, Sebastian, that is something I've never thought about before," she said.

"Oh, Merrill, you really ought to do that. For your husband's legacy, and for your children's sake. And I'd be happy to put you in touch with the firm I've used for years, ever since I started collecting."

Although he had made a valid point, one that she intended to seriously consider, Merrill was ready for this stranger to leave her office. "Well, Sebastian, perhaps you're right. I'll talk with my kids and get back to you," she said as she stood.

He got to his feet. "Great! I'll send you the information today." He stuck his hand out and she shook it. It was ice cold. "Good meeting you, Merrill." He headed toward the staircase, but looking over his shoulder at her, he had one more thing to say. "Keep up the good work!" The lighting on the stairway was horrible, but she could swear his crooked smile was more of a sneer. "Dig deeper!" he said, waving to her before he grabbed onto the old wooden bannister and climbed up the library stairs.

CHAPTER THIRTY-ONE

RETIRED LIBRARIAN

Merrill made a cup of coffee, hoping to warm up. Holding the steaming mug in both hands, she sat in front of her laptop and replayed in her head the unexpected encounter with Sebastian Crowell. The guy was an eccentric, as a lot of art collectors, in her experience, seemed to be. She had attended dozens of gallery openings and several auctions in her years with Richard and she'd met many colorful characters. But she sensed an intrinsic melancholy in this stranger that made her want to reach out and comfort him somehow. He had lost someone he loved he had said, and so she imagined that they might be kindred spirits because of their grief. Perhaps she would owe him a debt of gratitude for nudging her toward the appraisal and insurance of Richard's works.

She had to will herself to stop ruminating about Sebastian Crowell. She didn't have time for it. Her laptop awaited her. She set her coffee mug on the table and settled down to work. An hour later, her phone vibrated. She wasn't going to answer it until she saw that it was Joanna's number.

"Hello, Merrill." The tension in the woman's voice could not be missed.

"Joanna. I'm so glad you called. I'm working on your mother's case right now. I wanted to ask you…"

"Stop!" There was a thickness in her voice, as though she had been crying.

"What's wrong, Joanna? Are you okay?" Merrill asked.

"I want you to stop. I can't take it. I thought I could, but digging it all up again, it's killing me."

"Is this about your father's visit this morning?" Merrill heard the woman on the other end suck in her breath.

"In part, yes. He's angry at me for asking about my mother. About their marriage. And he's furious with me for getting you involved."

"I'm sorry, Joanna."

"No. I'm sorry. I should have left it alone. It was selfish of me. I didn't even think to ask my father if he would be alright with my being involved in the reopening of her case. He and I really don't talk that much anymore, but I should have known that he wouldn't approve."

"But she's *your* mother, Joanna…"

"And she was *his* wife! This horror happened to him and to my brothers, not just to me. You've been amazingly gracious and accommodating, but for my family's sake, I'm asking you to stop. Please, stop digging. Goodbye, Merrill," she said with a finality that Merrill couldn't ignore.

What little natural light that filtered into the library basement was gone by the time Merrill came back from the walk she desperately needed after Joanna's call. If she had had her running shoes with her, she would have walked to the high school and run the track. Instead she strode through the village to its outskirts and kept walking. The anger the two members of the Phillips family had provoked in her began to subside. By the time she reached the Mill Springs Mall, her head was almost clear.

Instinctively, she walked around to the back of building to what Rosemary Luiz claimed was the most likely place that Grace and the Ski Hat Man had emerged. Merrill stood with her back to the emergency exit door and stared out at the almost empty employee parking lot and the vacant fields bordering the furthest point of the lot. Beyond them stood six or seven houses on a dead-end street. An elementary school, which had been converted to senior apartments a decade ago when the new school was built, stood in the middle of the block. For some reason, the school playground with its outdated metal swing set, slide, and teeter-tauter remained behind the brick building.

Merrill turned her back on the distant street and stared at the mall's emergency door exit. Where had Grace gone that day, she wondered for the hundredth time. Was she under her own power or had the Ski Cap Man forced her out that door? Dan Phillips wanted her to stop looking for the answer to that question, and so did Grace's daughter. But what about Grace? What would she want?

By the time she got back to the library, Merrill's clothes were clinging to her sweat dampened skin, but her head had cleared and she could answer that question about the missing woman's wishes. She wasn't going to stop looking for Grace Phillips. As far as she could tell, Merrill, along with a few of her listeners, were the only people on earth who truly cared to know what had happened to her. And Merrill was going to find the answer. Her curiosity had always driven her to discover the facts of most matters she set her mind to, and she felt confident that, if she dove deep enough, she would find the truth about Grace's fate, too.

Merrill switched off the glaring overhead fluorescent lights and pulled the chains on the three glass-shaded lamps in her podcast studio. She draped her jacket over a chair, rolled up her sweater sleeves and sat down at her laptop. She read over all the notes she had made. Then she put on her headphones and listened once again to her recordings of Brad Childs, Marlene Niche, Joanna Phillips, and Crystal Karolidis. Grace's lover, her co-worker, her daughter, and her confidante. They were the people who perhaps knew Grace best.

Merrill typed frantically until she had accurately summarized their accounts and was satisfied that she had a much clearer profile of the victim than the official investigation had produced. Next, she listened to the interviews with the only eyewitnesses who had come forward because of her *Deeper Dive* podcast, Cory Brooks and Rosemary Luiz. Through their words, Merrill could summarize Grace's actions at the Mall that day, and more importantly, those of the mystery man who most likely led her to her ultimate fate.

An hour later, Merrill read over what she had. Where would she go from here? She needed to make certain that she hadn't overlooked other potential witnesses. She reached for the folder that Johnny had given her containing information on Jack Woodhall. Making notes on his arrest record, she compared his violence and criminal activities to Marlene Niche's description of him as a capable student teacher and friend to Grace. Johnny said he was working on getting the man's contact information. Merrill hoped he had it by now.

She flipped to the two sheets at the back of the file. It was Jack Woodhall's employment record that the school district required before he could begin student teaching there. Years before fingerprinting and background checks were made mandatory for school employees, this record was the only required documentation of a person's past.

Merrill yawned and rubbed her eyes. It had been a long, emotionally draining day. She was looking forward to getting home, making a quick sandwich, and getting in bed with the novel she had started. She scanned the form that Jack Woodhall had filled out decades before. *Camp counselor, McDonald's, farm laborer.* Merrill's heart stopped as she read the final entry from the summer of '96, the one before he started student teaching in Marlene Niche and Grace's classroom. *Phillips Construction Company, laborer.*

Merrill's brain was firing on all cylinders. So the Jack Woodhall who had worked in the same classroom with Grace, who had commuted to college classes with her, and who had run interference for Marlene Niche when she felt that the faculty suspected there was something inappropriate about Grace's relationship with Brad, *that* Jack Woodhall had been employed by Dan Phillips! Johnny needed to hear this news, so he would make it his business to speed up the hunt for Woodhall. She had to talk to him. Now!

He picked up on the first ring. "Where have you been?" he shouted. She was taken aback by his tone. He wasn't simply worried about her, it was raw anger she heard.

"I'm at the library, working," she said.

"I was at the library this afternoon! You were nowhere to be found, even though your car was there." He was trying to sound calmer, she could tell, but his strained voice told her it was taking a massive effort. "I asked every staff member and some patrons where you were. No one knew."

"I took a walk," she said. "I didn't realize that that would be a problem for you…"

He interrupted her. " I've made three trips to your house in the last hour, in spite of the fact that I'm on duty," he said, making no effort to hide his anger now. "I'll tell you something, Merrill, you *have* become a problem for me!"

"Johnny, does this have to do with Dan Phillips…"

"You're fired, Connor."

"For what?" she demanded.

"For conducting police business without the Sheriff's Department's permission or direct supervision. I need you to turn in all of the evidence files belonging to the department by Monday morning," he said. She was stunned. What the hell did Dan Phillips have on Johnny, or the department, or both? "Merrill?" he said. "Stop the digging and go back to your real life," he said.

Jesus, she thought, Dan Phillips had said the same thing to her this morning!

"Have I made myself clear?"

"Not really. But I understand that my skills are no longer needed by the department," she said. "Have a good evening, Johnny," she added, and hung up.

CHAPTER THIRTY-TWO

BADASS

AFTER THE DISTURBING events of the previous weekend, Merrill had been looking forward more than she usually did to this Thursday night at Larry's. Throughout the years, she and her friends had spent hours at "their" corner table, discussing child-rearing, health issues, politics, their jobs, their marriages, their divorces, and grief. The topics through the decades depended upon where each woman was in her life at the time. There had been tears shed, but mostly there had been explosive laughter, the kind that good friends instigate and join into with wild abandon. In the background, the beautiful old mahogany bar, the '70's music playing on the jukebox, and Susan, their cantankerous waitress, the familiarity of all of it gave Merrill and the other three women the sense of having a safe harbor. She waited until her friends finished their wings to break the news to them, since she hadn't wanted to bum them out and spoil the evening.

"Oh, Merrill. How terrible!" Jenna said after she had told them. "First the husband, then the daughter tell you they want you to stop looking for Grace!"

"And then the detective! Ohh, that Johnny Lovallo is going to be SO sorry he fired you!" Sherry said, making a fist and shaking it.

"And he did it over the phone! Of all the gall!" Kate said.

"Chicken shit move," Sherry agreed. "The guy must not know who he's dealing with. Have you seen him since he lowered the boom?"

Merrill took the last sip of beer in her glass before she answered. "No. I haven't seen him. He wasn't in his office when I returned the files on Monday. I put my incomplete report on his desk, too, even though he didn't ask for it. I don't think he'll be able to resist reading it, though." She decided that she wouldn't tell the women that the report did not include her discovery that Jack Woodhall had been on Dan Phillips's payroll. She didn't feel guilty about leaving the fact out in her report, since it could be found in the document that Lovallo himself had attained. It would be right there in front of him, if he wanted to find it.

As Susan began clearing their table, Sherry said, "Well, I for one am disappointed in Johnny Lovallo on several levels. As a police professional *and* as a potential boyfriend for our amazing friend."

"Please don't go there, Sherry," Merrill said, and her tone conveyed to everyone at the table that it wasn't a plea, but an order. "I'm disappointed in the guy, too, mainly because I thought he genuinely wanted to solve the mystery of Grace Phillips." She could see that Sherry was embarrassed by her mild scolding. To make up for it she added, "And I did enjoy his company the few times we were together. But people aren't always who you think they are, right?"

Her friends nodded in agreement. "So now that the case seems like it will remain cold forever, what's next for you, Merrill? What direction is *A Deeper Dive* going?" Kate wanted to know.

"Well," Merrill began, her smile widening as she talked. "I'm glad you asked. My next episode is about women in our age group reinventing themselves. I want to feature ladies who are bold enough to have forged new paths during the latter chapters of their lives."

"Cool," Kate said.

"Timely," Sherry added.

"And convenient," Jenna said. "The three of us are your next guests, aren't we?"

"If you'll agree to it," Merrill said, "which of course, you will, right?"

The three friends consulted their calendars on their phones, and one by one, they told Merrill that they were happy to oblige. Jenna ordered another pitcher of Southern Tier 8 Days A Week to seal the deal.

A few minutes later Kate said, "I'm thrilled you've asked us to do the podcast, but I have to say, Merrill, that I'm sorry to see you drop your audience's participation in helping to solve the Grace Phillips disappearance."

"Oh, I'm not dropping it," Merrill said. Her smile grew wider at the shock that registered on each woman's face.

"Wait. What do you mean? You were fired by the Westfield Sheriff's…" Sherry began.

"I was," Merrill interrupted her. "But almost every new discovery in this case since 1997 came from or because of my podcast listeners. With the blessing of the Westfield Sheriff's Office, at least initially. So what I choose to do with that information, and I believe there's much more to be uncovered, is my business."

Kate broke the stunned silence. "Badass!" she said.

"Reinvented badass!" Jenna added.

"The best kind of badass!" Sherry said.

A week later, the four women sat at the big oak table in the library basement. Jason had ordered a third commercial grade microphone and two new headsets. "It's my gift, Mom. Besides, once you start getting some better paying advertisers…"

"Who said that was happening?" Merrill asked.

"The whole county seems to be buzzing about A Deeper Dive with Merrill Connor these days. Hell, my college roommate is listening to you in Syracuse! Don't you ever check your social media?" Jason asked.

"I have enough trouble keeping up with the comments on the podcast website and my emails," she replied.

"Time to hire an assistant. Or maybe ask for a "Diver" volunteer?" Diver was the name that had become an organic label for fans of the podcast over the last few weeks.

"I don't see that happening, but again, I never dreamed this hobby would become my passion, either."

Jason and his sisters were thrilled with their mother's apparent conquering of the debilitating symptoms of her grief. They knew how much she missed their father, but their sibling consensus was that the podcast was giving her a renewed sense of purpose in this world. A world that, sadly, her true love and partner had left, but one that she had thankfully rejoined, in large part because of the three women who sat in her studio this evening.

"Hello, Divers," Merrill said, as Kate's theme song played and then faded in the background. "And thanks as always for listening. Today I'll be talking to three women who have reinvented themselves, to their benefit and for the benefit of others, as well. Kate Sterns, who taught public school music for twenty-five years before her transformation to studio musician and composer. Jenna Berlin, who sold her highly successful restaurant, The French Goose, ten years ago. That's when her new journey began. She was always an avid beach glass lover, but with the restaurant world behind her, she began in earnest, walking and swimming at our beaches, collecting glass and designing beautiful jewelry. And Sherry Lawton, who left her job of many years in the accounting office at the college to open her own custom travel company, *Yellow Brick Road*. Welcome to *A Deeper Dive*, ladies."

Merrill wanted this to be an intimate discussion. She had thought about setting up in the back room at Larry's or in the Shed at home, but she had decided against taking the women out of her library studio. She felt that her decision was a good one when from the moment they started, her friends did not disappoint. What followed her introductions was a lively discussion about how each woman had faced her fears and changed the course of her life by pursuing a passion.

"May I ask how old each of you were when you made your transformation, if you don't mind sharing that with our listeners," Merrill said.

"Fifty," Sherry said.

"Fifty-seven," Kate said.

"Sixty," Jenna said.

"Did any of you have any doubts about your choices? Did you ever think of turning back on your decision?"

"Many, many doubts, yes," Kate said. "And I made numerous mistakes, too. But I was having too much fun to turn back. I was

honing my artistic skills, putting into practice the music theory I had taught to my students all those years. And I love working in Nashville and LA! I've found that it is really thrilling to create and perform."

"And you, Sherry. What was your journey like? No pun intended," Merrill said.

"I've been fortunate throughout my life to be able to travel extensively. I had always dreamed of creating my own agency, so I took a large portion of my savings and a month-long leave of absence from work. I needed the time to plan. Once I had settled on exactly what I wanted to offer through my agency, which is a travel experience that is customized to the client's desires, I began researching a wide range of destinations. The initial investigations themselves took me on wonderful explorations, both virtual and real. I was so into it, I never thought about going back to the college," Sherry said. "I was also taking a couple of business courses at the same time. So I was so busy and immersed in making the change, I didn't have time to look back. And I'm so glad I did it."

"What about you, Jenna? You made a huge change in your life with your reinvention. Were you at all worried about making such a momentous move?" Merrill asked.

"It was scary, for sure. But I did have my husband's support. He knew how unhappy I was those last few years of owning and running the restaurant. You really are married to a business like that, twenty-four seven," she said. "I loved my customers and my employees, but in those last years, I was exhausted most of the time. Now, I get to play all day! When the weather's good, I'm gathering material at the beach. And in the winter, I spend my time designing and making jewelry. A lot of boutiques around the country are buying my pieces, and my new website is drawing a lot of interest, too. It's a real thrill to see friends as well as strangers wearing my jewelry."

"It sounds as if you each have had a second calling. Something *that you were almost compelled to do, am I right?"*

"Absolutely," Sherry said. "I stopped daydreaming about it and took out a small business loan."

"You could say that it was a calling for me too," Jenna said. "I'd always been a fanatic about sea glass. I thought it was more beautiful than any precious stone or gem. And even though I was very nervous about taking my first-jewelry making class, I forged ahead. That's what's great about reaching this age. Because you've had so many life experiences, you gain confidence. You know you're probably not going to die if you try something new, even if you fail." She paused a second and then added, "Unless it's skydiving."

"I wanted to make music more than anything," Kate said, after the laughter died down. "For years, I had encouraged many of my talented students to go into some variety of performance training in college and beyond, and eventually I started listening to my own advice. I would say that by the time I left the classroom, I was obsessed with the desire to play and compose."

As the hour drew to a close, Merrill thought about how happy she was that she had invited these three. Their recountings of their experiences was riveting and inspirational, just as she had known they would be. And they had set her up beautifully for the announcement. The last five minutes of her podcast would be a monologue, which was unusual, but a necessity.

"So Divers, my three guests, dear friends all, may have motivated you to make a change yourself, take a risk, follow a dream, no matter your age, or maybe because of your age, as they each have. They were instrumental in my own change in my life's course. In my case, they pretty much saved my life by encouraging me to live again after my husband's death. And this podcast, although a year ago I wouldn't have been able to imagine it, has added so much richness and satisfaction to my life. My natural curiosity and research skills have been put to use again and provided me with an audience I could have never dared hope for. From my first episode,

you listeners have given me feedback and suggestions that I've taken seriously in order to deliver a podcast that you would want to hear.

And that brings me to some exciting news. Your emails and phone calls, your willingness to help find Grace Phillips, have inspired me to take one more turn on this road I've been on over the last few months. You've helped me to decide that A Deeper Dive will be, from this time forward, a vehicle for gathering information about, and perhaps even solving cold cases that have been dormant for some time. Future episodes will focus on these cases from our region of Western New York, and my research tells me there are many, many of them. I will look for your support and input to help me bring some new insights, and possibly, solutions to these mysteries.

Tonight, I want to bring you back to the Grace Phillips case. Because of your reactions to that episode, I've come to have a clearer picture of who Grace was. What her life was like before she went missing. Because of you listeners, two eyewitnesses who were at the mall that day have come forward with facts that were not in the official police records. That day in March of 1997, each of them saw Grace Phillips sitting on the ledge of the fountain in the center of the mall. She was with a man. A man who wore glasses and a red ski cap, who bought her an Orange Julius, and then walked her to, and presumably, out of the emergency exit door. She appeared to need his assistance to walk. She had only one shoe on, and seemed to be inebriated, or drugged. If you have any more information about that day or about this man, please reach out to me on the Deeper Dive website.

Thank you to my friends, Jenna, Kate, and Sherry for your guidance and inspiration. And I wish all of you Divers happy reinventions of your own."

The three women sat in silence and stared at Merrill. Kate pulled off her headset and said, "You've got balls, woman!"

Chapter Thirty-three

INTO THE APRIL EVENING

AFTER MERRILL HAD said goodnight to her friends and reorganized the studio for her next podcast session, she smiled as she walked out of the library steps and into the April evening. "That went well, I think," she said softly, reaching for her car fob and unlocking the Nissan. "Until Lovallo gets wind of it." Talking to herself was something she did frequently these days, especially when she needed some kind of affirmation for a decision she'd made.

Ever since her termination from the police department last weekend, she had been planning tonight's announcement. She knew she had no other choice. Her innate, hyper curiosity had not been satisfied. In spite of the fact that Johnny Lovallo wanted her to cease and desist her work on the case, she couldn't. It went against her intrinsic nature. When Richard was alive, and her children were still at home, her family knew that when Merrill was working on a research project, she became almost impossible to live with, especially when she was searching for some elusive piece of the puzzle. Now that she was a widow with adult children, she knew she couldn't live with *herself* until she found and investigated every possible lead to discovering Grace Phillips's fate.

She started the car. Immediately, her phone rang and a number she didn't recognize appeared on the Bluetooth screen. She laughed out loud when she thought of a comment Kate had made tonight about how she was thinking of adding "Potential Spam" to her contact list. "He's the only one who calls me on a regular basis. Everyone else, texts." Merrill pressed the End Call icon on the screen. She had yet to pull away from the curb when her phone rang again, and this number was not familiar either. She declined it. Unsolicited marketing seemed more and more to be a night-time occupation, she thought to herself.

After what she had been through last weekend, Dan Phillips's threats and Joanna's ordering her to stop the investigation of her mother's case, not to mention Johnny's angry phone call, why was Merrill musing about Spam and cold-calling advertisers? She answered her own question. Random thoughts were her specialty when she needed a distraction from the unpleasantness of reality. She turned the radio up so that the images of a furious Johnny Lovallo would stay further at bay.

Even though her front porch light was on, she didn't see the package lying at the top of the steps until her headlights revealed it. As she turned into her driveway, she wondered what it could be. She couldn't recall ordering anything lately, but Jason was really passionate about finding more podcast equipment, especially the great buys to be had from EBay. If he kept shopping, the Prenderson staff would soon be kicking her out of her little space in the basement.

She climbed the deck stairs, unlocked the back door, and turned on the kitchen light. In the first year after Richard's death when she walked into her house she was crushed by a sudden, almost violent sense of loneliness. During that time, her senses were heightened and alerted, especially to the random sounds the empty house made, the clicking of the thermostat, the slow drip of the bathroom faucet. Until she identified the source of each noise, a rush of adrenaline would send prickles to her scalp. As she forced herself to move through the rooms, certain objects looked out of place, too. When did I move that pillow onto the couch? I could swear I put that coffee cup in the dishwasher before I left this morning. Had someone been here while she was gone? No, she thought. No one had been here. No one was here. And often during that time, the overwhelming sense of solitude would send her to bed with a blinding headache.

Eventually, after the grief group, the therapy sessions, her friends pulling her back from the brink, and her podcast, that marauding loneliness she experienced when she walked into her house had diminished. Tonight as she stepped over the threshold, she knew she was alone in her house. Alone, but not devastated. Not lonely.

What she did feel was exhaustion, but she managed to talk herself into a hot shower, anyway. She didn't give the two missed phone calls a second thought until she was sitting on the couch in her pajamas an hour later and saw that there were two voice messages on her home screen.

"Merrill, Sebastian Crowell here. Say, I've gotten ahold of my appraisal representative, who says he'd be delighted to assist you in getting the information you need regarding Dr. Connor's works. Would this Monday evening at 7 PM work for you? Please give me a call back, or shoot me a text and let me know. Hope all is well! Good night, Merrill."

So much had happened since this eccentric man had appeared in the library she had almost forgotten their having met. Yes, she would get back to him. Merrill was the custodian of this collection of Richard's work, and she needed to act responsibly on his behalf and her children's. The art was their father's legacy. She checked her calendar and texted Crowell, confirming the date and time and thanking him for his generosity.

The voice mail icon on her phone continued flashing. The second caller had left her a halting message. She played it three times to make sure she had heard everything correctly. "Mrs. Connor. It's…it's Brad Childs. From Salmon River? I wanted you to know that our meeting in December gave me a lot to think about…I've been sober since then…I've been going to meetings and I've been seeing a therapist up here…He thought it might help me if we got together again. I'm in Westfield helping my mother move into an assisted living community… That's another reason I'd like to see you…She told me something today that I never knew…Something I'd like to share with you…Okay. Let me know if you wouldn't mind getting together with me. Thanks."

Brad's call shocked Merrill. She had never expected to hear from him again. During their gorge hike, he admitted to having a sexual relationship with Grace, but that had never been corroborated by anyone else. She doubted that their getting together again would shed any new light on the case, but she felt sorry for him. After all, Grace was not the only victim in this tragedy.

Her call went immediately to Brad's voice mail. "Brad, yes, of course I'd like to see you. Let me know where and when."

The effort to leave a message seemed momentous, and she stood up, yawning loudly and stretching. It was almost 11 and still no angry call from Johnny. Good. Maybe he hadn't listened tonight, although she was sure that once he got word of the latest episode of *A Deeper Dive*, he would replay it. Then, she expected, all hell would break loose. She would worry about that tomorrow. Sleep was going to come easily tonight.

Merrill went to the kitchen for a glass of water, and noticed that the porch light was still on. That's right, she thought, I have a package. As she carried it back into the house, shaking it back and forth a little, she noticed it was much lighter than most podcast paraphernalia she owned. She studied the box and was surprised to see that there was no postage and no return address. The label was not a commercial one, instead, it was a generic white, crudely printed on in green Sharpie. It read, 'Merrill Connor, A Deeper Dive.' Merrill felt a shiver run up her spine and she was suddenly very much awake: someone had walked up the steps tonight and dropped this on her porch.

She carried the cardboard box back to the kitchen and ripped the packing tape off. Inside, there was something wrapped in a large wad of green tissue paper. Merrill lifted it out of the box. Ignoring a sheet from a yellow legal pad lying in the bottom of the box, she began to tear the tissue paper apart.

When all of the paper lay on the floor, she could barely resist the urge to throw what she held in her hands across the room. Instead, she carried the object very carefully and set it down on the kitchen table. Grabbing her phone off the counter, she took several pictures of what had been sent to her. It was missing part of the heel and a mate, and even though the once bright blue fabric was faded and torn in a few places, Merrill recognized Grace Phillips's lost shoe.

Her heart raced as she retrieved the paper lying at the bottom of the box. Scrawled in the same green ink was a short message.

"Dear Ms. Connor. I listen to *A Deeper Dive*. My daughter found this at the Green Street Elementary playground. She was probably 7, so that would have been in '98. I didn't know this until I was cleaning out the attic and found it in her old toy box. I asked her about it and she told me she remembers carrying it home that day. I hope it helps with the cold case."

Merrill read the note again and again. She picked up the shoe and turned it over, inspecting the interior, the sole and the broken heel. She didn't know what she was looking for. Retrieving her phone from the Shed, she went to her contact list and pressed Call.

"Yeah?" Johnny Lovallo barked.

CHAPTER THIRTY-FOUR

TOUCHED

U NTIL SHE EXPLAINED the reason for her call, that primary evidence in the Grace Phillips case had been hand-delivered to her, Johnny was less than civil. But he defaulted to his official police tone, the one she recognized from when they had first met at the Gibb Farm. The day they found Sarah Ingham. "That's very good news, Merrill," he said. "I'll swing by your place tomorrow and pick it up."

Merrill was formulating a plan as he spoke. She would have to stall Lovallo for a few more hours to carry it out, though. "No," she answered, "don't do that." The lies came rolling off her tongue with her goal in mind. "I'm headed to my daughter's at the crack of dawn. She has a doctor's appointment and I want to be there. I'll be back in the afternoon, and I'll bring the evidence to the station on my way home."

"But…"

"Johnny, the damn shoe has been missing for twenty years! Another half a day won't change anything," she said.

She could hear him breathing on the other end. "Yeah. Okay. Bring it to the station. I need to have you sign some papers anyway."

"Ah, the infamous walking papers," she said.

"Very funny, Connor," he said.

"Admit it. You're going to miss my keen sense of humor, aren't you, Lovallo?"

He ignored her question. "Can you be here by three?"

"I'll try. See you then."

"And Connor…"

"Yes. I'm still here," she said.

"Don't touch the…evidence, if you can help it," he said.

"You realize I already have, right? The box *was* addressed to me."

"Well, do your best not to handle it from this point on!" he shouted.

"Yes, boss! I mean, yes, Detective Lovallo." The hang-up came simultaneously, as though they had planned it.

Merrill carried the box with the shoe inside, glimpsing at it one more time before setting the package on her bedside table. She walked into the bathroom and brushed her teeth and washed her face. Exhausted just an hour ago, as she slipped under the covers and turned off the lamp, she realized she was wide awake. Reaching for her phone, she set an alarm. She'd have to be on the road early to pull this off. Should she text Kate or Sherry and ask one of them to come along? Jenna was heading to a Buffalo boutique tomorrow, so she was out. No, this was going to be a solo mission. She set her phone down and lay back on her pillow. As she started making a mental list of what she would need to bring, backpack, latex gloves, notebook…she was asleep before she got any further.

Merrill's torso was wrapped in some kind of tourniquet. A violent, violating bear hug of a squeeze was rendering her powerless. As she staggered closer to the door, she looked up at whoever, whatever, had her in this crushing grip. No matter how hard she tried, her eyes refused to focus. It was getting more and more difficult to breathe. Dread washed over her. She was being forced to go somewhere she did not want to go. She felt the grip tightening even more, and at the same time, she heard a sickening click as her shoulder broke loose from its socket. A human hand, a man's, she thought, pushed the door open, and loosened the vise-grip somewhat as the two stepped into the daylight. Why was she wobbling? Was she drunk? Her legs were giving out, and she looked down at her feet. She had only one high heel on. She wanted the man to let go of her, to stop leading her forward. She needed her shoe. She looked up at the man, who was a dark blob, and muttered something indistinguishable. It felt as though she had cotton in her mouth and she couldn't decipher the word she uttered, but she knew it was a question. She asked it a second time and she heard her own voice. "*Who...?*"

Merrill sat straight up and opened her eyes. Her bedroom was pitch dark. Her heart was pounding in her chest and her shoulders ached. Someone had been talking. In her bedroom. She grabbed the little flashlight from the bedside table drawer and turned it on, tracing an arc around the bedroom walls. No one. Nothing. She climbed out of bed and shone the flashlight downward as she walked into the bathroom. Looking at herself in the mirror, she realized she had woken herself up. It was her voice that had asked the question.

It was 5:30 and the sun wouldn't rise for another hour or so, but Merrill went into the kitchen anyway, made herself a cup of coffee, and toasted an English muffin. As she sat at the table, she thought about the strange dream. And her sleep talking.

Yes, she was creeped out that her subconscious had cast her in Grace's place. It was only a dream, but through it, she had experienced the hopeless vulnerability of a victim. Yes, she would go through with her plan today. After she surrendered the blue shoe, Johnny would likely submit it to a crime lab for DNA testing, but in this past year, Merrill had become aware of alternative investigative methods.

She dressed, packed her backpack, and by 9 AM, she was driving through the towering iron gates. As she turned onto Cleveland Street, she rolled her window down. It was late April and birdsong was the only sound she heard. No traffic, no people talking, even Cassadaga Lake was still. She had called Victoria an hour before. Once again the medium did not seem at all surprised to hear from her. April was not a busy month, she said, and of course, she would see Merrill.

A shadow of guilt climbed into the Nissan with her as she thought about the woman's kindness. During the prior visits with the medium, Merrill had been downright uncivil. "You can be a skeptic without being demeaning," she said aloud as she drove over the hill from Mayville. Talking to herself again, she thought, and now she was talking in her sleep, too. Merrill resolved to mind her manners today and be gracious, no matter what.

When she opened her front door to the sunroom, Victoria appeared to be genuinely happy to see her. The woman seemed to own beautiful caftans for every season. This one had a bright, paisley menagerie of butterflies and birds. "Come in, Merrill! How nice to see you! Would you like to leave your backpack in the living room? It will be safe there."

"No, thanks. I'll need it for our session." Once again, the sarcastic Merrill had a smartass comment, but she resisted saying out loud, *but you should know that, shouldn't you?*

A stick of incense burned and the overhead light was already off as Victoria led Merrill into the small reading room. Before the medium was settled in her chair, Merrill was unzipping the backpack. "I think we can skip the prayer today," she said. "I'm here in an official capacity, not a personal one. And we probably don't need to bother Richard with this, either, so I'm keeping my ring on."

Victoria frowned and said, "I think you know that we won't be skipping the prayer."

Merrill tried to be unobtrusive as she pulled the cardboard box out of the backpack while Victoria asked for guidance from Spirit. When she finished the prayer she said, "So tell me about your goal for today's session. How can I help you?" She watched patiently as Merrill pulled on a pair of blue vinyl gloves. The woman remained unfazed as her client passed another set to Victoria.

"Do you mind putting these on? I've brought a piece of primary evidence in a criminal investigation. I have to be careful not to contaminate it with fingerprints," Merrill explained.

"Is it the Grace Phillips case?" Victoria asked, as she blew into a glove and pulled it on.

Merrill's jaw dropped. "How did you know?"

Victoria's face lit up with laughter. "From listening to *A Deeper Dive*! I'm a fan of your work, Merrill."

"That's great! I can skip all the backstory then." She lifted the shoe out of the box. "The gloves won't dull your sense of touch, will they?"

"I don't think so," Victoria answered.

Merrill passed the shoe across the table to Victoria. "You know what this is, don't you?" she asked the medium.

Victoria's eyes widened as Merrill passed it to her. "Grace's shoe. The one she had on when the man in the red hat took her."

"Do you think you can get in touch with Grace? Like you did with Richard those times I was here?" Merrill asked.

If Victoria Erikson had an ounce of ego, she might have shown some smugness in that moment. The skeptic across from her had just confirmed that she believed in Victoria's gift. Instead, she said, "That all depends upon Spirit, Merrill." She began turning the shoe over and over, passing it back and forth in her hands. She closed her eyes and began to touch every surface of it, the broken heel, the toe, the interior, the sole. Then she sat back in her chair and became perfectly still. It seemed to Merrill an eternity before Victoria spoke again. "She's here."

The blood rushing to Merrill's head almost caused her to faint. Her voice was a whisper. "Can you ask her some questions?"

"More than likely not. I'm a witness to Spirit, Merrill. Not a prosecutor," Victoria explained.

"Alright. What are you witnessing?"

A moment passed before Victoria responded. "She's walking, stumbling really, through a field." How did she get from the mall to a field, Merrill wanted to ask, but she knew she mustn't interrupt the medium. "A man is holding on to her by her raincoat, pushing her forward. It's difficult for her to walk through the mud."

"What man?" Merrill asked. "Who is pushing her?"

"I see him, but not clearly." Merrill noted that Victoria's eyes were still shut tight. "The man in the red cap. He wears glasses. He's holding a gun to her back." Again Merrill wanted to intercede and ask if Victoria could tell what kind of gun it was, but she decided against it. "He's pushing her into a black truck."

"What kind of truck?" Merrill asked.

"I'm not sure. A van, really, a delivery style van. There's white writing on the side."

"Can you read it?"

"No. I can't make it out. The man is sliding the door closed and walking away."

Victoria's eyes were shut tight. As Merrill stared at her, she was reminded of the mask Richard once sculpted of an Egyptian goddess. Beautiful, inscrutable. It felt like ten minutes had passed, when the medium finally spoke again. "It's pitch dark now."

"In the truck?" Merrill asked.

"No, I don't think so. I can't see her, but I hear her voice. There's an echo. She's praying….For her children, for Brad." Victoria's voice is breaking. "She asks God to forgive her. She says, 'When it's done, they bring me back to the field.'" Victoria's trance broke with a sob and she opened her eyes. "She's gone, Merrill," she said. "I can't see her anymore."

As Merrill drove away from Lily Dale, she was full of questions that Victoria hadn't answered. Did Grace know her captor? What field had she been in? Whose panel truck was it? Why was she returned to the field?

Merrill parked the car in the employee lot outside of the emergency exit and stood as she did the other day, looking across the lot. It ended at the sidewalk on 7th street and there was no field, but there was a playground. The one her listener wrote about in her note. Where her child had found the shoe.

Merrill walked across the lot to the back of the transformed elementary school with its old-fashioned metal swings and slides. The merry-go-round was covered in graffiti, and the steps to the slide were rusted. Merrill turned around and stared in the direction of the mall, where there had once been a field. Where there was now a parking lot.

Merrill's next stop was the library where she searched the maps of Westfield dating back to the 18th century. She wouldn't need to go back that far. She grabbed the atlas containing the 1990's charts. Turning to the 1996 map of the east side of town where the mall was built, she studied the page carefully. Behind the Mill Springs Mall extending to 7th street, there was an open field. The January 1997 chart showed a paved parking lot that had replaced the field.

She had left her laptop at home, so she climbed the stairs, avoiding the librarians and patrons. With her head down, she sat at one of the work stations and began her internet search of the *Westfield Herald* archives. The date range and subject she entered was "March to April 1997, Mill Springs Mall." The links to dozens of articles appeared on the screen. She glanced at the antique clock that hung above the card catalogue. She was late for her meeting with Johnny. There wasn't time to do the searching she needed to do. She copied the search links and sent them to her email.

A few minutes later, as she entered the police station, she was anxious. It was probably from the lack of sleep, she told herself. Or it could have been the appearance of a dead woman at her session with Victoria this morning. She wished Richard were alive so that she could call him and say, "Look what this diving deeper has done to your predictable librarian wife. I've become a believer in the paranormal, and I'm no longer a law-abiding citizen."

The receptionist at the desk told her that Johnny was expecting her. She carried the small box into his office and set it down in front of him. The detective greeted her with a formal handshake. "Good afternoon, Mrs. Connor."

"Hello, Johnny. Sorry I'm running late. I took my daughter out to lunch after her appointment and the construction traffic on 90 West was bad." Before she had finished her lie, he was pulling on gloves. He reached into the box and pulled out Grace's blue shoe.

"It looks right," he muttered to himself.

"It's actually the left one," she joked. She couldn't resist pulling his leg for the last time.

He paid no attention to her remark and pulled out the note from the sender. When he finished reading it he said, "Well, Merrill, in spite of all the trouble you've caused me, your podcast seems to have brought this key evidence to the surface." He placed the note and the shoe back in the box, pulled off the gloves and told her to have a seat. From his desk drawer he pulled out a clipboard and slid it across the desk along with a pen.

"Before I sign off here, can you at least answer a couple of questions?" she asked him.

"Maybe. Depending."

"What will you do with the shoe?" Merrill began signing her resignation papers as he answered.

"Send it to the lab. They'll screen it for touch DNA evidence. What's your other question?"

"Two more, actually. Did you find Jack Woodhall's current info? I really think he could tell you a lot more about Grace."

"I can't answer that one. Sorry. What's the final one?"

She finished signing the papers and looked him directly in the eye. "Just what does Dan Phillips have on you, anyway?"

Johnny stood and indicated the door with his eyes. "Goodbye, Merrill. Have a good life."

When she sat down at her laptop that evening, Merrill began reading through the dozens of articles from *The Westfield Herald* chronicling everything from the breaking of ground for the mall by a Cleveland investment group to the ribbon cutting by the Chamber of Commerce and other county officials in 1995. When she zoomed in on that picture and the caption, she was startled to see a young Dan Phillips, village board representative, standing in the last row. The guy seemed to be ubiquitous in those days, she told herself. She continued looking through the headlines: *Mill Springs Mall to Sponsor Annual Easter Egg Hunt, Breast Cancer Awareness Walk at Mill Springs Mall Saturday, Senior Mall Walkers Reach the Thousand Mile Mark.*

Merrill continued scrolling, but she found that her researcher mind was wandering off on a tangent about malls and their dual function in small towns like hers, particularly before the advent of Amazon. They were commercial trade locales, but they also took the place of the village square of centuries before. A headline and short article from March 2nd, 1997, put an end to Merrill's random stream of thought.

Employee Parking Lot Under Construction at Mall.

"Patrons of the Mall are reminded that construction will begin next week on an expansion of the parking lot. It will extend to the 7th Street side of the building. Work will start next Monday, April 15th. A spokesperson for P Asphalt, a division of Phillips Construction, said they hope to complete the work within two weeks."

Chapter Thirty-five

PECULIAR WEATHER WE'RE HAVING

MERRILL STOOD ON tiptoe and stretched her arms toward the ceiling. She had sat at her laptop for so long, she hadn't realized that a late April storm was brewing. Western New Yorkers had enjoyed a premature warm-up that day with the temperature climbing into the 60's, but the warm rain had suddenly turned to hail and then to fat snowflakes in the coolness of the evening air. Merrill circled the Shed, turning on all the lamps to counteract the dying natural light. When she finished, she hurried to turn on the porch light for Sebastian Crowell and the appraiser who were due any minute.

She had been so engrossed in researching touch DNA, she lost track of the time. One of Richard's colleagues in the Biology Department had sent her in the direction of the latest research on the subject. She was determined that her questions for Lovallo regarding the blue shoe would be well-informed ones, based exclusively on the most recent science. Her plan was to wait a few more days and then reach out to the detective for any updates on the possible evidence left on Grace Phillips's shoe. She reasoned that after all of her hard work, he owed her at least that.

She would also withhold from Lovallo her findings regarding the transformation of the field behind the Mill Springs Mall done by P Asphalt Co. in 1997. She had a strong hunch that her discovery would be useful leverage in her future dealings with the sheriff.

As she walked back to the Shed, a sudden sensation swept over her and stopped her in her tracks. She stood absolutely still on the threshold of the room. What was this? *Richard.* She felt his presence so powerfully in that moment, her eyes began to seek him in every corner of the room. From the time they were newlyweds, all the way into his last days of battling ALS, this was where he spent the majority of his time when he was home. His essence was still here. She willed her breathing to slow and the feeling abated.

Stepping back into the space, Merrill marveled as she always did at the beauty her husband had created. She turned the art lights on, the ones that highlighted each photograph, every sculpture and painting. Standing in front of the watercolor that had inspired her own transformation from librarian to podcaster, she stared at the diver's face. Merrill had never been able to pin down the emotion the woman was experiencing the moment before she reached the depths. "Is she scared or is she excited about what she's about to do?" she asked Richard near the end of his life.

"I'm not sure. I change my mind about that every time I look at it. I think the ambiguity has to do with the limitations of my technique. The method I was stuck with by the time I got to her expression," Richard had said, alluding to the fact that he had used his mouth to create the brush strokes that formed the enigmatic emotion on the diver's face.

What an amazing person and artist she had shared so much of her life with! As she stood gazing at "A Deeper Dive," Merrill realized that she was experiencing a real breakthrough, one she had read about and discussed in her grief group and therapy sessions. In this moment, three years after her husband's death, she was not feeling the familiar cutting edge of grief. No, she was actually smiling. It was not sadness, but pure gratitude that washed over her as she thought about Richard tonight.

The doorbell interrupted her epiphany, and she left the Shed and went to the front door. Standing on her porch, collapsing a huge golf umbrella, was Sebastian Crowell. Behind him, Merrill saw the signs of the brutal storm still raging in the night sky. "Come in, Mr. Crowell. I'm sorry you had to brave these elements to see me tonight."

"Not at all," the man answered, setting his umbrella down on the porch and picking up a briefcase. "I wouldn't have missed this opportunity for the world," he said. "Mr. Shields, the appraiser should be here soon. He's coming from his office in Buffalo."

Merrill hoped this meeting with Crowell and the appraiser would not take more than an hour. She was expecting someone else tonight. Brad Childs was finally feeling like his mother was stable enough to be left in the care of the ICU nurses. "My father was a control freak, which I knew from the time I was a young kid," he had said on the phone. "But my mother has shared some details of her life with him that were soul-crushing for her. She never dared to challenge him. That's one of the reasons I wanted to see you, Merrill. There's something you need to know."

"Would you like some coffee or tea, maybe?" she asked Sebastian Crowell as she took his damp raincoat and hung it on a hook in the hallway.

"Coffee would be lovely," he said, fumbling in the bottom of his briefcase for something. The phrase "nervous and jerky" came to Merrill as she watched him. "I seem to have left my phone in the car. May I borrow yours? I'd like to find out when we might expect Mr. Shields."

"Of course," Merrill said, handing it to him. "Perhaps you'd like to look around Richard's studio while I make the coffee."

"Could I?" he asked, delight washing over his face. "I promise not to touch anything, but I've brought gloves in case Mr. Shields needs any assistance."

"Certainly," Merrill said. "It's right this way." She waited until he had pulled the vinyl gloves from the brief case. She guided him to the entrance of the Shed and asked, "What do you like in your coffee?"

"Black would be fine," he answered.

As she carried the tray with the two mugs back into the Shed, Merrill heard Crowell say, "Amazing! What a treasure you have here!"

"Yes. I love every piece, though I've never thought about the insurable value. Until I met you, that is." Merrill set the tray down on a corner table. "Have you talked with the appraiser?"

"I have," Sebastian said, picking up his coffee. "He's on his way. The storm has slowed him down a bit, but he'll be here soon."

Through the bevel-paned windows, a huge flash of lightning lit up the Shed, followed by several loud volleys of thunder. The rumbling was the rare weather phenomenon that, as the temperature fell rapidly, warned not of rain, but of snow. Sebastian traversed the studio, undisturbed by the storm. "I think his sculpture is my favorite mode of your husband's. But his photography is amazing, too." The man stood in front of Richard's final work, a look of rapture on his face. "Ah," he said, "and here is the famous "*Deeper Dive*," your podcast signature."

Another bolt of lightning illuminated everything in the room, and in the following seconds, the power went out. "Damn!" Merrill said. "Let me get some candles. And I'm sure Richard had a flashlight somewhere around here. May I have my phone back, please? I'll use the flashlight app to find the lantern and some candles."

"Of course," Crowell answered. "I set it on that corner table."

She retrieved it and slid it into her jeans pocket. Before she could go on her quest for more light, the doorbell rang. "Oh, here's the appraiser!" she said.

"May I use your lavatory, please, Mrs. Connor?" Sebastian asked.

"Of course. It's down the hall on the left," she said, surprised to see that the man lit his way with a phone. He must have forgotten that he had it with him after all. He was a strange fellow, she thought to herself. She pulled her own phone from her pocket to light the path to the front door. "Damn," she said, trying but failing to find the flashlight app in the pitch darkness. She walked slowly, feeling her way along the wall that led from the Shed to the front porch. As she opened the door, another flash of lightning lit up the sky and the blowing snow, and Merrill found, not an art appraiser standing there, but Brad Childs.

"Hello, Merrill," he said. "I know I'm early, but my mom wasn't feeling well tonight, so the aids suggested I leave while they got her ready for bed." He stepped inside and brushed the snow off his jacket. "I tried to call you, but your phone went right to your voice mail. I'm heading back north tonight, but I wanted to see you before I left. I hope it's alright."

Merrill explained the situation to Brad. "Can you stay until the appraiser is finished? Then we can talk."

"No. I can't stay that long. The weather is crazy here, but it's already snowed six inches in Salmon River with more to come. I don't dare hang around. I need to tell you something that my mother shared with me. It's about Grace."

"What is it, Brad?" she said, forgetting all about Sebastian Crowell and the appraiser.

"She told me that the night before my dad forced me to go on that fishing trip, he got a phone call from someone who refused to identify himself. He told my father that Grace and I were having an affair. He said that if my father cared about my safety, he would get me out of Westfield for the weekend. He said, if he didn't, he couldn't guarantee that our whole family wouldn't be in danger."

"And after Grace disappeared, your father, your mother, never told the police about this phone call?"

"Never. They were afraid." The light in the hall flickered. A brown-out, Merrill thought. The light went out entirely before she could comment on it. "But my mother always suspected she knew who the caller was, even though my father never verified it."

"Who did she think it was, Brad?"

"Dan Phillips. Or someone who worked for him. My father's window company was a sub-contractor of his. My mother knew how much weight Phillips carried. If he told my father to jump, he jumped. So I was dragged up north by my dad, more than likely so I wouldn't be around and would have an alibi when Grace went missing."

Brad and Merrill turned toward the footsteps that were coming nearer to them in the dark. Sebastian Crowell's phone flashlight suddenly came on, illuminating the pistol in his right hand. "What the hell…" Merrill said as the man came closer.

"Back to the Shed, Merrill," he said, prodding her under her ribs with the weapon. "You, too," he said to Brad.

"Wait. I know you," Brad said. "Coach Woodie? What…"

"I said, keep moving! Back to the studio."

"Sit down, both of you," he said, moving two wooden chairs to the middle of the room. He never took his eyes off of the two of them as he reached into his briefcase and pulled something out. Merrill couldn't make out what it was in the dark. In the brief flashes of lightning, she saw the angry face of the man who was not Sebastian Crowell.

"You called him Coach?" she said turning to Brad, who nodded. "You're Jack Woodhall!" she said, taking a step in Woodhall's direction.

The man's cordial tone and pleasant demeanor of minutes ago had undergone a radical change. "You're brilliant, you know that lady? Here, take this," he said to her as he handed her a cable tie, the plastic kind that Jason used in her podcast studio to keep the cords neat and out of the way. Merrill knew that they locked tightly when you pulled on them. You had to cut them with scissors or a knife to get them off. "Childs, put your hands together, like you're praying. Which you should be doing, right about now." Brad followed his former coach's order. "Mrs. Connor, take one of these ties and wrap it around his wrists. Pull it as tight as it will go."

Merrill was shaking, but she tried to clear her head so she could follow his directions. She knew both of their lives depended on her ability to think clearly. She managed to tighten the tie around Brad's wrists.

"Coach, why are you doing this?" Brad asked.

"I don't take any pleasure in this, Childs. But you've brought nothing but trouble in my life from the day I first laid eyes on you. You were a spoiled little shit, entitled, I guess they say nowadays. Thought because you could throw a decent pass, you could have anything you wanted, including Grace Phillips. The two of you were such fools! You were thinking with your dick, as most seventeen-year-old males tend to do. And she…she was a total mess! To think you believed that you could get away with having, whatever it was you were having…"

"I could sense that you were watching us. I tried to tell Grace that we had to be careful around you, but she didn't think you were a problem," Brad said.

"Oh, no. *I* wasn't her problem. I knew that she was a disgusting whore, for sure…"

"But she thought you were friends," Brad said.

"That's the way he wanted it."

"He? You mean Dan Phillips wanted it that way. You were working for him, weren't you?" Brad said.

Jack Woodhall came closer and checked the tightness of the ties. He seemed satisfied. "From the time I was seventeen and sweating over his fucking hot asphalt," the man sneered. "After he bribed somebody on the parole board in Genesee County for my early release, I thought that our association was over. And then a month ago he ordered me back to this godforsaken place. Put your ankles together, Childs. Bind them, Mrs. Connor. Same way as the wrists."

She did as she was told. From her kneeling position, she looked up into the barrel of the pistol. A weird calmness washed over her as she asked him the question. "Were you with Grace the day she disappeared?" Merrill asked.

He didn't answer. Instead he ordered her to sit next to Brad. "Did you call her from school that day?" she persisted, as he began binding her wrists together.

"You know, lady," Woodhall said, as a bolt of lightning lit up his furious face, "you wouldn't be in this position if you had kept your goddamn nose out of this! But you just *had* to dig up a couple of eyewitnesses and then broadcast the details of a 20-year-old dead-end case to most of New York State and beyond!" He knelt in front of her, wrapped the tie around her ankles and cinched it. "And your friend Brad wasn't supposed to be here tonight. You got yourself *and* him into this predicament."

"What did you say to her, Jack? On the phone that day?" Merrill had entered her zone of stubborn determination, in spite of Woodhall's obvious intention to shut her up for good. It would be impossible for her to back down now.

Woodhall stood and looked down at her, shaking his head at her persistence. But he answered, in spite of his disgust with her. "I told her that Childs had been badly hurt at baseball practice. That I was taking him to the ER, but that the kid wanted to see her first. Told her that I would bring him to the field behind the mall so they wouldn't be seen. You know she was going to break up with you, right?" he said, turning to Brad. "She told me that on our way to class that same week. You were both such damaged goods. I tried to convince Dan that it would blow over and it would be like it had never happened between the two of you. But he said it was too late. There was no turning back."

"So Grace trusted you," Merrill said.

"I guess you could say that," Woodhall answered. A bolt of lightning was reflected back at her from his glasses.

"And you murdered her," Merrill said.

"You're wrong about that, lady. I told Dan I didn't have the stomach for it. At least, not at that point in my life. No, I didn't kill her, but she trusted me enough that she believed I would take her to her precious Brad. Told her I would grab him an Orange Julius to drink on the way to the hospital. Of course, I put something special in hers. By the time we got to the emergency exit, she was a mess. She was so out of it, I had to practically carry her across that field and put her in the van."

"That's when she lost her other shoe, right?"

"With my assistance. Her being hobbled like that didn't help, so I pulled it off."

The thunder snow rumbled and rattled the windows. "Is she buried under the mall employee parking lot?" Merrill asked.

"I have no idea," Woodhall answered.

Merrill closed her eyes, and in that total darkness, she had a horrible vision. It was the smashed face of George Simpson, Woodhall's former roommate. She knew in that moment that he was capable of the worst kind of violence.

She watched as he reached into the briefcase and pulled out several pieces of rope. After he tied each of them to a chair, he pulled out a roll of duct tape from the case. He gagged Brad first. As he placed the tape over Merrill's mouth he said, "Thanks for trusting me with Dr. Connor's works, Merrill. Which ones do you want me to leave behind? Of course, it really won't matter once you're dead. But I have to make this look like an art heist, which of course, it isn't. And a double murder, which it will be."

After he gagged Merrill, Woodhall began removing several of the smaller photographs and paintings from the walls around the Shed. Of course, Merrill thought. The gloves he wore would keep his fingerprints from being discovered. He dragged the easel holding the *Deeper Dive* watercolor and set it in front of Merrill. "Here. You can look at this and consider where it got you as I pull the trigger."

The April thunder crashed as Woodhall carried Richard's creations down the hall toward the front door. Guilt washed over her as she thought about how naïve she had been to let a murderous stranger into her home. Another bolt of lightning illuminated the room. Brad Childs twisted toward her and Merrill saw the look of regret and misery in his eyes.

The light coming through the Shed windows suddenly flashed red.

And the booming thunder snow was replaced by wailing sirens.

CHAPTER THIRTY-SIX

LIGHTS ON

"I'M SORRY, MERRILL, but this is really going to hurt," Johnny Lovallo said, kneeling at her feet.

"God damn you to hell, that hurt!" she hollered into his face.

He shone the flashlight on her and saw that the bruising had started. "I'm so sorry," he said again, balling up the duct tape. The sheriff walked on his knees to Brad and repeated the same painful operation.

"Where is Woodhall?" Brad asked the detective after the tape was removed.

"In the back of my squad car with my lieutenant," Johnny answered. As he worked on cutting their cable ties and untying the ropes, another officer entered carrying two of Richard's photographs.

"How did you know?" Merrill asked Lovallo as she attempted to stand. A sickening wooziness swept over her and she fell back into the chair.

"I didn't know. I've been calling you for over an hour. Your phone went right to voice mail, which was very annoying." As he spoke, Merrill pulled her phone from her pocket. "I thought maybe the storm had taken out a cell tower, so I..."

Merrill interrupted him. "It won't turn on. That bastard must have removed the battery when he asked to borrow it."

"When I pulled up, I saw someone loading what turned out to be some of your husband's art into a car. It didn't look right. As soon as I turned on the flashers, the creep started to run. I called for back-up and one of my guys got him two blocks away. They ran his prints and because he's had prior convictions, we found him in the system." Johnny's sheepish tone was better than an apology, Merrill thought. "His name's Jack Woodhall. The guy you wanted to talk to about the case."

Suddenly, the lights came on and the lamps and the art fixtures illuminated the Shed. The first thing Merrill saw was *A Deeper Dive* on the easel in front of her. Something in her broke at that moment, and she put her hands to her face and began to sob. Immediately, Johnny Lovallo knelt in front of her once again.

"Aw, kiddo, don't cry, please," he begged, as an officer carried in the rest of Richard's works.

Merrill lifted her head and took a deep breath. She hated to appear this vulnerable, especially in front of the tough cop. Brad silently held out a handkerchief and she blew her nose. She had a sudden impulse to tell him what a good man he had become, in spite of what adults had done to him when he was a child. Instead she turned to Johnny, "What was so important that you had the urgent need to talk to me?"

"The Touch DNA report came back a couple of hours ago. Jack Woodhall's genetic material was on that shoe," he said. "He was in the Codis Index System because of his prior arrest. So the match was 99.9%."

Merrill made a move to stand again and Johnny helped her to her feet. "The shoe is crucial to the case. It would have never been found without you and your podcast, Merrill. I wanted to tell you the results myself and to apologize for taking you off the case," he said and she could tell he meant every word. "Because of you, we very likely have Grace Phillips's killer in custody."

"An accomplice, yes, but probably not her killer," Brad said. For the last couple of minutes Merrill noticed that he had been looking at his cellphone. He pressed it and turned the volume all the way up. Jack Woodhall's voice filled the room.

"I don't take any pleasure in this, Childs. But you've brought nothing but trouble in my life from the day I first laid eyes on you…"

"Oh my God," Johnny Lovallo shouted, "you recorded him???"

"Just before Merrill tied my wrists, I pressed what I prayed was my voice recorder," Brad said.

The three listened to the rest of the recording which ended when Brad and Merrill were gagged. Johnny took the phone from Brad and replayed the last exchange between Merrill and Woodhall.

> *"So Grace trusted you."*
>
> *"I guess you could say that."*
>
> *"And you murdered her."*
>
> *"You're wrong about that, lady. I told Dan I didn't have the stomach for it. At least, not at that point in my life...*

After he replayed that portion a third time, Johnny pulled his own phone from his front pocket and hit a button. "Yes, Kathy, John Lovallo here. Put me through to Judge Domakowski's cell phone, please. Yes, right now... I know it's late, but he'll pick up when he sees it's me. And Kathy, stay at the precinct. I'm going to have to file an affidavit, and I'd like you to work on it with me."

Merrill finally felt that she could stand without being overcome by dizziness. She began walking around the room, inspecting Richard's pieces that Woodhall had taken. One photo of Jason as a child had a tear in it, but Merrill knew she could have it replaced using a negative that her husband had saved and filed. The paintings seemed fine, and so did the two sculptures that "Sebastian Crowell" had so admired.

"Are you okay, Merrill?" Brad asked.

"Yes, I'm alright. What about you, Brad? It must have been terrible for you, seeing Woodhall again and being confronted with his part in Grace's disappearance. And the fact that he used you as a lure to get her to leave the mall," she said.

"I'm okay," Brad answered, "At least I think I am. I'll be better when I get back to my camp. Tell Sheriff Lovallo to give me a call when he needs me to come in," he said, as he watched Johnny walk toward the kitchen.

Merrill accompanied Brad to the front door. "You're sure you're okay to drive?"

"Yes. We'll be in touch," he said.

"I'm sure of it," she answered.

She heard Johnny's side of the phone conversation when she joined him in the Shed. "Yes, Craig. You heard me right. I need two warrants: one for the arrest of Jack Woodhall and the other to bring Dan Phillips in for questioning. In the next hour, if you can manage it."

As he slipped his phone back into his front pocket, Johnny walked toward Merrill. "How are you feeling?" he asked, genuine concern supplanting his usual sarcasm.

"Fine," she said. She stood in front of *A Deeper Dive,* staring at the woman's face. "So, have we just solved a twenty-year-old murder case, Lovallo?"

"Not quite. We need to find a body before we can say it's really over."

"I think I can help with that. Can you get your hands on some ground penetrating radar?" she asked.

"Yes." His furrowed brow signaled that she was still able to surprise him. "You think we can find Grace Phillips with it?"

She nodded, silent.

"How do you know that?" his more customary tone of voice filling the room.

She answered the question with a question. "Have you ever been to Lily Dale, Sheriff?"

CHAPTER THIRTY-SEVEN

YOU STRETCH OUT YOUR HAND

Richard's funeral three years earlier was the last one Merrill had attended until today. At her husband's graveside, she had been sickened by grief, overcome with sorrow. Her three children, frightened by their tough mother's vulnerable state, had held her up through the entirety of the service. Today, her emotions were very different. She had awakened this morning with a feeling of resolution and finality. And peace. Grace Phillips was finally being laid to rest.

On this clear June morning, the minister had to shout to be heard over the celebratory birdsong that was coming from the old oak trees surrounding this section of the cemetery. As Merrill followed along with the program that the funeral director had handed out, she saw that the brief service was coming to an end. Richard's ceremony had lasted an eternity in her memory. He had been so loved by so many. She had not had the presence of mind to count his funeral goers, but her children told her that there were more than two hundred people there.

She and the few dozen others who were gathered at Grace's graveside today bowed their heads and read aloud a final passage of scripture that Joanna had chosen for her mother's service.

> *"Though I walk in the midst of trouble,*
> *You preserve my life;*
> *You stretch out Your hand against the anger of my foes,*
> *With Your right hand You save me."*

As she scanned the mourners, Merrill wondered how many of them were ever angry with the deceased woman, perhaps still angry with her. Several of the gathered had never met Grace, including Merrill herself. Jenna, Sherry, and Kate never knew her; they were here to support Merrill. Sheriff Lovallo, in civilian clothes today out of respect for Joanna and her brothers, had never met the dead woman. She glanced across the aisle and saw Roberta Luiz, the mall janitor, and her daughter Rosemary. Behind them sat Cory Brooks, the Orange Julius worker who had walked the mall with Merrill. These women had not known Grace, although two of them had seen her once on what was likely her last day on earth.

Besides Joanna and her brothers, who stood close to the casket that would soon be lowered into the ground, only Crystal, her hair stylist, Marlene Niche, her colleague, and Brad Childs, her student and victim had truly known the woman. As an adolescent, Joanna had hated her mother, but without her daughter's ultimate act of devotion, which was calling on Merrill for help, Grace Phillips may never have been found. Brad was in touch with Merrill on a regular basis now, and through therapy, he was gaining a realistic perspective on the relationship he had had with his teacher. He knew she was culpable, but he told Merrill that he could never hate her. No, Merrill could count no foes of Grace here today.

The dead woman's true enemies, Jack Woodhall and Dan Phillips, were awaiting their trials in the Chautauqua County jail. Bail had been denied to both men. Once the police played Brad's recording for him, Woodhall confessed. He insisted that Grace was alive when he put her in the black van, but he added a detail that was crucial in implicating Dan Phillips. He admitted that he knew the owner of the van. On the side of the vehicle he had seen the words *Village of Westfield*. When Johnny combed through the village records from the spring of 1997, he came across a sign-out sheet for the van. On the day Grace went missing, Dan Phillips, a village board member, had signed it out for an approved visit to an Erie County water treatment plant like the one Westfield was planning to build. When Johnny called the supervisor of that center, the man could find no record of Phillips having visited that day.

Although he had hired an expensive legal team from New York City, they could not prevent the investigation of Dan's involvement in his wife's disappearance from going forward. Johnny was convinced, with Merrill's urging, that the employee parking lot that was excavated and asphalted by Phillips's company two weeks after Grace's abduction likely held her corpse. After a week of the crew using the ground penetrating radar on the four acres of asphalt and finding nothing, Merrill discovered an article about how useful the instrument could be in probing what lay beneath concrete. She sent Johnny a link to the piece.

The following morning she stood next to the sheriff in the employee parking lot as the two lamp posts at either end were removed from their bases. As Merrill and Johnny watched the process, he told her that the standards were constructed with nine inches of concrete and twenty-seven inches of stone beneath that. The excavation depth for each base was five feet, more than two feet deeper than the asphalt lot.

The team ran the underground detection system over the concrete standards, and within an hour, the operator waved Johnny and the police investigators over. "We've got something," Merrill heard him say. Within minutes the backhoe began its work, and Merrill felt a wave of nausea sweep over her.

"I'm leaving. Call me," she said to Johnny.

An hour later, her phone rang. "We found her, Merrill. She was buried below the lamp base on the north side of the lot. We've sent the remains to the crime lab, but off the record, it looks like she died from one bullet to her left temple."

Merrill grabbed a kitchen chair and sat down. She was overwhelmed with an amalgam of emotions. Dread for the family, relief for the family, too. And gratitude. She was grateful to her *Deeper Dive* listeners, and ultimately she was grateful for her husband's encouragement, throughout their life together. And after.

"Merrill? Are you still there?" Johnny asked.

"Yes. I'm here."

"I just got off the phone with the Mill Springs Mall corporate headquarters. They have documentation to prove that, not only the employee parking lot, but the light standards were made and set by Phillips Construction."

The sound of the crank lowering Grace's casket into the ground interrupted Merrill's thoughts. She watched as the Phillips children, middle-aged people now, slowly approached the edge of their mother's grave. One by one, each of them threw a shovel of rich, brown dirt on top of their mother's coffin. A shiver ran down Merrill's spine as she realized that today for a second time in the past twenty years, Grace Phillips's body would be buried.

Trying to hold back the tears that threatened, Merrill concentrated on the minister's final words and fixed her stare on his face. Over his shoulder, standing back by the line of cars with their black flags waving in the mild breeze, stood someone who, in a way, also knew Grace.

The service was over and people began to slowly mill around talking quietly to each other. Merrill set her purse down on her chair and turned to leave. "Where are you going?" Kate asked her.

"I have to say hello to someone. I'll be right back."

Victoria Erikson gathered her black knit maxi dress so she would not close it in the car door. It was the first time Merrill had seen her wearing something that was not a splashy print. "Victoria, wait!" Merrill said, trying not to shout, given the solemnity of the circumstances.

She walked faster. Victoria smiled at her and rolled down her window. "Get in," she said as she unlocked the passenger side door. Merrill slid in. "I hope you're not upset with my being here, Merrill. I've been following the news since they found the body. I read about the funeral in the paper. I just wanted to pay my respects, even though I never met Grace."

"But you did, Victoria. I can't explain it, though believe me, in the past couple of months I've spent hours researching the ability of mediums to contact the dead. But you did know her. You met her that day when you held on to her blue shoe. She told you where she was. You're responsible for the discovery of her body after twenty years of being lost."

Victoria shook her head. "I'm not the one who convinced the police to use ground penetrating radar to look for her under that parking lot."

It was true that she had used her leverage over Johnny Lovallo to make that happen. After all, he had almost gotten her killed. Plus, Dan Phillips's complaint to Johnny's commanding officer that Merrill had been hired by him without having taken the required civil service test had been the reason he had to fire her. Even though he had apologized numerous times for having terminated her because of Phillips's influence, she used his embarrassment to her advantage.

"It turns out the field would not have been excavated as deeply as a grave would need to be," Merrill told Victoria.

"And when they didn't find her there, I'm willing to bet it was you who insisted they keep the equipment in spite of that. How did you know that the lamp post bases would have to be dug much deeper than the parking lot?" Victoria asked.

"Research," Merrill said.

"Of course," the medium responded.

"And a bit of woman's intuition," Merrill added.

Merrill got out of the car and came around to the driver's side window. "I'm glad I got to see you in person to thank you. I expect I'll be seeing you again sometime," she said.

"Yes, you will," Victoria answered.

As she walked back to the graveside of Grace Phillips, Merrill watched as Jenna, Kate, and Sherry, with Johnny following behind, climbed the small rise to meet her. "Is it too early to go to Larry's?" she asked the group. "A listener got in touch recently with an idea for my next podcast. I'd like to bounce it off all of you."

Johnny had caught up to her. "Me too?" Seconds passed without a reply. "I wanted to talk with you about an upcoming civil service test."

"We'll see about that," Merrill answered.

ACKNOWLEDGEMENTS

Thank you to my beta readers, Kathy Holser, Susan Penn, Gary Madar, Joe Pace, Susan Breon, and Marjorie Switala for their astute and constructive advice.

I also owe a huge debt of gratitude to the libraries and librarians of my past and present. The Dunkirk Public Library and The Barker Library in Fredonia, where as a child and a teen I wandered and read while I waited for a ride back to Sheridan. SUNY Fredonia's Reed Library, where I learned research techniques and wrote dozens of papers on my way to receiving my degrees. Westfield's wonderful Patterson Library where my sons grew from Story Hour tots to teen skateboarders launching off her beautiful steps. The Patterson staff also welcomed me and hundreds of my 11th and 12th graders over the years on their research journeys. Last but not least, I'm thankful for the Bemus Point Library, where I currently serve as a board member. I imagined Merrill doing her due diligence in each one of these places.

I'm indebted to my siblings for their support and for their expertise concerning subjects that I explore in A Deeper Dive. My sister Dina Volante, who worked for the New York State Division of Youth, informed me of the type of facility in which a minor, such as the Gibb boy in my novel would more than likely be placed. She and her partner Jeff built a wonderful camp on Kasoag Lake, which I had in mind as I wrote about Merrill's Airbnb destination. My brother Joe Pace, a social worker and therapist, provided me with information regarding the life-long consequences of molestation by an adult on a young boy, such as those suffered by my fictional character, Brad Childs. My sister Mary Beth Pace, fisherwoman extraordinaire, checked my details for accuracy in the salmon fishing chapter. Thanks also to my sister Sheila Hardie, who believes in Bigfoot and in my psychic powers and kept me laughing over the five years it took me to write the book.

Special thanks to my friend since 7th grade, Kathy Holser, who patiently listened as I attempted to explain what the cover of my book should look like. I'm so happy with the design she created!

Thanks to my husband, Gary for his love and support throughout the years as I wrote and rewrote A Deeper Dive.

Thank you, Doug Breon, for sharing your "concrete knowledge"!

My multi-talented son, Jesse Stratton, created my very cool new website and I love it! Thank you, Jesse, for your hours of work.

Lastly, to my faithful readers through the years. Thank you for telling me, "Your book made me think." Thank you for asking me, "When is your next book coming out?" Thank you for recommending my books to your family, friends, and book clubs. Your support through the years has inspired me. And for those of you who have asked, "Is there going to be a sequel?" I can finally answer, yes. You haven't seen the last of Merrill Connor.

ABOUT THE AUTHOR

Deborah Madar is a native of Western New York and lives with her husband Gary in Bemus Point. They have four children and nine grandchildren. Debbie taught high school and college English for many years before opening her laptop and her imagination to the "what if's" that she loves to explore in her books. A DEEPER DIVE is her third novel.

CONTACT DEBORAH
http://www.deborahmadar.com
On twitter - @Deborah Madar
Facebook.com/DeborahMadar
Instagram.com/debmadar
Goodreads – Deborah Madar

Made in United States
North Haven, CT
25 July 2023

39498212R00134